LOVE ME ANYWAY

LOVE

ME

ANYWAY

TIFFANY HAWK

THOMAS DUNNE BOOKS
St. Martin's Press ≈ New York

This is a work of fiction. All of the characters, organizations, and events portrayed in this novel are either products of the author's imagination or are used fictitiously.

THOMAS DUNNE BOOKS.
An imprint of St. Martin's Press.

www.thomasdunnebooks.com
www.stmartins.com

ISBN 978-1-250-02147-2 (hardcover)
ISBN 978-1-250-02282-0 (e-book)

St. Martin's Press books may be purchased for educational, business, or promotional use. For information on bulk purchases, please contact Macmillan Corporate and Premium Sales Department at 1-800-221-7945 extension 5442 or write specialmarkets@ macmillan.com.

First Edition: May 2013

10 9 8 7 6 5 4 3 2 1

For Aimee and Jennifer

ACKNOWLEDGMENTS

So many people helped bring this book into the world. My agent, Rachel Sussman, for your tireless efforts, unwavering belief, and inestimable publishing savvy. I couldn't have a better champion. Plus, this journey wouldn't have been half as fun if I hadn't shared it with you.

Margaret Brown, my editor. I am in awe of your ability to transform a book with the lightest touch imaginable.

The late Lynn Ferrin for helping me believe I could be a writer. Kim Fay and Justine Amodeo for giving me my start. Susan Segal, Jessica Forsyth, Joanne Wyckoff, and Stephanie Cox for moral support and for reading the earliest drafts of this story, which thankfully ended up right where they belong—in the rubbish bin.

All of the outrageously talented and generous instructors at the hottest MFA program in the country, UC Riverside, Palm Desert, especially Tod Goldberg, Mary Otis, David Ulin, and Elizabeth Crane, with special thanks to Mark Haskell Smith and Deanne Stillman, who have gone over and above the call of duty at every turn. I owe you a lot of drinks at the lemonade stand. Gratitude should also go to my fellow students whose talent intimidated the heck out of me and made me push myself harder than I knew I could. Andee Reilly and Debbie Graber, the other two-thirds of the three-headed writing monster. I don't know where I would be without you. You continue to inspire me and keep me sane and make me laugh through it all.

My flight attendant family from the good old days at United.

It was one hell of a party. For a while anyway. Kara, Jory, Terri, Paula, Amy, Andrea, Gail, Gordon, Sue, Jennifer, Aimee. I love you. Always.

I also want to pay tribute to the rest of the flight attendants out there. The traveling public can complain all they want, but you are the most pleasant and hardworking group I have ever come across. It continues to astound me that out of the thousands of crewmembers I flew with, at two airlines, exactly two people were ever a challenge to work with.

Reanna Hawk Wolberg for simply being one of the best people on the planet, and Charles and Linda Hawk for inspiring my love of books and travel, for providing tremendous support, and most importantly, for not being like the parents in this book.

Matt. Where do I even start? You are my happy ending.

JULY 2000

1

Into the Frying Pan

As the working crew crams bags into overhead bins, I nestle into an extra-wide first-class leather seat. I may only make twenty grand a year, but, space permitting, I can travel in style to anywhere United flies. Tonight, after a day off, I'm trying to get back to my base at San Francisco International Airport before I go on call at midnight.

Predeparture Dom Perignon flows freely to the rich and powerful passengers seated around me, but being on call, I have to turn it down. I close my eyes and try to block out the fluorescent lights and the angry coach passengers who shuffle down the aisle and grumble about delays and a possible cancellation. If we don't make it to SFO tonight, no one will be more screwed than me.

As a new flight attendant, one slipup will get you fired. We live in constant fear of termination, but it's not about the money. If you can relocate anywhere they tell you to, then spend twenty nights a month in twenty different hotels, you're not just earning a paycheck, you're running away.

A pilot steps into my row, stooping so he doesn't hit his head on the overhead bins. He holds his hat in one hand and loosens his blue-and-gold United tie with the other. His light brown hair is brushed forward, perhaps attempting to hide the inch or two of slippage that is just starting to shine through. I'd guess he's about ten years older than I am, probably somewhere in his early thirties.

He looks down at me and smiles. I sit up a little straighter.

"Hi, I'm Rick," he says and lets his hand linger as he shakes mine.

"I'm Emily," I say without smiling back. If I've learned anything in my first few weeks on the job, it's that flight attendants don't flirt with pilots. Like crossing a picket line, it's just not done. There's a joke that demonstrates the party-line position on cockpit crew:

How many pilots does it take to screw in a lightbulb?

One.

He holds it up in the air and the world revolves around him.

"Emily what?" asks Pilot Rick.

I hesitate and then reluctantly say, "Cavenaugh." The name has been attached to me for two years, but I'd like to step under a power washer and blast it off.

Rick pulls a small stack of clothes from his bag before stowing it in the overhead. "I'm gonna slip into something more comfortable." He laughs at his own attempt at humor and tells me he's commuting home.

As he heads for the lav, I reach up and twist shut the vent that has been whistling above me, dislodging wisps of hair from my otherwise perfect French twist. I smooth the flyaways back down to comply with company appearance regulations. In training too many wisps would get you a tap on the shoulder and a private grooming consultation. When you work for an airline, seniority is everything. You have to earn the right to get fat and disheveled.

When Rick emerges, he's tucking the last corner of a blue golf shirt into a pair of khakis. Golf is a surprise. His swagger suggests he's more the motorcycle type. Still, the shirt is an improvement over the polyester uniform jacket that had been hiding his well-toned arms, deeply tanned, probably from layovers in Maui and Miami. I make sure to look away before he catches me staring.

The lead flight attendant, or purser, comes up behind him with a pen and pad that both say MARRIOTT. Blond wisps are escaping from her ponytail in every direction, so clearly she has finished her first six months of probationary employment and has union protection.

She follows procedure and starts with me, the window seat. "What would you like for dinner this evening, Ms. Cavenaugh? The chicken Parmesan or the salmon with lemon and capers?"

It's my first time riding up front and I'm psyched, but still I say, "I'll have whatever's left over."

She winks at me in appreciation. I won't be the kind of flight attendant who morphs into a self-important corporate type when I'm sitting in first class for free.

Rick shakes his head and says he already ate. When she reaches the last row and I hear what must be the tenth request for chicken, I know I'm having salmon.

"So where are you based?" asks Pilot Rick.

"San Francisco."

"Ah, I'm based at LAX," he says, "but I commute to Denver. At least for the moment. Tonight I have to connect through SFO. You like San Francisco?"

I nod and don't tell him that although I have a bunk in a crashpad by SFO where I stay between trips, I've been using my flight benefits to commute home to a husband and condo in Bakersfield, the odiferous central California cow town where I grew up. I'm not sure it matters now, anyway.

We're interrupted when the purser leans over to offer me a hot towel and turns to face Rick, placing her cleavage squarely in his face.

I feel the chocks release and the plane eases away from the jet bridge. Finally, I'm going somewhere.

After the purser carefully blows into the tubes of the demonstration life vest, she sets her hand on Rick's shoulder and asks him to put his seat in the upright position. She once again leans across him, this time to pick up his predeparture mimosa. She must be what they call a cockpit queen.

The plane creeps along the taxiway, repeatedly turning and rhythmically smacking the same pothole every few minutes.

"Recognize this box pattern?" asks Rick.

I shake my head.

"We're going to be here awhile. When the ground controllers don't have room for another jet in the takeoff line, they keep us moving. They have a motto." He pauses for effect. "A moving airplane is a happy airplane."

I laugh and shift in my seat. I look up at him. When he laughs, the lines around his eyes seem to smile, too.

"So how long have you been flying?" he asks me.

"Six and a half weeks."

He looks me up and down, nodding. "I thought so. You're so regulation."

I widen my eyes. "What do you mean by that?"

He leans across the armrest and says into my ear, "Maybe someday we can get you to let your hair down."

I suspect he may be flirting, but I'm not certain enough to play along. "If it's below our chin we have to have it pinned up." I touch my tightly formed French twist. Then I smile just in case.

I hear my cell phone ring from inside my purse. Carl again. This is the eighth time he's called tonight, each message increasingly angry. I turn the phone off and stuff my purse back under the seat in front of me.

Rick's arm bumps against mine on the double-wide first-class armrest between us. I can feel its warmth, and I'm caught off guard by how soothing I find it. I have an urge to press my arm fully against his. Immediately, I want to pull it away, but that, too, would seem awkwardly deliberate. I sit straight forward, frozen in position, staring at the graying leather seat in front of me, its texture rubbed smooth from wear. I slide my eyes to the left to see my hand next to his, my ring finger ringless for the first time in two years. I slipped my wedding ring into my purse this afternoon as I walked away from Carl outside the therapist's office. It's just an experiment to see what my hand feels like without its weight.

I turn to look back into Rick's eyes, pale glass-like blue eyes that appear open for anything. I wonder what he's thinking about before I notice that he's watching the purser, who is standing in the galley repeatedly plunging a bag of tea into a Styrofoam cup.

Eventually the box pattern becomes a straight line.

"Finally," says Rick.

A voice over the PA says, "Flight attendants prepare for takeoff." As if I were on the jumpseat, I shift into brace position for takeoff, legs together in front of the seat, hands tucked at my sides, head facing forward. We hold short at the end of the runway, and when I hear the engines spool up, I begin my silent review. No matter how routine this job gets, we still rehearse for an evacuation with every takeoff and landing.

We race down the runway, gathering speed. Rick pulls the *Hemispheres* magazine out of his seat pocket as I mentally review throwing open doors and rushing people down slides. The plane hums louder and louder as we get ready to slingshot into the air. We're about to lift off and *bang!* The noise is so loud it's as if we fired a missile from our right wing. I'm thrown forward, pressing into my seat belt. The brakes scream and the whole plane slides from side to side.

"Holy shit!" says Rick. "Our gear collapsed."

The forward force is so powerful I have to press against the armrests to hold myself back in the seat.

Rick looks at me and then, so loudly that the passengers in

front of us turn around, he says, "We're full of fuel. We'll catch on fire."

He has the entire first-class cabin's attention. A man across the aisle unbuckles his seat belt and the woman next to him screams at him to put it back on.

We continue to whip from left to right as we screech down the runway. I'm thrown back against my seat when we finally slam to a halt.

Just as I'm about to shout my first command, "Release your seat belts and get out," a voice booms over the PA, slow and clear.

"Ladies and gentlemen. This is your captain speaking. There's nothing to be alarmed about. We just experienced what we call a compressor stall. We'll pull off the runway for a few minutes so maintenance can inspect our engine."

In time with the passengers seated around me, I whip my head around to look at Rick.

"I guess it wasn't our gear," he whispers.

Thank God he wasn't in uniform or 163 passengers would have been rushing the doors and scrambling out window exits.

"What was it?" I ask, still pressing into my seat.

"Just an engine failure."

I look at him with concern.

"There are two kinds of pilots," he says. "Those who have had an engine failure on takeoff. And those who will."

I give a sarcastic half laugh.

"I'm hoping that was my one and only," he says.

I hope so, too. I wouldn't have wanted Mr. Cool Under Pressure in the cockpit for that one.

As if reading my mind, he says, "Sorry about that. I'm kind of on edge right now." He shrugs his shoulders and says, "Personal stuff."

I offer an "Ah," intended to let him off the hook without an explanation.

"My wife wants a divorce," he says, shaking his head. "Fuck."

I search for an appropriate response, something better than the "Why are you telling me this?" that springs to mind. The best I can offer is a blank stare, which, I realize, is even worse. I thought jumpseat therapy was just for flight attendants.

He snaps his fingers and points his index finger out like a gun meant to say gotcha. "Too much information. I know. I'll shut up."

"Is it because of the job?" Before I accepted the job, someone told me that it would either make my relationship stronger or end it faster than I could imagine. I promised Carl it would make us rock solid, but now I wonder if I was hoping for the alternative.

Rick shrugs his shoulders.

I feel bad for him. He seems so nice, but people would probably say that about Carl, too. He's always the one to laugh extra hard at your joke, even if he doesn't get it. *Especially* if he doesn't get it.

I wonder what might actually lie behind Rick's agreeable appearance. I can't imagine he would kick his wife out of the car and leave her on the side of the road late at night just for reminding him to turn on his headlights. I highly doubt that his wife flew into town to meet with a marriage counselor today only to watch his frustration build until he said, straight to her face, that he did nothing wrong, that getting physical is "sometimes what it takes."

Rick says, "Let's change the subject. How about you? Do you commute?"

I shake my head.

"Must be nice being young and single with no responsibilities."

"Yeah." I laugh.

"How old are you?"

"Twenty-three."

"Ah, the good old days."

He reminisces about pilot training in the Navy, spending his days studying and his nights partying at Pensacola Beach bars with groupie chicks who were looking for Maverick from *Top Gun*. He misses getting hammered and stopping for pizza at 2 A.M. on his walk home.

I nod along as if he's describing my life. In reality I'm so straightlaced that the first time I ever caught a buzz was at my college graduation. I was proud to have summa cum laude stamped on my diploma, even if it was just Cal State Bakersfield. Only it wasn't joy that led me to drink. It was terror. I had no idea what to do next. Would I say goodbye to my high school sweetheart and move to New York to make worldly new girlfriends and work a fast-paced job in a skyscraper?

No. Only weeks later, I stepped onto the white aisle runner covering the lawn at the local rec center. Carl squinted into the sun as I swept one foot toward the other, staring down at the hideous stargazer lilies that capped each row of seats. I suddenly hated the stargazer lilies. I had chosen them because they were the cheapest option and I was tired of making decisions.

Rick envies my youth. "You must be living it up," he says. "Flexing the flight benefits, flirting with passengers, flitting around the world all carefree. Drinking cosmos in Manhattan and absinthe in Prague with men who are wrong in all the right ways."

I haven't actually been called up for an international yet, but my training flight to London two months ago was enough to show me that if something in my life had to go, it wouldn't be the job. We hadn't even landed yet and I knew. About five hours after we left Chicago, the captain called me up to the cockpit.

"I want to show you something," he said as he sprayed two pumps of Binaca in his mouth and turned off the lights. Then he told me to kneel and look outside. Thirty-seven thousand feet over Greenland, I pressed my face against the 777 cockpit windows and watched the northern lights shoot miles above and below us, rising and falling, bursting and disappearing as abruptly as the equalizer bars on a stereo. It was several minutes before a radio call from Reykjavik Air Traffic Control broke the silence and I was sent back into the cabin to refill gin and tonics.

No matter how early in the morning or late at night, whenever I put on my uniform, I feel that moment's exhilaration. I see the rest of the world every time I glance at a departure board. I taste my freedom every time I glide, rollaboard in tow, through the neon tunnel at our O'Hare hub while hidden speakers play "Rhapsody in Blue," United's theme song, the new soundtrack to my life.

Rick turns and looks straight at me and says, "Don't ever get married."

"I won't."

He says his wife, a pharmaceuticals rep, is screwing one of the doctors she sells to. I don't know what to say, so I turn away, lean against the glass and look back toward the tail of the plane. I can see a truck parked out there but no mechanic. We were on the runway, for God's sake, we better not cancel now. If I'm late to work, I'll be sacked for sure.

I can understand the hard line the company takes when it comes to tardiness. A late crewmember can start the proverbial snowball rolling—one delayed flight turns into another and another at each subsequent destination, and in the end, it could mean hundreds or even thousands of missed connections, all of those passengers needing to be slotted into already overbooked flights. The final cost could be more than my annual salary.

Rick apologizes again for unloading all of this on me. I know it's really a request to continue, so I ask him if he suspected anything.

He did. But he hoped it would pass, until he opened the door to his crashpad this morning and a process server threw a manila folder at him and ran down the stairs.

"You know what they say we carry in these, right," he says, kicking the black boxy flight bag stowed under the seat. It's topped with a sticker that says, I LOVE THE SMELL OF JET FUEL IN THE MORNING.

"Your divorce papers." I laugh, proud of myself for knowing the joke. Then I catch the rudeness of this response. "I'm sorry."

"An anonymous process server? What did she think? That I was going to hurt her or force her to stay with me or pull out a gun and shoot her and then myself?"

"Maybe."

"What do you mean by 'maybe'?"

"Nothing." I wave my hand as if to brush the comment away. But it is good to know she didn't have to confront him with a divorce herself. I imagine her putting on a kick-ass pair of shoes, confidently walking out of their home, and never looking back.

Rick starts flipping through the *Hemispheres* magazine on his lap. He doesn't stop on any page long enough to read more than the title.

I wonder if he had a big wedding, if hundreds of family members came out to support his vows, promising to help them stay together for better or worse. His wife probably doesn't care what other people think. I wish I didn't.

I turn toward him. His eyes are so gentle. They look safe. I'm tempted to tell him everything.

He looks up, perhaps feeling my stare. "So. On to a happier subject," he says. "Are you seeing anyone?"

I shake my head. Seeing anyone? I married my first boyfriend. Since then I have worn the turtlenecks and baggy sweaters he prefers, and true to form, they have vigilantly kept other men from checking me out.

At first I was devoted to Carl, and later I was even more devoted to avoiding a blowout. But I could never get that right.

A few weeks ago, I was running late and forgot to call. When I got home, Carl was in the kitchen slamming cabinets.

"I'm sorry," I said.

He grabbed a Calphalon frying pan and held it over his head.

"Who the fuck," he said as he slammed the pan into the top of the stove, "do you think you are?"

I saw an inch-deep dent on the edge of the stove and the frying pan was no longer round; he had completely flattened one side. I started to back away, but he ran past me and stood in the doorway with his arms out, blocking the exit from the kitchen.

I tried to squeeze by but he grabbed me by the shoulders and pushed me up against the pantry door. He pulled back his right fist. I closed my eyes and turned my head as if I had always known this day would arrive, the day he would move from hitting walls to hitting me. But his knuckles flew past me and slammed halfway through the hollow door.

I squirmed out from under his left hand, but he grabbed me again, his hands pressing into my shoulders and shaking me. I looked right into his eyes, surprised at my nerve. *He could kill me*, I thought. But it was as if I was on Valium. I couldn't get that near-death rush. I realized that I wasn't afraid to die because I was already dead.

He pushed with all his strength. I flew back and crashed into the floor and cabinets. The physical pain hit immediately—my head throbbed, my elbow burned, my wrists ached. I lay on the floor looking up at him.

He stared down at me, both of us expressionless.

Before I could react, he dropped to his knees, shaking, sobbing.

I didn't move. I lay crumpled against the cabinet and felt the last ounce of respect I had been reserving for him drain away. It was so after-school special that I could almost see the camera on him as he ran through his lines.

"I'm sorry, I'm sorry, I'm sorry," he repeated.

I said, "It's okay." And what I meant was that I would be okay. By escalating to physical violence, he had given me a gift. I could hardly suppress a smile.

For years, I'd been afraid to leave a water ring on the coffee table or a speck of toothpaste on the mirror, afraid to buy the wrong brand of shredded wheat or wash a shirt on the wrong temperature setting.

All of that evaporated. I was filled instead with an enormous sense of freedom.

I had to go to work that night, but I promised I'd fly home to see a counselor, which he had offered to do. Before I left for San Francisco, I furtively packed the few photos and mementos that mattered to me. At the last minute, when he wasn't there to see, I took the frying pan too.

"Ladies and gentlemen, your captain here again. Maintenance has given us the all clear, and we're going to try again."

"Try?" I say to Rick.

He smiles and winks.

I feel the parking brake release, and once again we are moving.

We turn toward the runway. Outside the window, I see a blinking trail of commercial jets from twenty-seat props to the double-decker 747s. We take our place in line and inch our way forward.

I look around at the silent cabin. We could probably hear each other breathe if it wasn't for the hum of the air-conditioning. I've heard that when a flight suddenly becomes "eventful," you won't see the chaos of a scene from *Airplane!* You'll see quiet passengers squeezing their armrests and facing forward as if turned to stone. Well, unless you're seated next to Pilot Rick.

"Flight attendants, prepare for takeoff."

I hold my breath and grip my armrests, surprised at the nervous energy jolting through my body. I'm afraid, I'm afraid to die, and the feeling makes me want to sing with joy.

The airplane trembles as it builds up power, a windup toy about to be released, and we're screaming down the runway again.

No bang, no brakes, we lift off into smooth, quiet air.

I'm alive.

2

Unaccompanied

You know, dear, you look just like Marilyn Monroe," says a wheezing antique of a man as KC stands on her toes to fasten his oxygen tank into an overhead bin.

KC interprets that to mean she's fat. She finishes with the tank and hurries into the first-class galley before anyone can see her cry. An unfortunate downside to traveling the world is discovering new vices. Her list of addictions now includes clam chowder, cheesesteak, pulled pork, oysters, and sweet tea.

She smacks the bags of ice so hard with the rubber mallet that she rips holes in the plastic. After a deep breath, she reminds herself why she took this job—free tickets to places like Paris and Hawaii.

Normally, flirting with unattractive older men is a hobby for her. Just yesterday she stared across the moving walkway and into the eyes of a fanny pack–wearing husband for so long he stumbled over the end and nearly ate carpet.

But today, all she wants is to be invisible. This morning, she popped a button on her uniform, and it's the worst possible time for a fat day. She's tentatively planning to meet Max Valentine tomorrow for the first time in almost ten years. She needs to look perfect. Not like Marilyn Monroe, who was huge by today's standards.

"Knock, knock," says a voice from just outside the aircraft door.

A Chicago ground supervisor with a white carnation on his jacket is holding the hand of a little boy, maybe seven or eight years old. "One more special," says the agent. "Who's in charge?"

Kevin, a former Marine who still looks enlisted with his buzz cut and oversized torso, is their purser for the day. He waves his hand as he walks up to the supervisor, who immediately starts whispering in his ear. A man with a bushy beard and tie-dyed Grateful Dead T-shirt, presumably the boy's father, points his son's attention to the cockpit and all its glowing buttons and lights. As the boy stands mesmerized, his dad tries to make eye contact with KC, but she looks away as if she doesn't notice. What kind of creep would try to pick up a woman with his son at his side?

Although KC can't make out what the supervisor is saying, she hears Kevin mention her name and knows she's getting juniored into UM duty. She's only been flying for a few months, so this morning she was also juniored into the passenger-facing jumpseat and was told she's up if anyone, such as oxygen man, needs CPR.

The agent looks back and forth from the boy to Kevin as he continues whispering, which can't be good news. They must already know this kid's gonna be a handful. Just watch, they'll pass him off to her and he'll torture her all the way from Chicago to San Francisco.

The father pats the boy on the head and turns back toward the terminal.

Kevin waves KC over and confirms that the boy is an Unaccompanied Minor and her charge for the day. He smiles at the agent and says, "Let's give him the pretty flight attendant so he can have one nice memory from this flight."

KC does not appreciate or trust Kevin's frequent compliments. The second they met in briefing she could smell the machismo venting from his pores. He rolled up his sleeve, flexing as he showed off an Eagle, Globe, and Anchor tattoo. There is nothing worse than a guy who tries that damn hard.

KC grabs the boy's red-and-white-striped paperwork out of Kevin's hand and folds it into her pocket. Kevin tells her to be nice and treat the kid as a VIP.

"Whatever you do, don't get off the plane without me. Okay?" she says to the boy. "And don't lose this"—she taps the red-and-white UM button pinned to his shirt—"until we hand you off to, um, um . . ." She reaches into her pocket for his papers.

"My grandpa," he says while looking at his shoes.

"What's your name?"

"Ross. I'm nine."

When he looks up, she says, "KC Valentine. I'm twenty." She sticks out her hand for him to shake. She was raised to treat children like adults.

He wiggles her arm up and down.

"First rule. Never, ever get up when the seat belt sign is on." She walks him back to his seat to explain the exits and oxygen masks and life vests.

He scoots into his seat and says, "Thank you, ma'am."

KC looks down at him for a moment, internally debating the merits and dangers of the call button, but then points up at the orange button and says, "If you need me, you can call me by pushing this."

He asks her if she'd like to see his Pokémon backpack. She'd rather not, but by the way the agent and Kevin were whispering about him, she fears he's the tantrum type, so she nods. When he holds it up, he says he got the entire luggage set for his birthday because he's going to be a frequent flyer.

She laughs politely but he says he means it, that this is already his second time flying by himself since his parents got divorced. This one was a surprise trip because his mom really misses him. She's working though, so his grandpa is picking him up.

"In San Francisco?" she asks.

"Nope. My mom lives in Modesto, so I have a little airplane after this."

"You're connecting all by yourself?"

He nods and twists his hands up in the pocket of his sweat-shirt.

She thinks of his loser parents and shakes her head. Who wouldn't be the tantrum type in his situation? At least when her parents first split they both still lived in Albuquerque so she didn't have to get on a plane and risk diversions and missed connections and emergencies and cancellations all alone at the age of nine. Who would make their kid do that?

For the first time in her life, she's thankful for the Peter Piper Pizza parking lot where her parents made the weekend exchange along with every other broken family in town. Everyone who was anyone in the spousal reject pile chose Peter Piper's. KC heard her friends' parents call it the Bad Meat Market. She would slink down in the seat of her dad's Ford Ranger while he chewed tobacco and smiled at the single moms who were checking him out. It was disgusting.

Poor Ross.

After she seals up the galley for takeoff, she feels around her tote bag for the Reese's Peanut Butter Cups she bought on a whim from the vending machine in the domicile. She brings the candy to Ross and tells him he's earned it for being such a good flier.

He looks out the window and says, "But we're still on the ground."

She assures him he deserves it, and he smiles at the prize. She wants to sit in the seat next to him and explain how to survive divorce. She wants to say that even if it's scary and weird if

his creep of a dad has sleepovers with a new "friend," it's okay.
But she'd be lying.

A few minutes after takeoff, when they've almost reached a
workable angle, a flight attendant named Raj climbs his way
uphill to the mid-galley and KC's jumpseat. He leans against
the bulkhead with one leg crossed over the other. He's so slick
with that mischievous smile and a whirl of black hair moussed
to perfection. He's definitely the best-looking guy on this
crew. If she told her roommates she was flying with three
straight male flight attendants on one plane today, they'd never
believe it.

"Yo, KC, the captain called back and said we're going to need
an air sample." He hands her a plastic garbage bag.

She unbuckles her harness and stands up before saying, "I'm
new but I'm not stupid." At training, their instructors warned
them about the most common pranks tried on rookies. If she'd
fallen for the air sample gag, she would be walking through the
cabin holding the bag over her head to collect sixteen gallons of
air for the pilots.

"Didn't your mom ever tell you that boys always tease the
girls they like?" he says with a raspy laugh.

She tells him he's pathetic and turns back to the coffeemaker. Then she smiles. Maybe she does still look all right.

It was actually KC's dad, not her mom, who told her about
boys and teasing, back in the fifth grade when Jimmy Szybowski
called her "big bones." That was almost ten years ago, right before she had to tell people her dad died.

When he first disappeared, she thought she could find him
and even checked out a detective tool kit from the school library. Learning how to lift fingerprints didn't help because the
police wouldn't run them, and the innovative facial identifica-
tion system was worthless because she already knew what he
looked like.

When he stopped coming for KC on his weekends, her mom

suspected that the rumors were right, that he and the big-titted bimbo ran off to Hawaii. There's only one thing harder than watching your father die when you're eleven years old, and that's admitting that he up and dumped you.

So she killed him off. She told people all about his funeral and how they burned his body and stuck his ashes in a cactus-shaped urn and how she wore a black dress from JCPenney's.

She felt a little guilty, and a little good, that she might somehow jinx him into dying for real.

"Hot towel? Hot towel? Hot towel?" KC is the floater, so she's helping Kevin kick-start first class before moving back to economy with Raj and Tien, the guy working the galley. She dumps the empty trays that held the hot towels onto the counter and reaches for the manifest of passenger names so she can properly address the guests. She feels Kevin behind her, moving a little too deep into her required three feet of separation. He brushes against her and she smells a whiff of Drakkar before she slips back into the aisle.

She looks down the aisle and sees Raj and Tien setting up beverage carts in the back galley. When Raj looks up toward her, she puts her hands together in prayer as if to say, "Get me out of here." The interphone chimes. Kevin picks up, brushing KC's shoulder, and says, "Fine, Raj, you can have her," and she jogs aft. As soon as she hits the other end of Raj's cart, she smiles at him over the bucket of pretzels. Now if *he* were to brush up against her . . .

"They didn't give us any lemons or limes today," Raj says as he pushes the cart out into the aisle. "So people are just going to have to do without."

Four rows in, KC reaches a woman with a sequined USA cap. She asks her what she'd like to drink and the woman checks her watch, pretending she doesn't know the time. They all do this, and then if it's too early, they'll order a Bloody Mary or screwdriver as if it makes it more acceptable to drink in the morning. *Get the scotch if you want it.* As if she's one to judge.

After debating her timing, USA lady says, "I'll have a Manhattan."

"I'm sorry, ma'am. We don't have Manhattans," says KC. "May I get you something else?"

The woman pulls reading glasses out of her seat-back pocket, slips them onto the end of her nose, and asks KC to show her the labels of each spirit that is available.

KC pulls out the liquor drawer and presents one of each liquor they sell, from Johnnie Walker to Kahlua to Courvoisier. The woman asks for a better look, so KC holds the drawer over the woman's lap and waits.

"We also have red wine and white wine," says KC.

"That's a bit vague. What type of red or white wine?"

KC reaches into the cart and presents six-ounce splits of Redwood Creek Chardonnay and Cabernet Sauvignon.

The woman studies the labels for several minutes before looking over her glasses at KC. "This is uncivilized. If you can't make a Manhattan, I guess I'll have sparkling water."

"Of course, ma'am."

"With lime."

"I'm sorry. We didn't get any limes today. Or lemons," she adds in case the woman decides to switch citrus.

"You little . . ." The woman trails off. "You know I'm a Premier-Exec, don't you? I'm going to write a letter about you and your huffy little attitude."

KC is astounded by how much energy some people are willing to invest in a beverage. The woman's attitude shouldn't bother her, but she feels a burning in her throat. Then she gets mad at herself. Years ago, she mastered the ability to appear strong when facing a crisis, but she doesn't have enough energy left for the little crap, so it's the stupid stuff she ends up crying over.

Raj pushes the cart up and gets right in front of the old lady and says, "Ma'am. Next time you're in a bar, see if they can fly your ass to San Fran."

As the woman gasps, KC turns away to hide her smile and says she's going to check on Ross.

She finds him hunched over his tray table scribbling in a notebook with colored pencils. He says he's having an awesome time. He loves airplanes so much he wants to become a pilot when he grows up. His dad wanted to be a pilot but he works at a computer store.

That's funny, KC's dad always wanted to be a pilot, but she doesn't know where he works. His profile just says sales. A little less than a year ago, KC found him listed on Classmates.com.

Apparently her mom was right. He wasn't dead. Not that she had ever really, really believed it, but it was only when she turned nineteen and the charade suddenly seemed totally immature that she was ready to give it up. KC got online at night when her mom was bartending at the Wooden Nickel Tavern. She was religious about deleting her browser history so no one would know that she was looking for her dad or that a man by his name was indeed living in Hawaii. She was too chicken to call the number, but then she found his e-mail through Classmates.com.

Ross hands her a picture he drew. It's of an airplane in the clouds. Floating outside the plane is a stick figure with blond hair pulled into a bun like hers. "It's you," he says. The figure is surrounded by at least a dozen hearts.

She thanks him and promises to hang it up on her wall. She means it. She walks away to finish the service, but then she turns back and ruffles his hair. "Don't forget you can call me with that orange button anytime."

A hundred and fifty-eight beverages and bags of pretzels later, she reaches the back galley. All three of the guys are there.

Kevin and Raj are trying to look serious, but she can tell they're holding back smiles. Tien is breaking down the carts, putting away leftover pretzels and napkins and Styrofoam cups.

"The cockpit called," says Raj.

Tien shakes his head.

"They said we're all being drug tested," says Raj as he points at three plastic cups filled with a dark yellowish-brown liquid. Each cup has a name—Raj, Tien, Kev—written on a blue piece of tape torn from the cart labels. "You'd better start chugging water."

Tien puts his hands up in surrender and says he had nothing to do with it.

"What the hell?" says KC.

"Oh jeez, never mind," says Kevin as he dumps the cups into the trash cart. "It's just apple juice. It was supposed to be funny."

She knew it wasn't real. It couldn't have been. But the FAA can test them for drugs and alcohol at any time, and she wouldn't pass right now. She knows she can't drink within twelve hours of reporting for work, but she's quitting smoking and she can't quit everything at once.

She tells them about the UM and why he's flying cross-country alone.

"That's usually the case," says Raj, with all the compassion of a bartender who's heard too many stories.

"One time I had a twelve-year-old girl on a flight who was supposed to go home to her mom in Sydney," says Tien. "She was coming from her dad's house in Dallas, but she had to connect in San Francisco. Only we canceled at two in the morning on the runway at SFO. The girl didn't know a soul in town, so she had to spend the night at the Travelodge with a customer service rep."

"Yikes," says KC, shaking her head in disbelief.

Tien closes a stainless steel carrier with emphasis. "My kids will never get stuck spending the night with a gate agent."

"Are you married to their mom?" She noticed his wedding

ring the minute they met in briefing. It wasn't because she thinks he's cute, especially being several inches shorter than her, but checking for a ring, or a tan line, has become a habit. She wishes she was attracted to the responsible, haircut every few weeks kind of guy. Someone with sweet, nurturing eyes like Tien who probably loves to cuddle. There's just something irresistible about a tall, cocky, swashbuckling guy. She wants to tangle with that confidence. Raj is clean-shaven because of United's appearance regulations, but she bets if he could, he would rock that five o'clock shadow.

"Of course," says Tien. "Going on eleven years."

No one KC knows has married parents. She wonders if they're happy or if having kids ruined everything. So she asks if he's happy.

He puts a fresh packet in the coffeemaker and starts filling a cup with sweeteners and swizzle sticks. "Yes, we're happy. My wife is a great person."

KC can't fault his response, but she hopes her future husband will see her as something more enchanting than a great person. "Was it having kids?"

"What?" He turns away from the coffee tray to face KC. "Oh, no. Having kids is great."

Yep, having kids ruined everything.

But at least he's sticking around. His kids aren't going to have to stalk him online and send him a drunken e-mail saying, "Hey, Max. I think you're my dad. Write back if you want."

She rubs her temple and remembers that night. After deleting "best" and "warm regards" and "see you soon," she thought of this contractor Rocco her mom once dated and went with "take it easy." Rocco used to bail out on plans so often that KC suspected he was married. But her mom was always obsessed with men she couldn't have, so they analyzed Rocco's every word for hidden meaning. No matter what he said in the body of an e-mail, if he signed off with "yours," they agreed that he was definitely falling for her mom. One day he used the "take it easy." There was no spinning that. That was a definitive blowoff.

Take it easy, Dad.

She's still waiting for a reply. She has his number, but she hasn't gone as far as calling him. Her mom would kill her if she knew about the e-mail. Or that every time she has a few days off and flies home to Henderson, the Las Vegas suburb her mom will never leave, she would rather be in Waikiki with the sand between her toes. Every time she gets off work, KC stands in front of the Hawaii gates watching pasty families and lovers fly off to paradise. She looks down at her write-your-own tickets and up at the departure boards. Time after time she sees LAS VEGAS, LAS VEGAS, LAS VEGAS, flashing for last call, and she gets on, goes to the hospital, hands her mother tea roses, and asks the nurses about IVs and catheters and morphine doses.

With each visit, her mom looks so much worse that KC can't believe she thought she looked bad the last time. She considered quitting the job and moving back home, but even if it means sneaking around, she has to keep the possibilities in Hawaii alive.

A few weeks ago she almost found him. She took her roommate Emily, got on the plane, and flew five hours over the Pacific. When they touched down in Honolulu, she inhaled the warm sticky air as if it could give her life. They took the Wiki Wiki bus into town, and at first KC was excited. She kept reaching into her pocket to feel the note she'd written his number on, imagined punching those keys over and over and over. But hopping on the plane that morning had been a whim and she didn't have a plan for rejection. What if he didn't want to see her? She decided it would be weird for him if she had a friend along, so she lay in the sun and took surf lessons instead.

It wasn't a total loss. She got to spend time with Emily, who she admires for taking charge of her life, making bold decisions. It had been pathetic watching her in training, constantly answering calls from her husband and accounting for her time. The rest of them were crying because they didn't want to be there, spending sixty hours a week in class, living in a dorm with four girls and one bathroom, fighting fires, jumping down slides, building bomb stacks, all while maintaining a perfect coif and double-coat of red lipstick. But as they got closer to finishing, Emily started crying because she didn't want to go home.

Thankfully she decided to leave that jerk for good. In Hawaii, they sipped mai tais to celebrate the great escape. As they swung their bare feet from bar stools, KC decided she would make it her mission to add some excitement to the girl's life.

"It's gonna be a wild one tonight, right?" Kevin says while nudging Raj. "So, KC, are you going to party with us in the city tonight?"

"Sorry, guys. Can't do it. I'm on call at five A.M."

"But you would if you weren't on call?" asks Raj.

She shrugs her shoulders.

"She's probably a Mormon," says Kevin.

But she doesn't fall into this trap. She doesn't get angry and tell him that when she's not on a plane or at a hospital, she's staring into a glass of vodka. She doesn't inform him of the sad fact that she could drink him under the table.

"Oh come on, we're all going. Even my man Tien's going out."

"You are?" she asks. He doesn't seem like a partier. He's the innocent Asian stereotype, nicely combed and recently cut hair, a few wrinkles around the eyes, totally straight and narrow. Only minutes after they met in briefing he mentioned his kids. He's even good with the passengers. While most of them head down the aisle with their eyes on an imaginary spot at the back so they don't have to make eye contact with the passengers, Tien slowly sweeps his head back and forth to see if he can anticipate any needs. He even did an extra coffee service.

He says maybe.

"See," says Raj. "And he never leaves his room. Tonight's our chance to break the quiet, law-abiding old man out of his shell."

"Hey, I'm only thirty-six," says Tien.

"Exactly," says Raj.

So she shrugs her shoulders again and says, "I would if I wasn't on call." And maybe she would if she could. As a reserve, she's never flown with the same person twice, so it's cool to her that these guys are senior enough to have a set schedule and have been working together all month.

"Well, you're in luck," says Raj. "I'll call my cousin who's a supervisor at the SFO crew desk and get you out of it."

"Are you serious?" she asks. If he really can get her out of early morning check-ins, he's worth getting to know. But if he calls this supervisor cousin, he'll find out that she lied to him and she's off work for the next three days. But she's not available. She's going to Honolulu. Or Las Vegas.

Raj pulls out his wallet, then his credit card and swipes it through the jet phone in the last row of seats.

KC looks down with hands on hips as if to say, "Yeah, right." But he does spend the three dollars a minute and at least pretends to speak to someone at the crew desk, a.k.a. "screw desk." He hangs up and says his cousin isn't working.

Once again she shakes her head and tells him he's pathetic. She does it jokingly, almost flirtatiously, but Kevin says, "Wow. Shut down," and turns to go check on first class.

A call bell lights up at 21A. Ross. She goes to check on him.

"KC?" he says. "Can I have an apple juice?"

She tells him it's her favorite drink too, and when she comes back with the plastic cup of Mott's, she flops down in the empty seat next to him. It's her job to comfort him, but she's also thankful for an excuse to get off her feet.

"Do you like flying?" he asks.

"Oh, I love it. It's the best job I've ever had." She pulls the inflight magazine out of the seat-back pocket in front of her. "I

get to visit all of the cities I always saw on TV when I was a kid."
She flips to the route map and starts pointing at all of the places
she's been. "Chicago and Albany and Omaha and New York and
Miami and Denver and L.A. and Atlanta and Philadelphia and
Hartford and Boise—"

"Do you ever get homesick?" Ross asks.

She bites her lip as she considers the question. She hasn't had
a home in so long she wouldn't really know what it feels like to
miss one. After KC's dad left, her mom moved every time she
got backed up on rent or dumped by a guy. "You get used to it,"
she says. "It's easier if you keep busy."

Ross nods.

The seat belt sign chimes and she stands up to go check the
cabin for fastened belts. "Don't worry. Nothing is as bad as it
seems."

KC makes her way up the cabin tapping shoulders and pointing
at seat belts. When she reaches the first-class galley, she sees
Kevin plating the just-defrosted Mrs. Fields cookies. She sets her
hand on his arm and begs him to save one for Ross if there is an
extra. She wants to do something special for him, but she can't
give him a free cocktail so she's hoping someone in first will refuse their cookie.

"Sure," Kevin says and starts back on his course. But he
turns around and puts his arm around KC. "Did he say anything
weird?"

"What do you mean, 'weird'?"

"I wasn't sure if I should tell you this," he says quietly. "But
since you're the one handing him over, maybe you should know.
The UM—"

"Ross," says KC.

"Yes, Ross is on a bereavement fare because his mother died
yesterday. But anyway, he doesn't know yet, and we aren't to

mention anything about it. Just so you know when you hand him to the next crew." He pats her on the shoulder, looks down to the ground as if in a quick prayer.

"That's not funny," she says.

He shows her the passenger manifest to verify. "The agent who brought him on told me it was his mom. Car accident. His granddad will tell him when he gets there."

His mom is dead and he's excited about the surprise trip. KC wants to punch his father in his furry face. What kind of dad can't spring for the flight to accompany his child to his own mother's funeral? *Take out a loan from the Mafia if you have to, asshole.*

"Sucks, huh?" says Kevin.

"Of course it sucks, Kevin. How would you feel if your mom died?"

He looks down and says, "Sorry. You're right." Then he points to the liquor drawer and asks her if she wants anything.

She shakes her head.

"Take some in case you decide to come out with us tonight. Oh no, wait, you're not coming, that's right."

"I have to fly in the morning," she says, even though she doesn't. Going out and getting wasted and lighting the wrong end of her cigarettes and passing out and missing all of the flights to Vegas or Honolulu would not be the healthy new KC she's going for.

"Oh come on. You're no fun," says Kevin.

No fun? A girl who was no fun wouldn't have woken up at the Hilton this morning to a $126 minibar bill. A girl who was no fun wouldn't have bought leather pants and a leopard-print top at Express on Monday after accidentally falling out of the stall and showing her bare ass, new palm tree tattoo and all, to the entire store. That fucking palm tree. What was she thinking?

The second he leaves the galley, she kicks open the liquor cart, pulls out four bottles of vodka, and pours them into an

empty water bottle she'll hide in her purse. There's nothing waiting for her in Vegas or Honolulu and she knows it. So she really
has no excuse not to go out tonight. She could show Kevin and
Raj a thing or two about passing time on a layover. She could
show them all about pounding shots of Bacardi 151, tell them
what it's like to down eight of them after a hard flight to Kauai,
an island only 117 miles from your so-called dad, dance on top of
the bar, and then lie down under a rasping needle that permanently scars you with the symbol of everything he has and you
don't.

She slams the bottle on the counter and comes up behind
Kevin as he carefully places a warm chocolate-chip cookie on the
linen-lined tray table of 1B.

She leans into his ear and whispers, "I'll be there. I'll show
you fun."

3

Fun

I heave my suitcases up the concrete stairs to my apartment near the airport, a boxy two-bedroom with off-white walls, popcorn ceilings, and six roommates. Fast fog blows past me as if I am still in the clouds. I open the door to our apartment, already looking forward to my own bed.

A cluster of suitcases sit next to the door and several pairs of black leather heels are piled against the wall. After living with a micromanager, the mess makes me happy. I can rest easy knowing that no one here is going to lose their temper if I don't get the vacuum lines straight or the hospital corners flush with the edge of the mattress. No one will throw away a book because it's monopolizing my attention. It's amazing how free I feel just knowing I can leave my hairbrush on the counter and buy whatever I want at the grocery store.

Six of us fit in this small apartment because it's rare for more than two of us to be in town at the same time. More space would be nice, but thanks to the dot-com boom, rents are nearly double what they should be and vacancies are hard to come by. When we got out of training and found out we would be based at SFO, they told us to take any place that came up, sight unseen, which is what we did. KC and I walked into the rental office as a young couple was turning in their notice. Sensing a quick transaction, the manager let us take over the lease despite a six-page waiting list.

KC sits on our garage-sale denim couch, still in uniform, pouring mini bottles of Finlandia vodka into a giant red Tupperware cup she calls her "fun cup." I'm surprised she's home since I know she has tomorrow off. She's really close to her family and flies home every chance she gets, so I rarely see her. One of these days, she says, she'll take me down to Las Vegas for a traditional Valentine Sunday dinner.

I liked KC the minute she walked into our dorm room at the training center, shook the snow out of her hair, and threw a suitcase onto the twin bed next to mine. We were both deliriously happy to be experiencing winter for the first time, even though it was technically spring. We put our clothes in the shared closet and went down to the World Headquarters parking lot where we spun around in the falling snow with our arms out and our mouths open, welcoming the cold taste of a new world on our tongues. KC squealed with joy. For her, picking up and heading to Chicago meant she was a grown-up. For me it was proof I was young after all.

For the next six weeks, we spent twenty-four hours a day together. I helped her memorize aircraft systems and evac procedures. She highlighted my hair. Being over twenty-one, I bought the bottles of Smirnoff at the nearby Jewel-Osco. She snuck them into the training center.

Her eyes are redder than an all-nighter, so I ask her what's wrong.

"Nothing," she says and takes a swig. "I'm just tired."

Lori Lee, our resident nut job, saunters into the living room dressed for a flight to Sydney. She gets the good trips so often that even she jokes about the secret room behind the crew desk where she offers blow jobs. She laughs, so I'm pretty sure she's joking.

She tells us she flew with a straight male flight attendant

yesterday, her first, and early in the trip he made a joke about a girl who nicknamed her boyfriend Grand Marnier because he was a fancy liquor. "Licker, get it?" he said. Then on every leg of the trip he asked her, "Can I interest you in some Grand Marnier?"

KC and I agree that the rumor is true. All male flight attendants are gay, married, or completely weird.

Despite the consensus, KC's going downtown to party with three straight male flight attendants she met on the plane.

"They all wear blue ties and buckles," she says.

Though not foolproof, there is a fashion code to determining flight attendant sexual orientation. Red ties and lace-up shoes means gay, blue ties and buckles means straight.

She wants me to go with her, but I've never "partied" in my life. Carl and I decided to go steady on the bus home from a marching band tournament in tenth grade, so I've never really dated let alone met up with strange guys in downtown bars. In college, I actually studied.

"You can't let me go alone. What if I do something stupid?" she says.

I get in her car. It smells like KC—a mix of smoke and CK One perfume.

Although I should feel bad that the Las Vegas flights were full and she can't get home, I'm happy to be able to spend time with her. For the last few years, I've fantasized about living in the city with a best girlfriend. We'd have crushes on boys and silly misunderstandings like best friends on a TV sitcom.

That fantasy died the minute Carl and I drove away from the rec center with cans clanging behind our car. Then when KC and I moved in together, I thought my dreams were coming true. Now even though we share a bedroom, we hardly see each other. One of us is either flying or she's in Las Vegas with her family.

As KC drives to the city, my phone rings. Carl. I concentrate on the plastic hula girl that swings her hips on the dashboard.

"Don't answer," says KC.

She's been a huge support for me. When I told her I hated that Carl had my new address, she suggested a restraining order. She knows about these things. Apparently when she was four-teen, she talked her mom into one after a live-in boyfriend pulled out a gun and started playing Russian roulette in front of them both. It's hard to imagine KC having been through anything like that. She's usually so upbeat.

If it wasn't for her, I might not have made my escape. She's the first one who mentioned the word *divorce*. Our five weeks of training in Chicago were almost over and I was terrified that the minute we graduated I would lose all of my new friends and my newfound independence. I had barely left Bakersfield and there I was in Chicago, seeing snow and tornadoes and elevated trains and meeting people from all over the country. It was more than I had ever hoped for and we hadn't even gotten started yet.

My dad and Nancy, who has been my stepmom for as long as I can remember, had raised me not to take chances. They lectured me that expecting too much from life would only lead to disap-pointment. They had me convinced that doing what you love was only for people with money or connections or both. They talked me into majoring in accounting because it was practical.

KC makes me want to try anything. She makes me believe I can have a rewarding career, a full passport, and true love. If I'm going to fail, I want to fail trying.

The phone rings and rings before finally going to voice mail. Through the windshield I watch the landing lights of a 747 com-ing in over the bay. I delete Carl's message without listening to it.

We find the Hotel Richelieu on the corner of Van Ness and Geary, a mid-size Victorian hotel on the edge of the Tenderloin district that United books in entirety every night of the year. The company gets a bulk rate, and our out-of-town crews stay in a flight-attendant-only hotel. KC asks for a guy named Raj, and the front desk points us in the direction of his room.

We knock on the door and hear a cheer from inside. A slick-looking Indian guy in a dress shirt with the top two buttons undone answers the door. He jokingly bows and beckons us into a small room with a double bed covered in a shiny floral bedspread. An old-fashioned cherry dresser by the door is stacked with every kind of liquor mini imaginable, from Jack Daniel's to Drambuie, along with plastic cups, stir sticks, United napkins, and a full complement of lemons and limes.

"That's where the garnishes went!" says KC.

She hugs each of the guys hello as if they had all known each other for longer than one flight. She stands close to Raj as she introduces me to Tien and Kevin.

She gives me eyes like she thinks I should consider Kevin. No. He's looking me up and down, making me feel like a piece of meat. Plus he smells like Drakkar and looks like a bully with his overblown muscles and rigid posture.

They take us across the street to Koko's, a dive bar topped with a red neon martini glass.

There are only three other patrons. Rancheros, probably in their mid-forties, in cowboy hats and tight jeans, who sit on stools near the jukebox and nod along to "One of These Nights." They whistle when KC walks past them.

Raj makes his way to the bar where two female bartenders in slinky knit dresses are laughing and speaking Korean. He orders shots of tequila for each of us. I shake my head and KC drinks mine and hers.

Raj sits on the edge of the pool table with one foot up and an arm on KC's shoulder.

He looks at me in the sequined turtleneck I dressed up in and says, "You're a nice girl. How did you end up in this job?"

I don't know if it's a compliment or an insult, and I struggle to come up with a clever response.

KC says, "What does that make me?" He pinches her cheek.

Kevin rubs his much-too-thick neck and says he thinks I'm the wild one. "The quiet ones always are." He laughs and nudges Raj and says, "Right, right? Don't you think she's really a wild one?"

"Sorry to disappoint you," I say, only no one is more disappointed than I am. I'd love to have KC's confidence and sense of freedom. Half the reason I married Carl is because I was ashamed of having slept with him and thought I could shove the cart back behind the horse and restore my virtue.

Britney Spears comes on the jukebox, and KC says, "Oh, I love Britney." Maybe to prove that *she* is indeed the wild one, or maybe because she had already started drinking at home, she pushes herself all the way onto the pool table. She sways back and forth, mouthing the words "I'm not that innocent," and tugging at the button on her low-rise jeans.

I choose a bar stool next to Tien, the older married guy, who I know won't hit on me. Even though I left Carl minutes after he said violence is sometimes the answer, I still identify with married people, people who don't go to bars and dance on pool tables like KC. I love that about her, but I don't want to dance on tables.

Tien and I laugh at KC and he tells me he's normally a slam-clicker, the kind of flight attendant who goes to his hotel room, slams and locks the door, and doesn't emerge until morning. Basically, a bore.

"Me, too," I say. "I don't have her energy. Not with this job."

"It'll get easier when you get off reserve and don't spend twenty-four hours a day on call. I promise." He's been flying for ten years so he has a line, which means he gets a schedule of trips to fly all month long. Everyone wants a line. Like all the new hires, KC and I refuse to believe the seasoned reserves who say that when the screw desk calls, they don't even ask where their flight is going. They just say, "Tell me what time to be at the airport."

"At least there are cell phones and answering machines now," he says. "Back in the old days, if the stewardesses wanted to take a shower, they had to call the crew desk and tell them they wouldn't be able to pick up for X number of minutes. Then their shower couldn't last longer than X number of minutes."

"I'm on call right now," I admit.

"You're crazy," he says, shaking his head.

KC starts singing "Hit Me with Your Best Shot." She gets louder and louder and dances more and more wildly until she's bending over and dangling her blond hair toward the floor before she jerks back upright, letting it fly into the air. We all cheer her on.

She looks gorgeous up there, swishing around and showing off her curves. I wish I could be more uninhibited like her, believe in myself like she does and live for the moment, never worrying about what people think or what might happen next.

But then before the song is over, she says, "Oh God, I need to throw up," and climbs off the table.

Kevin brings Tien a beer. "Do you know what a blonde's mating call sounds like?"

Tien shakes his head.

"'I'm *so* drunk,'" says Kevin, laughing out loud at his own joke.

Ignoring Kevin, Tien tells me he has two daughters and spends most of his time coaching softball and packing lunches and playing Mr. Fix-It. Right now he's halfway through painting the trim on his house. If he finishes that before it gets too cold, he'll start drawing up plans for the patio cover he's going to build.

He seems proud and happy as he describes his domestic life. Warmth and peace radiate from him, and despite the anxiety I have been carrying all night, I feel myself relaxing into easy conversation.

"It must be hard being away from your family," I say.

"Sometimes," he says. "But it's great for the kids. I stay home

with them all week while my wife works. Then I fly Friday afternoon to Monday morning and she's home with them."

As someone who was palmed off on day care providers shortly
after being born, I immediately respect him and his wife. I envy
his children.

"Was it love at first sight? The first time you met your wife,
did you just know?"

He looks away, considering the question. Kevin is at the bar
slamming down another shot of something. KC emerges from
the bathroom looking surprisingly refreshed. She takes a swig and
buries her head into his shoulder while giggling. The rancheros
stare at them from the corner.

Still Tien doesn't answer. I'm disappointed. I want to know
someone who has found real love, the kind I bypassed for Carl,
the seemingly safe choice.

Tien looks at me for a while in deep consideration, a teacher
trying to figure out a student's strange question.

"Don't worry about love," he finally says. "You'll find the right
person."

That wasn't an answer, but I decide that he's right anyway. I
will find love and when I do, I'll never let it go.

I feel comfortable telling him all about Carl and the frying
pan. He rubs his chin as he listens. He is taking me as seriously
as if it were his job. No, more seriously, as if he actually cares.
He pats my hand and says he's sorry to hear all that.

I tell him that my dad thinks I should go back to Carl.

He shakes his head as if I'm lying.

"If it was my daughter, I would kick his ass," he says, whispering the word *ass*, which makes me think ass-kicking is not in his
nature. He looks like he could do some damage if he wanted to
though. He's not big, only a few inches taller than I am, but he's
got the lean, toned body of a kick boxer.

KC and Raj make their way over to our table and she hands
me a tall glass of clear liquid with ice and a lime.

"I got you another glass," she says and sets it down next to the water I just finished. Before we got here, I told her I couldn't drink because I was already well into the twelve hours before possible flight time in which all alcohol consumption is prohibited.

The water burns as I suck it down. "Oh, God, KC. What was that?"

"Vodka tonic," she says. "Didn't you like it?"

I stare at her in disbelief. I was trying to be good, sitting quietly talking with Tien.

"I want you to have a good time," she says, shrugging her shoulders innocently.

"I *was* having a good time."

Soon I'm having an even better time. And another vodka tonic.

Kevin yells across the room and tells me to dance with him.

He walks over to the jukebox, and I look to Tien for help. He grabs my hand, drags me up, and says, "Sorry Kev, Emily's dancing with me."

When he says my name with his accent, it sounds like Em-Lee, two syllables instead of three. I like it. EmLee sounds strong.

I let Tien pull me close. I feel the warmth of his body against mine.

I step on his toes as he spins me around the room. We laugh together, and I feel guilty for being with a man other than my husband. Then I remind myself the guilt is just a reflex.

I try to stop spinning when the song ends, but I'm too dizzy.

Tien grabs me and holds me up. I stare at his smooth bronze skin.

The music slows down. "So Far Away" by Carole King. *Doesn't anybody stay in one place anymore?*

Tien's hand is still on my waist. I put my head against his chest and notice that even though he looks strong like Jet Li, he smells like vanilla. We slowly shift our feet, almost dancing, almost not.

I pull back and look up at him.

"What?" he asks.

"Nothing."

I long to say that meeting him reminds me of my best friend from first grade, Hope Staddler. When we moved across town, I was the new kid and Mrs. Casper asked Hope to show me around. By the time we got to the hopscotch squares, we were best friends.

The song changes. It's a fast song and somebody starts a conga line. The rancheros sit in the corner and nod along with the music. One of them raises his bottle of Miller Lite to me. I smile.

Even when my phone rings and it's the crew desk, I'm happy.

They assign me a 4:45 A.M. check-in, so I drive to the airport really, really fast. This is the first time I've ever been drunk, but I've heard drunk drivers get caught by driving too slowly.

I think of Carl's obsession with tracking gas mileage, the insistence on logging my miles before each fill-up, and I joyously press the trip meter over and over and over at random intervals.

I reach SFO by 4:30 A.M. The Hawaii flights are just coming in, and sunburned tourists wearing leis are quietly leaving the airport. Only two weeks ago that was me. When KC and I realized we both had three days off, she suggested doing something together. I mentioned a movie. She said let's test drive the flight benefits. Forty minutes later we were sitting in first class on a 747, sipping mai tais and heading to Honolulu.

I still have a hell of a tan.

I rest my head on the schoolroom desk in briefing room seven, a gray office like any other except that it's filled with matching zombies in blue dresses, little blue scarves, and well-polished black heels.

I shield my eyes from the fluorescent lights. I'm so tired that it hurts to breathe.

"All right, kids, we're fully booked," says the man who will be our purser. "How sweet it is."

According to the flight paperwork he is passing out, he has only a few years of seniority despite the over-tight skin at his temples that suggests a face-lift. He's wearing the red uniform tie. I look down at his shoes and note the laces. Definitely gay. I wonder if he is the type who had a wife, three children, and a picket fence before a midlife awakening pulled him out of the walk-in.

"But don't forget it's Saturday morning," he says while rubbing his hands together like a cartoon villain. "So, as always, people will sleep in and the loads'll drop off. We'll surely be half empty. How sweet it is."

He says "how sweet it is" six more times during the briefing, so already nobody likes him. Luckily, as a reserve flight attendant, I will never fly with him again.

We board a 767 and I sandwich myself between two other flight attendants in the middle seat of a three-way jumpseat behind the lavs. It's a tight squeeze for three people and our wool uniforms brush against each other with every bump and turn on the taxiway.

Alcohol, smoke, and sweat vent from my body. I wonder if they can smell me. I'm making myself sick. I must be killing them.

I wave my hand in front of my face and look at the lav in blame. The flight attendant to my left asks me if I had a late night. I nod. She compliments my makeup, but I'm not wearing any. It must be hanging on from yesterday.

I didn't even brush my hair before I pinned it into a French twist and swapped my smoky jeans for a blue-and-burgundy United Airlines dress.

The girls on my jumpseat say their first few years of flying were their party years, too. Party *years?* Last night was a one-time thing.

I pass out coffee and water and orange juice. The people of Denver are very thirsty and always want all three. After just a couple of months of flying, if I was blindfolded and stuck on a plane, I would know where I was headed just by the passengers' drink orders. Hot waters go to Vancouver, breakfast soda pops go to upstate New York, sparkling waters with lime go to Orange County, and the $140 liquor tabs go to Vegas and, for some reason, Kansas City.

Two hours later, we land and watch our crew split up, all of us headed for different gates. I enter the one that says CHARLOTTE, NORTH CAROLINA.

I check into the Quality Inn, flop onto the bed, close my eyes, and dream of last night. The dive bar with its blacked-out windows and floor sticky with stale beer. Tien.

In Chicago the next day, I am in the neon tunnel between concourses when my phone rings. It's Carl, of course. I send it to voice mail. When the message beeps through, I know I should delete it, but without KC by my side, I am conquered by habit and listen.

"Hey, babe. It's me," he says all nonchalant as if he's having a great time at a football game and just thought to call and tell me about a good play. "I was just wondering if it's everything you dreamed of." He lets out a laugh that turns into a cough. I suspect he's drunk. "Have you 'found' yourself yet? Are you ready to come home?"

4

Girl, Corrupted

In two weeks, I've seen the windswept plains of Omaha, the snowcapped peaks of Colorado Springs, and the congested freeways of Los Angeles. I've sweated in the overheated air of Atlanta, listened to brass bands in the streets of New Orleans, and tasted both red and green chile in Albuquerque. But nothing is as unique as what I find at home tonight. A familiar face.

KC drags me to a San Francisco club to meet Raj and Kevin, or Straight Kevin as we've taken to calling him since he has no attribute more noticeable than his blatant heterosexuality. The best we can figure, he's sick of people assuming he's gay just because he's a flight attendant.

"You clean up nicely," he says, looking me up and down.

I feel like a fraud wearing KC's sparkly tank top and strappy four-inch heels, which are nearly impossible for me to walk in.

I wobble behind her into the body-to-body room where people have to yell to be heard over the bass, where various colognes and perfumes compete with the inevitable blossoming of sweat, where lovers don't even bother to find a dark corner before they start making out. Part of me is thrilled to be here, the other part would rather be safely reading a book in bed.

"I'm gonna corrupt you yet, little missy," she says. She laughs, but I think she's serious. Sometimes I can't tell if she wants to change me because she cares about me, or so she'll look more respectable without the shy girl standing next to her in contrast. I'm not sure the makeover plan was working tonight anyway since she is dressed even more "fun" than usual in a pair of black leather pants and a tight-fitting leopard-print top.

She says she'll lend me the top for my stepsister's wedding in Bakersfield tomorrow, an event I'm dreading. It will be the first time I've seen my family since I left Carl, and instead of worrying about what people will be saying about me, KC thinks I should turn up drunk and half-naked and wrestle the best man into a closet. That would show them I'm not going back to Carl.

KC looks at home as the center of attention in this sweaty, overcrowded bar in downtown San Francisco. She grinds against various men and crouches near the ground like a stripper.

At least Straight Kevin is not targeting me tonight. At the moment, he's trying to schmooze a couple of girls that seem to be an actual couple since they're holding hands and swinging their arms. I wonder if they're actually gay or if they're just trying to get rid of him.

Before long the girls are rubbing up against each other. As Kevin stands next to them gaping, they pull him closer.

If he has some potent appeal, enough to convert lesbians, I certainly don't get it.

"They're not real lesbians," says KC. "They're just trying to seem slutty so Kevin will like them. Girls do that shit all the time."

"Oh," I say, feeling tremendously ill-equipped to start dating again.

"Tien!" yells KC.

I turn to see Tien pushing his way in our direction and realize I'm nervous. He's better-looking than I remember with that dark skin and warm smile. When he reaches us, he inadvertently touches my arm, and suddenly he doesn't seem so easy to be around like last time. I quickly look away.

I've thought about him over the last couple of weeks—the way his hand held mine so gently as we danced, the way his voice turned soft and serious when he said my name. Letting his warm memory comfort me as I bounced solo around the country was easy when I was sure I would never see him again.

"This isn't my kind of place," he says. "But I wanted to get out of the hotel."

I consider telling him I'm glad he came but think better of it.

"I'm glad you're here," he says.

I feel my face brighten and hope he doesn't notice.

"It's a relief to see another sane person who won't be pounding shots and dancing on tables."

I nod in agreement.

As the night wears on, KC's voice gets louder and louder, Raj's walk turns into a shuffle, and they work themselves into a frenzy dancing. We hang back, quiet and responsible.

Even our corner is body-to-body crowded, and at some point, a guy with sagging jeans and a black hoodie moves from groping me with his eyes to trying to grope my butt with his hands. I gasp, and he mutters something I can't understand.

"Hey," says Tien.

The guy lifts his chin and grins at him. But it isn't a friendly smile and I'm suddenly very worried for Tien.

With complete calm, Tien says, "She's with me." Then he puts his arm around me. I set my head on his shoulder to complete the effect.

The guy lifts his hands up in surrender.

Tien softly kisses the top of my head. I know it is only for show, but it feels so safe and reassuring and the second he lifts his lips, I wish he would do it again. I try to imagine what it would be like to be here for real with someone kind and patient and mature like Tien.

I look around the bar at the guys downing shots and circling like sharks, and as much as I want to be free, the idea of throwing myself at anonymous men in cheap bars is hardly more palatable than being with Carl.

I see Kevin leave the bar with his new friends.

When the bar closes, we go back to the Richelieu, but instead of turning toward her car, KC says she's going to Raj's room. She takes the car keys, blows me a kiss, and turns on her heel. As they disappear into the hotel, I am left alone with Tien. We stand there looking at each other awkwardly.

Tien takes a deep breath.

He better not think I'm the kind of girl he can just have his way with. I may look like KC tonight, but I'm not like her.

"I'm not going to your room," I say.

He laughs. "No, I didn't think you would want to do that."

I wonder if plenty of girls, gutsier girls, have gone up to his room.

Tien makes a point of looking up and down the nearly empty street. To the left there is a stumbling drunk and to the right a homeless person bedded down in the doorway. "I can't leave you out here alone."

I would say I can take care of myself, but staying out here seems even more dangerous than going to his room.

"Let's go for a walk," he says.

We stroll up and down the steep streets of Nob Hill. It's cold and quiet and the streetlamps cast an eerie, glowing light through the fog. The curbs are lined bumper-to-bumper with parked cars, but the city looks and sounds deserted.

We peek into the windows of closed stores—a bakery with a fake wedding cake in the window; a vintage clothing shop with half-naked mannequins; an Asian market with burlap sacks overflowing with herbs, gnarled roots, and dried fish.

"This place reminds me of being a kid. They have everything there—galangal, mung beans, cardamom. Sometimes I pick up ingredients here and bring them home to cook with."

I don't want to admit that I don't know what any of those things are. "Do you lay over here a lot?" I ask.

"Almost every trip. It's like a second home now. I like that you don't know where the Asian and American sides start and stop. Kind of like me."

He points across the street at a second-floor restaurant with an elaborate wrought-iron terrace. "The best Thai place in town."

"I've never tried Thai food."

He stops walking and looks right at me. "You have to be kidding."

"I assure you, I'm not."

"We'll have to remedy that sometime."

"We?" I ask.

He smiles crookedly. But before I can decide if he's suggesting something he says, "No. You're right. *You* will have to remedy that."

It hits me that maybe he was just making conversation and I am the one who turned it into a flirtation.

Either way, he brushes it off and starts walking again. "I always wanted to be a chef. I chose business because it was practical."

"I can relate to that." I point to myself. "Accounting major."

"Yuck. I never liked accounting."

"Me neither."

"Lucky for us the only numbers we have to deal with at United are the liquor proceeds."

"Yeah, I can always measure the extent of my sleep deprivation by how difficult the simple arithmetic becomes."

"Tell me about it. Stay awake long enough and two times five somehow gets recorded as twenty. Thank God no one in management pays attention or they'd think we'd been drinking it, not selling it."

"So have you always loved cooking?"

"I got it from my mom. She was an incredible cook. She would take me to the bay first thing in the morning. We would push our little boat out and fish with big white nets that you don't see in America. We'd take our catch to the market and come home with rice and meat and things I rarely find anymore, like green papaya."

I've never heard of green papaya. "So where was that? Where are you from?"

"Vietnam," he says.

"Why did you come to America?"

He hesitates before saying, "It was probably before you were born." We walk at least half a block before he continues. "When I was ten years old, I escaped. I haven't seen my parents since the fall."

I realize he means the Fall of Saigon and feel stupid. What did I think he was going to say? That his family wanted to be closer to Disneyland or that they heard there was good money in dry-cleaning American clothes?

"I worked with a pilot the other day," Tien says. "He told me he flew over Vietnam back in the day, as if we come from the same place. I said, 'Oh, that was you up there. Dropping bombs.'"

An SUV pulls up to the intersection, so we stop at the corner in front of a bar with black walls and covered windows, a neon sign that says THE RED DEVI LOUNGE, the L in *devil* burned out.

I look at the faint scar above Tien's eyebrow and wonder where it came from. He has experienced so much more of the world, good and bad, than I have.

I hear voices behind me and turn to see the red double doors of the bar swing open. An enormously buff man with a

well-polished bald head pushes a guy with a bloody nose out
onto the sidewalk. The guy stumbles and nearly falls backward
before righting himself.

We start walking again, and I ramble about living in the same
town most of my life, never having left the state before this job.

"I think that's nice."

"You do? Why?"

"I do enjoy traveling, but I would have loved to have stayed in
one place with family nearby."

"I'm ready to experience as much as I can."

He tells me about Paris, where two of his brothers live, and
all of the places he got sent when he first started flying—Milan,
London, São Paolo, Santiago. "The first thing you notice in the
southern hemisphere is that the night sky is completely unfamiliar. The Big Dipper and Orion are upside down, and there are
new constellations like the Southern Cross."

I pump him for information on Brazilian food and Italian
fashion.

"I'm sure that when you get to those places they'll be quite
changed from what I saw ten years ago. Sometimes I miss it, but
now that I can hold a line, I like my San Francisco routine."

"So how did you become a flight attendant anyway?"

"Yeah, everyone wonders why a straight guy becomes a flight
attendant."

"There aren't that many of you."

"It was supposed to be temporary. I thought I'd move up to
management, but then my wife started making good money, and
it made sense that I would stay home with the kids during the
week."

"Mr. Mom," I say with a laugh.

He squishes up his nose in disapproval. "Maybe. But with a
tool belt. I can build a mean deck."

"I'm sorry. That was probably rude."

"No, don't worry. This is nice," he says. "I can't think of the last time I had fun like this."

"Me, too. It's the perfect distraction, too, because tomorrow, well, in a few hours, I'm headed home for my stepsister's wedding and I'll have to face my family for the first time since the divorce."

He doesn't say anything, and I'm tempted to lighten the mood with a joke about Bako. Before I can, he reaches out and squeezes my hand.

A comfort spreads over me. Though he says nothing, I feel him telling me I'm going to be okay.

A few moments later, I stop to rest. I've been walking all night in these stupidly high heels and the balls of my feet are in flames.

I look into Tien's eyes. As the seconds pass and he continues to hold my gaze, I can feel my heart speeding up.

He steps toward me. So close I can feel his breath on my face. Sirens echo and fade from across town. My resolve weakens as he puts one hand on my cheek and brushes my hair out of my face with the other. I breathe in his sweet vanilla scent. It smells like home.

We lean toward each other so gently that although he doesn't seem to move, he is pressing against me. I can feel his heart beating.

I close my eyes and suddenly he is kissing me. I want to be disgusted with myself, but I'm thrilled. I'm kissing him deeply, slipping into another life, tasting the other side of the world.

He stops, takes a step back. I can see a change in his eyes, and am sure that I've already become a regret. With one kiss, my world opened up and his began to crumble.

Where I felt comfort and desire, I am now flooded with embarrassment and shame. "What would your wife think?"

Tien looks at his shoes.

I try calling KC, but she doesn't pick up. I can't run in her high heels, so I walk as fast as I can back to the Richelieu and through the halls to Raj's room. I bang on the door. Light from a TV flickers in the crack of the curtains, but no one answers the door. I bang and bang. And still no one answers.

I tell Tien I'll *sleep* in his room but that's it.

I follow Tien back to a room on the fourth floor with a bay window that overlooks Van Ness and collapse on top of the comforter with my clothes and shoes still on.

He leaves a foot of space between us and lies down on his back.

I try not to move so I don't disturb him if he falls asleep. Every so often, a car passes by and a triangle of light moves across the ceiling and disappears, leaving only the green glow of the clock radio.

This is not where I expected to end up.

Twenty, thirty, forty minutes tick by on the clock radio as I think about Bakersfield and the family and the questions that will surely come. I watch Tien's chest slowly rise and fall. I crawl over, lay my head on his shoulder, and think, this is not who my family expects me to be.

Tien is awake. He kisses my forehead. Then my right cheek, then my lips. I'm not drunk anymore, but the room is spinning. He runs his fingers up and down the inside of my arm, kisses the length of it. I feel a sick pride that I am irresistible to a man who should be resisting me.

He stands at the end of the bed, lifting my foot and unbuckling my sandal.

I sit up and say stop.

"You want to keep your shoes on?" he asks.

"Yes."

He carefully rebuckles the strap, sets my foot down, and pats my leg.

I say, "I can't."

He shakes his head. "Don't feel bad, I'm the one who's wrong." He moves over to the armchair and tells me I can sleep in the bed. He slowly crosses his legs and folds his arms over his chest.

Once again I am watching the clock radio, aware of my breathing, the sound of the sheets if I move just an inch. I wonder if he is beginning to nod off.

I roll onto my side and close my eyes, wishing I hadn't ended up here tonight. Actually, I wish I had ended up here, but as a bolder woman. I might have discovered how being with a man is supposed to feel.

5

Living the Dream

When a man carries you over the threshold to his hotel room, it can only mean one thing. You're not too fat to lift. And that, KC decides, is a beautiful thing.

If she thought more highly of men, she would let herself believe that by picking her up and carrying her through the doorway, Raj was hinting at a fairy-tale future.

In spite of herself, she imagines that future. She pictures the day she'll have enough seniority to get off reserve and she and Raj can buddy-bid their trips and fly around the world together. She can see herself plating meals in the business-class galley on the way to Hong Kong or Buenos Aires while he mixes drinks beside her.

Not that she would ever admit to needing a man. She's proud that while other girls from her high school are trying to find sugar daddies, whether high-roller boyfriends or regulars at bars and strip clubs, she's self-sufficient, name on a lease, current on her car loan, and safely enrolled in a group health insurance plan.

The door slams behind them and Raj tosses KC onto the bed. It may have taken a couple of weeks, but she knew he would call her. It's not technically a date since he invited her and Emily to meet up with his crew again, but it didn't take much to get him alone. She almost felt bad taking the car keys and stranding Emily with Tien. Almost.

Skipping all small talk, Raj pounces on top of KC. She runs her fingers through his hair, tugging enough to show him how fiercely she wants him. She's determined to blow his mind.

Raj lifts her shirt and kisses her stomach. She can feel his tongue through her lacy bra as he caresses her nipples.

She parts her lips in a well-practiced seductive pout. KC has spent years training herself to be too hot to be forgotten.

Raj frantically starts tugging at the zipper of her leather pants. She tries to help him pull them down over her hips, but before she manages, her phone rings.

It's 3 A.M., so there's only one person it could be. Evil Debbie at the crew desk.

Legend has it Evil Debbie hates flight attendants because her husband ran off with one. KC doubts the rumor—it's too cliché. But she acknowledges that Debbie *is* evil. She calls her at 3 A.M. and gives her god-awful trips—like six legs to Des Moines—and laughs about it. Even worse, she never releases KC early so she can go visit her mom, even when there are no open trips in the system.

Evil Debbie with her stringy blond hair and Lee Press-On Nails has total control over KC's life, and KC hates her for it.

She wrestles herself free of Raj and answers the phone.

"This is Debbie at the crew desk. I've got a trip for you."

"Hi, Debbie. How are you?" says KC, theorizing that maybe Debbie is mean because no one is ever nice to her.

"Be here at seven A.M. I put you on a Frankfurt." The phone clicks off.

KC's first international trip. She beams as she tells Raj, but he just shrugs his shoulders and says, "Frankfurt is blah."

Raj might not appreciate her luck, but KC can't wait to tell her mom all about Germany.

Hearing about KC's new life makes her mom happy, so every time she visits, KC lies about having seen the Statue of Liberty and the Smithsonian and Disney World. In reality, she would never have the time. Layovers are too short and she uses her flight benefits to spend every free day back in Henderson.

Back when her mom first got sick, she had taken KC by the hands and said, "I'll be damned if I'm going to let my daughter spend her life chasing tips in a casino bar." She unfolded a newspaper clipping and showed KC the ad that announced United was hiring.

She had said, "Just think, KC. You could see the real New York and Paris and Rome. Don't let a lifetime go by without leaving the walls of the desert." KC promised to go to Paris and learn French and quit smoking and stand up straight and stop drinking and live life to the fullest.

Since then, KC has done her best to make her life seem easy and glamorous. Last time she visited, she found her mom lying in the dark with her eyes open, staring at the shadows on the ceiling. She looked gray—gray eyes, gray skin, sprouts of gray hair growing back.

KC held her mother's hand and found herself making up an entire Paris layover that never happened.

"My little girl is living the dream," her mom said.

KC resisted the urge to laugh. Even if she had been running around Paris and New York, well-rested and happy, all of that was more her mom's plan than hers. She has never mentioned the real dream—finding her dad.

She wants to make things right again. They were a good family once, sitting on the porch and dreaming up plans for a backyard with a dog and a swing set, sharing popcorn and Milk Duds at the movie theater, playing Frisbee in the park and dominoes in the kitchen.

KC shoves her phone into her purse and crawls back into bed with Raj. He starts twirling his finger in her hair and keeps staring at her like she's the most beautiful woman on the planet. He traces his fingers on her lips. She opens her lips, and he slips his fingertips into her mouth. She sucks on them, and he closes his eyes.

She's optimistic about his potential. With any luck, he'll invite her to hang out on his layovers in New Orleans next month. With even more luck, he'll bring her home to his apartment in Chicago.

Raj looks into KC's eyes so sweetly that she is about to ask him what he's feeling. She's sure she could fall for him if she let herself. She wants to let herself, to give herself over to someone strong enough to carry her.

Before she has a chance to ask, he grabs her hips and pulls her body toward him. He pushes his lips to her neck.

She closes her eyes, anticipates making love to this strong, grown-up man.

He growls playfully and slips his hand up her shirt. Seconds later she is helping him peel it off.

He tears off her pants and pulls his own down to his knees.

He turns her over and pulls her hair back as he slams into her. "I knew from the moment I saw you that you'd be hot and dirty. I love that you're so dirty."

She tries to focus on the word *love*.

Raj thrusts and grinds against her and says, "I'm about to come, come with me baby." She tries to make herself come so it will be over and they can lie in each other's arms again, but the harder she tries, the further it slips away.

And then it's over.

Raj flops onto his back with his arm behind his head. He lets out a satiated sigh.

He asks her if she needs a cigarette, and she shakes her head. Although she would love to satisfy at least one craving, she fears he would perceive it as an indication of his success.

She knows she could find Emily and go home for a nap before flying to Frankfurt, but a twisted sense of pride makes her stay the night.

She curls up next to Raj. While he snores heartily, KC spends the next few hours awake. She hears Emily knock on the door, but she ignores her. She's not ready to face the truth—that she's the kind of girl who dumps her friends for a guy. She doesn't mean to be that way. It's just that it's easier to get close to a guy.

Besides, leaving Emily with Tien wasn't just about getting Raj alone. Part of her hopes innocent Emily is the one making the biggest mistakes tonight.

When the alarm on her cell phone and the clock radio go off, KC is still awake, but she pretends to be asleep. She wants to let them ring until Raj wakes up. She's not going to slip away without a word no matter how much he'd like that.

He sits up and rubs his eyes.

"Sorry," she says and shuts off her phone. She can't help but notice that the hotel wake-up call still hasn't come. No matter what hotel it is, there's only ever a fifty-fifty chance they'll bother with it.

He pulls the clock radio off the nightstand, yanks the cord out of the wall, and drops back down into bed.

"Is that it?" asks KC.

Without opening his eyes he says, "It's five thirty in the morning."

If the sex had been good, she might have been willing to let him off that easy.

Now she has to add another one-night stand to her count and she didn't even come. Maybe if she had, she wouldn't feel quite so used.

She tries to think of what to say to make him want to call her or see her again.

He rolls over and pulls the sheet over his eyes.

"I can't stay," she says. "I'm going to Frankfurt."

"Fly safe."

She flips on every light in the room. She's sick of guys wanting nothing but sex. She refuses to be like her mom, clinging to a dead-end job and chasing after any man who promises to get her caught up on her debts, who will inevitably bail long before payday. KC doesn't need to be rescued. She's going places.

She packs up her stuff and then stands at the end of the bed, waiting to see if Raj will react. Sometimes she thinks maybe Emily had been on to something getting married right away. If KC had been a straightlaced girl from a simple place like Bakersfield, maybe she would already have a husband and a family, and she wouldn't have to deal with this bullshit. Not that Carl was a good candidate. He gave KC the creeps the one time she met him. She knew it wasn't right that he flew all the way to Chicago to check up on Emily when she was in the middle of training. Still, she wishes someone would need her that badly.

Raj sits up. "Okay, what now?"

She isn't sure what to say.

"Look. We had fun here, right?" he says. "Nothing serious."

She steps back from the bed and smiles like the blow-off is her idea. "Exactly. I'm all about fun."

"I know," he says. "Just wanted to cover my bases."

KC is actually nothing but serious. She slams Raj's door behind her.

She calls Emily's cell phone over and over and over, but there is no answer. KC hopes Emily isn't angry with her. Perhaps, liberated by alcohol, she actually is too busy having fun.

When she gets to the lobby, an airport van sits idling by the front door. The room is buzzing with flight attendants reporting for early morning check-ins after legitimate layovers. They wear starched blue suits and dresses, and as they pass, they each look at KC. Her hair is matted, her eyes are soiled with mascara, and she is wearing a leopard-print shirt and leather pants. She's sure they think she's a hooker.

6

The Parent Trap

Only four hours after leaving Tien at the Richelieu, my United Express turbo-prop lands in Bakersfield. I hold on to the rail as I carefully walk down the stairs that folded out of the door. My dad is waiting at the edge of the tarmac, white hair and beard shining in the sun. His coworkers call him Papa Smurf. I keep as much distance as I can during our awkward hug and wonder how long it will take before he starts pressuring me to work things out with Carl.

We meet my stepmom, Nancy, at the Boll Weevil, my dad's favorite burger joint. She's wearing jeans and a button-up tank top, but her hair is wedding-ready. It's been teased and lacquered into a crisply-parted 1960s bouffant. Her car is filled with bottles of bubbles that she's delivering to the church. She picks one up and shows me the personalized labels stuck on each side. One side says, TODAY I MARRY MY BEST FRIEND, and the other, TINA AND PAUL, AUGUST 9, 2000.

"Instead of rice," says Nancy. "Isn't that clever? Tina's always been good with details."

I suspect Nancy's been going overboard with this wedding—making the invitations by hand, dropping a month's salary on

Tina's Demetrios dress, tasting thirty-six cakes with different frostings, from buttercream to fondant, before choosing the perfect one—in an effort to make up for lost time with Tina, whom she more or less abandoned for my dad. They got married when I was five and Tina was eight, and for whatever reason, Nancy moved in with us and Tina stayed with her dad.

Tina hasn't exactly made Nancy's life easy either. In high school, she was constantly getting in trouble with boys and drugs and bad checks. Although I've never really liked Tina, I've felt bad for her as long as I've known her. By the time I started elementary school, I knew it wasn't right that I spent more time with her mom than she did or that I got praised for getting good grades while she had to go to special reading classes for her dyslexia.

My mom wasn't around either, but at least I had Nancy. I was too young to really remember much about my mom anyway. I once heard my dad telling Nancy I was better off. "There's no sense letting her dwell on some selfish beatnik that split when she was three."

"Children are resilient," said Nancy, oblivious to the signs of her own daughter's distress.

We go inside and slide into my dad's regular booth under the Tiffany-style Budweiser lamp. We've been coming here for years even though most of the town prefers Happy Jacks, which opened a few years ago. My dad appreciates the familiar, and Nancy and I go along with it because it's not worth arguing over.

Nancy stares out the window, keeping her eye on a teenager who she clearly feels is standing too close to her car. She must suspect he's going to steal her bubbles.

I recognize our waitress from high school. She was a few years older than me and was our star softball pitcher. She was offered athletic scholarships to colleges all over the country, but she stayed home to raise cattle, and apparently, serve it, too.

I've only been gone for a couple of months, but it feels strange to be back as an outsider, especially after severing almost every tie I had. I drifted away from my high school friends when I married Carl, who hated when I spent time with them. I did enjoy hanging out with his friends and their wives, but I know they've sided with him now. I don't want to air our troubles. It's easier just to walk away.

As my dad lifts the Steerburger to his lips for his first bite, he asks if I'm planning to come home or if I'm just going to abandon everything to be wild and free. He says the words *wild* and *free* as if they were spelled with four letters for a reason.

I exhale sharply.

Nancy whips her plasticized beehive head toward me. Dad sets the burger down.

"Em." He wipes his mouth with a paper napkin. "I've got news for you."

I expect he's going to lecture me again about lowering my expectations and give me the "life is no fairy tale" lecture. But he means real news.

"I talked to Mr. Davis at the refinery. I explained your situation, and he understands."

"Understands what?" I ask.

"He realizes that sometimes when you're young you need to chase pie in the sky for a while. He says you should come talk to him while you're down here."

"Why would I talk to Mr. Davis?"

"Aren't you listening? I'm pretty sure we can get you your old job back."

I should believe it, but I honestly can't believe he said that. I look around the restaurant and see nothing but men in torn jeans and trucker hats and women in sloppy Walmart T-shirts that look like pajamas. They spend almost all their time at soul-crushing jobs, and the Boll Weevil is as good as they can do with their day off. This is what my dad wants for me.

But existing in his type of world is no longer an option. That epiphany came six months ago at my annual gynecological checkup. I had spent nearly twenty minutes lying on a table with my feet in stirrups when the nurse practitioner came in and apologized for keeping me waiting. Without thinking I said, "I don't mind. The longer I'm here, the longer I'm not at work." By saying that out loud, I had slapped myself awake. When it's just a thought, it doesn't hit you that you shouldn't be thankful for a trip to the gynecologist to add variety to an otherwise dead life.

When she finished examining me, I returned to my windowless dungeon of an office at the refinery where Mr. Davis was on me to reconcile the crude inventory and calculate gross refining margins. There would be no leaving work until all prep for the audit was finished.

When I got home that night, instead of a hug or a hello, Carl welcomed me with his favorite introductory phrase—"In the future." He somehow thought he wasn't complaining if he said, "Emily, in the future you need to buy the generic toilet paper, not the name brand" or "In the future you need to fold the laundry straight out of the dryer."

That night it was, "Emily, in the future you need to start dinner by five thirty." It was a quarter to six and I had busted my hump to finish work on time.

I went to a United cattle call at the Sheraton the next day. I had been eyeing the ads in the newspaper travel section for months, but I didn't think I had the guts to go for it. Finally though, I was fed up enough to pretend I did.

After Carl left for work, instead of putting on my glasses, I put in the contacts I bought for our wedding along with the suit I wore to my job interview at the refinery. Then I called in sick for the first time in my life, gassed up the car, and drove three hours to the Westin LAX, where I smiled and smiled and smiled

until it hurt. It was thrilling to be in that elegant hotel with its
vaulted ceilings, marble floors, and black leather club chairs. Surrounded by the rush of travelers checking in and out and uni-
formed bellmen pushing luggage carts back and forth, it seemed
easy to act like the outgoing and self-assured type United was
looking for. Lucky for me, they bought it.

Recalling the power of that moment from inside our regular
burger booth, I decide to be unprecedentedly direct with my
dad. "I am not going to go back and work in accounting at the oil
refinery."

He folds his arms over his chest. "Now there's something
wrong with people who work at the refinery?"

It's just like my dad to make everything about him.

Nancy glares at me, visually begging me not to get him
started. In my entire life, I've never seen them fight. She always
rolls over. "His way or the highway," she often said to me when I
wanted to do something all the other kids were doing. I wonder
if Nancy has even once flirted with the highway boundaries.

"Look, Dad. I didn't leave here to make a statement about your
life. It's just that I like what I'm doing right now." I don't tell him
that the thought of living in Bako again makes me want to slit my
wrists. I'm not going to get into the whole "what's wrong with
people who live in Bakersfield" argument. He moved us back here
the minute my mom left and he'll live here until he dies.

As we congregate outside the church, people ask me where my
husband is. I do as Nancy asked and tell them Carl has to work.
Other people who have already heard the gossip say they haven't
seen me since, "Well, you know." They mean my wedding.

I see the groomsmen milling around in tuxedo shirts with
bolo ties and black Wranglers and laugh at KC's suggestion that I

wrestle one of them into the closet. We file into the pews to wait for Tina to sweep her way down the aisle to paradise. The preacher walks in holding his Bible, and for some reason I smile. I suddenly want him to look at my eyes, red from being up all night, and know I'm the practically divorced hussy who spent last night in the arms of a married man. Take that, God. You give me Carl, I'll up you Tien.

Out of the corner of my eye, I see my dad lift his hand. I turn to see who he is waving at. I hope it isn't Mr. Davis. Under the arched doorway, I see Carl. My veins freeze over, and in an instant I have gone from feeling irritated to feeling violated.

Carl starts down the aisle with long, purposeful strides. My dad scoots over to give him room next to me. He looks bad. His skin is pale and his clothes are baggy. He sits next to me without making eye contact.

I don't know if this is all an act for the sake of Tina's wedding or if everyone thinks I can just fall right back into place. I scan the room, but nobody even notices us. They're beaming up at Tina with watery eyes.

Carl shifts in his seat, and I can practically smell the mold of our old, dark condo wafting from his suit. I helped him pick it out when he was interviewing for the Bakersfield Police Department. I should have known something was amiss when he failed the psych exam.

Carl puts his hand on mine and whispers, "Em, I'm sorry."

The ceremony starts and he continues looking forward with a fake smile. His hand is still on mine as if it owns me, as if it isn't burning a hole through me.

I wiggle my hand out from under Carl's and wipe at my eyes as if I'm tearing up about the wedding. The first time Carl took my hand, we were sitting side by side at the Mann Theater watching *Silence of the Lambs*. Just like now, I stared forward at the screen, hiding my reaction, but that time it was pure excitement. I was thrilled to be out with Carl Cavenaugh. He was a junior at North

High, and I thought that would somehow elevate me from my sophomore world. He was cute then, tall and skinny, a swoosh of bangs always falling into his eyes. He smiled more, and his face was smooth and boyish.

By the time I was a senior, I found myself suffocated by his constant presence. I hated that Carl gave up his dream to move to L.A. and major in music, settling for an assistant manager position at Radio Shack. Especially because he said it was to stay near me. I should have been flattered, but I didn't want to be his excuse. And I longed to date Danny Brooks, a cute soccer player in my economics class.

It wasn't that I thought Danny was "The One," but every time he blazed onto campus in his red 300ZX, he made me believe that somewhere, somehow there would be someone more exciting than Carl. After a particularly encouraging conversation with Danny, I told my dad that I was thinking of breaking things off with Carl.

"No relationship is perfect, Em. Don't be the kind of girl who deserts people. You'll spend the rest of your life quitting and nothing will ever be good enough for you."

I knew he was talking about my mom and couldn't help but wonder if she had ended up happy. Still, I decided it was good advice at the time and let Carl become my fallback. Now I wonder what my life would be like if I were more like KC, fearless, the kind of girl who makes things happen.

If I were more confident and carefree, the kind of girl who could cause a scandal, cut class, drive over the speed limit, maybe I wouldn't be here sitting next to Carl, which is more than stifling, it's terrifying. Not because I think he'll hit me again, but because I'm afraid that he won't. If he really did commit to change, where would that leave me? When he told the counselor it was my fault and refused to take anger management classes, I was secretly thrilled. I had my excuse.

As I watch Tina and Paul exchange vows, I think of my new

life and of KC, who is on her way to Frankfurt right now. I wish she were here. Actually, I wish I were with her. We could run around Germany together saying, "*Guten tag*," and "*gesundheit*," to cute guys in lederhosen, sing drinking songs while sloshing beer steins as they urge us to "*trink, trink, trink.*"

Instead, I'm only twenty feet under a preacher's nose and I can't stop thinking that I should have had sex with a married man last night. I want to hold that up like an amulet that will ward off any righteous attempt to get me and Carl back on track. If I *had* had adulterous sex with Tien, everyone in this room, including God, would know there could be no going back.

"Love is patient, love is kind," starts the minister.

Tina and Paul stare at each other with goofy eyes, reciting their lines like new lovebirds who didn't already have a three-year-old. They each say I do, and the second it's over, I push my way out of the pew, up the aisle, and into the parking lot. I had to sit through the service, but I don't have to go to the reception. I'm afraid Carl will come after me, but when I look back, I see my dad jogging toward me.

I reach his car and pull on the handle. I want to get my stuff and walk to somewhere else, anywhere else, but it's locked.

"Emily Leanne," my dad says in his punishment voice.

"Don't even start," I say, still pulling on the car door handle as if it's going to give in and open. "I'm not the one ruining this wedding. You are."

"I was just trying to help."

"By blindsiding me with Carl? We're getting divorced, for God's sake."

His hand still in his pocket, he unlocks the car with the chirp of a key chain. I'm still pulling, so the door flies open, nearly knocking me off my feet.

As I lug my suitcase from his car, I am hit with an astonishing thought. I can call a cab. Until today that kind of freedom would have never occurred to me.

My dad stands there quietly. I know he's expecting me to apologize like I always eventually do.

"There are worse things than stability," he says.

As if life with Carl was stable.

"Trust me," he said. "You'll understand when you're older."

I am so offended by his willingness to sacrifice my sanity and my safety just so he can be right that I snap. "What would you know? You've never taken a chance in your life."

He takes a deep breath, but instead of losing it, he tries to act concerned. "I just don't want you to look back and feel like a failure because you couldn't make it work."

"It wasn't just one time," I say. "Carl was degrading and controlling and jealous and needy and angry all of the time and I can't live like that."

He bites his lip and shakes his head. "Just because a husband wants to be respected and wants to spend time with his wife—"

With his use of the words *a husband*, everything suddenly clicks. He never cared about Carl. He's afraid I'll give Nancy ideas.

I can tell by a flick of his eyes that he knows I've figured him out.

He looks at me and takes a deep breath through his nose. "Emily," he says and takes another even deeper breath. "Emily," he says even louder this time. I brace myself for the onslaught of yelling, but he turns his head away from me.

When he looks back I can see that his eyes are shiny. If I didn't know him better, I would think he was on the verge of tears.

I should feel sorry for him. Instead I suddenly think that maybe she wasn't just a "selfish beatnik" or a "flighty feminist." Maybe my mom had her reasons.

7

How to Be a Flight Attendant

There is only one way to survive life as a new flight attendant. Appear perfect. Luckily, this comes easy for you. You have been pleasing people all your life.

Arrive twenty minutes early for your 4 A.M. check-in. Carefully pin each strand of your hair into a wisp-free French twist. Buff your black high heels on the Buffmaster electric shoe shiner in the preflight groom room. Cheerfully welcome 312 passengers with a well-feigned enthusiasm for predawn departures. Try not to let the guy in 14E remind you of the last man you kissed. With twenty-six thousand flight attendants, the odds of running into him are slim.

Push the beverage cart down the aisle and pass out OJs and coffees and decafs.

Make sure to place the napkins faceup with the airline's logo pointed toward the passenger. You have to be careful. A girl was actually sent home from training for blowing this one.

Ask the man in 17H, "Can I get you something to drink this morning, sir?"

"I don't know if you *can*, but you *may* get me a sparkling water with lime," he says with a scowl.

Sweetly ask him if he would care for ice as you place a can of LaCroix on his tray table with another perfectly aligned napkin. Force a smile and roll on.

Say thank you when people hand you their trash. When the passenger in the middle seat is red-in-the-face angry about her botched seat assignment, compliment her shoes. It works every time. Enjoy giving, giving, giving. You don't ask anything of anyone. You are not in management, worrying about the bottom line. You get to be nice.

A man in business class asks you for an empty soda can. You have no idea what he could want with it, but you pour out a Canada Dry and give him the can. A few minutes later when you are collecting trash, he hands it back. But it's full. And warm. Thankfully, you manage not to drop it in the aisle.

Drink three cups of coffee on the next night's red-eye. On final descent, watch the little boy pressing his face to the glass as his mom leans over him, pointing out the landmarks of their hometown. Look out your window at the glowing Lite-Brite carpet below. From up here, the world is peaceful. The traffic lights cycle from green to yellow to red and there is no swearing or honking. A Ferris wheel quietly turns, no shouting ticket sellers, no screams coming from the neighboring roller coaster. You could get used to this untroubled version of life.

It's morning when you reach your hotel. Sunshine springs from the cracks in the curtains. Seal them shut using the safety pin that kept the gaping neckline on your dress from exposing your chest. Wash your dress in the bathtub and hang it on the shower rod to dry.

Accidentally say good morning when boarding the 7 P.M. flight.

Fly to Columbus and Atlanta and Dallas and Memphis and so many cities you have to check the hotel stationery each morning to remember where you are. Consider moving to each place you land.

—

Check his schedule and see that he will be in San Francisco on Friday. Conveniently arrive at the airport at just the right time. See him walking through the terminal with a girl you don't know. Wonder how many girls he kisses and wonder if he likes this girl with her out-of-date spiral perm. Watch her touch his arm as she says something. Think, *What a slut. He's married.*

But when he sees you, he stops and she doesn't. Smile.

Reciprocate when he reaches in for a hug. Feel the warmth of his body and want to press your head against his chest and be comforted by him. Before you are ready, he begins to pull away.

Look around the airport while trying to think of what to say. Find a place for your hands—try your pockets, then try crossing your arms.

Say, "I just got—"

But he starts to say, "So it looks like—"

"Sorry," he says and waits for you to talk.

Tell him your fake story—that you are there for a meeting with your supervisor.

"I was thinking if you're off tonight and, um, why don't you come for dinner?" he asks.

Suddenly think that if he asked you to dinner so casually, maybe he does this all the time. Begin to dislike him and hear yourself saying you can't because it's a really bad idea.

"I understand," he says, nodding.

Think, *You do?* But say, "It's not that I'm not happy to see you again."

He says that you're a smart girl and that he was so excited to run into you that he got carried away.

Realize that you're resistible. That if you were prettier or more interesting, he would be convincing you to come over.

He says that he's not That Kind of Guy, which makes him perfectly sensible and responsible and completely appealing.

"Well, if you change your mind," he says, trailing off.

Tell him you'll let him know.

Resist for a few hours, then stand outside the door of his hotel room and think about knocking. You don't want to be here, yet you want to be here more than anything you've ever wanted. All of your life, you have acted according to *should*.

Headlights from passing cars shine through the window at the end of the hall. Turn to look outside. Through the fog you see the flashing red martini glass atop the bar where you danced.

You definitely should not be here.

You have to be here. You need him to show you the want and heat and pain of life. One night with him and life will hit you with everything it has at once.

You are technically still married, your papers waiting with a judge, but no one knows where you are. No one is waiting up for you. No one anywhere in the world.

Double-check the number beside the door. 612. Just as you have written down.

Imagine him opening the door, wearing the same layover clothes—jeans and the black T-shirt that clings to his arms and chest. This time he will take them off. His chest will be smooth, hairless, brown. He will smell of vanilla like last time when you got drunk and he kissed you and you swam into that kiss's current with all your strength. Only he wasn't drunk and neither were you. You were pretending.

If you knock, another woman's husband will open the door and he will press you against the wall and slide his hands onto your hips. You will run your hands through his hair, this other woman's husband's thick black hair.

This time when he opens the door, you will let him lay you down on the bed. Let him press you so deep into the mattress you can't crawl out of the shame. He will tell you again that he is to blame. You will say no, no, I am not a good person. I am far from perfect. So love me. Love me anyway.

8

Surrender

KC steps out of the stairwell and onto the tarmac below gate 81. She closes her eyes and takes in the soothing aroma of jet fuel and morning fog. The familiar scent welcomes her back home to SFO, even if it is only for a two-hour sit between flights. The traveling should be fun, but some days, she longs to stand still. After spending her childhood trading apartment complexes and desert towns at her mom's every whim, KC is ready for a break.

She sits down on her suitcase and whips out her last pack of cigarettes. The faster she finishes the pack, the faster she'll be smoke free. She's determined this time. No more smoking, drinking, or eating. It's been two days since her last drink and thirty-six hours since her last meal, except for the coffee with two packets of Equal intended to convince her taste buds she'd had breakfast. Now all she has to do is finish this pack and she'll be able to decontaminate her lungs so she doesn't get lung cancer, too.

While aggressively sucking and puffing her fourth-from-last cigarette, she sits in awe of her own self-discipline and looks around to take in this moment of triumph. Unfortunately, it's not a festive ambience. The rising sun can't seem to cut through the fog, so everything is shrouded in gray—the sky, the mist-draped hills, the miles of concrete tarmac. The only flecks of color amidst the gloom are the blue lights along the taxiways and the fluorescent orange vests of rampers driving by on tugs and fuel trucks and baggage cars.

Out of habit, she checks her phone to see if she's missed any calls from Raj. He called her the other day and said he really liked her but that he was "sort of seeing" someone back in Chicago. Sort of, sure. From her experience, a girl overestimates her dating status, while a guy downplays his. If she says they're "dating," he tells people they're boning. So if Raj says he's "sort of seeing someone" she knows they're living together.

Of course he invited KC over anyway, but there is no way she's going to waste her time and self-respect with that.

A tug with a ramper hunched over its steering wheel speeds toward KC and stops abruptly in front of her.

The driver sits up and says, "Bum a smoke, babe?"

Reluctantly, she nods and digs for one of her three remaining Marlboro Lights. He's not cute, with weathered skin, mangled teeth, and fingerless black gloves, and it's probably sexual harassment, but she loves that he called her *babe*.

The ramper lifts the earmuffs off his ears and hangs them around his neck before getting up to pull the cigarette from her fingers. He clicks his tongue in appreciation and winks at her. They smoke in silence, and a few minutes later after an especially long drag, he lifts his cigarette into the air and says, "These things'll kill ya, you know."

Tell me about it, thinks KC.

The ramper leans back and blows an impressive chain of smoke rings.

KC smiles in approval.

"Just don't tell my wife. She thinks I quit."

KC thinks of his wife and can't help but wonder what else he's keeping from her.

"Where you headed? Somewhere glamorous?" asks the ramper.

"Everywhere. Nashville tonight, and then I don't remember what comes after that." She can't think past Nashville because tonight is the night. She and her dad have scheduled a phone call at 8 P.M. sharp. The thought makes her happy and queasy at the same time.

He finally e-mailed her the other day. It was only a few lines, but he said he was thrilled to hear from her and would have written back sooner if he were better at using the e-mail. He said he's a paper and pencil guy, but that he is indeed living in Hawaii and working in sales.

He said she must be beautiful and all grown up. Then he asked how old she is.

When the ramper is finished, he stomps the butt of his cigarette into the ground and says, "Thank you, ma'am."

She watches as he kicks his tug into reverse and then buzzes toward an outgoing plane that needs a push from the gate. She hates being ma'amed.

With only one cigarette left in her pack, KC takes the elevator upstairs to her briefing where she is told she's getting a "support ride" on her first leg to Portland, Oregon. In reverse-psychology management speak this means a supervisor will sit on her plane with a clipboard and jot down everything she does wrong. She prays it was a random assignment and that they haven't received some sort of complaint against her.

Before they even take off, she's already screwing up. While helping a passenger push his bag into an overhead bin, she doesn't use proper BackSafe form. She forgets to hide the seat belt extender up her sleeve as she hands it to the fat man in row ten. *And* she forgets to boot him from the exit row. Anyone who requires an extender is considered too unfit to open the exit and help evacuate the rest of the plane.

Dick, an aptly named local supervisor, sits in his first-class seat shaking his head and scribbling away on the clipboard. He's newer to United than she is and just got out of supervisor training a few weeks ago. He's five foot even and in his short tenure at United, has already told the entire base that he had always dreamed of being a flight attendant but didn't qualify because he's too short. "Not that I'm bitter," he jokes almost daily from the office where he reviews attendance reports and grooming demerits. Normally she just checks in with him at his desk when she arrives, but today she gets his "support."

She arms her door for departure and grabs her demo kit from the overhead bin. As the purser reads from the announcement booklet, she pulls the oxygen mask completely over her nose and mouth this time instead of holding it out in front of her to avoid other flight attendants' germs. The extra gesture backfires when multiple wisps of hair begin slipping out of her bun.

When she leaves the lav after fixing her hair, she remembers to lock it off for departure so it can't swing out in an emergency and block an exit. She picks up Dick's glass of ginger ale with a smile.

Back on her jumpseat and out of Dick's view, she begins to calm down. It's not going *that* badly.

Then it is. The captain calls back and says they're on a hold from air traffic control and it could be a while. They can't be late. She can't miss her dad's call.

An hour later, they're finally in the air. KC tries not to worry about the delay as she loads the beverage cart with ice and coffee and OJ. A line starts to build in front of the lav, and she realizes she forgot to unlock it after takeoff. She sees Dick standing in the aisle jotting, jotting.

The service quickly falls apart. The other girl in economy is new and so, so, so slow. Plus, with Dick there, rather than handing out whole cans, they have to pour each beverage into a cup, which everyone knows is something you only do in training.

They run out of chicken and then orange juice and then tomato juice. How do you run out of tomato juice? Nobody ever wants that.

They're two-thirds of the way through the cabin and still passing out meals when the call bells in the first rows start going off. The people are sick of sitting with their empty trays. Now, she starts to get really worried. As ambivalent as she is about her future here, she cannot, absolutely cannot lose this job. She has no fallback, no one to take care of her. Getting fired would mean no paycheck, no apartment, no distraction from her mom's condition, and no Hawaii. She has to find her way back to Hawaii.

The second they finish passing out food, she grabs her purse and pops into the bathroom. She meant to quickly touch up her lipstick for Dick's sake, but once inside, away from the clamoring masses, she fears she's going to cry, so she puts the lid down and sits with her head in her hands.

Just one drag. That's all she needs. She stands up and puts the toilet seat up, opens her purse and stares at the cigarette. Fuck it. Before she can think about it, she pulls out the cigarette, sticks her head in the toilet, reaches up, and holds the flush button while she lights up next to the hole.

One, two, three drags and she pulls her head out of the bowl and flushes away the evidence. Then she thinks about the dry flush. What if the butt ignites down there and the plane goes down in flames? She sprays her CK One perfume on herself and into the air, then washes her mouth out with a little pump of soap since she doesn't have any mouthwash. If Dick smells her, she can say the hotel stuck her in a smoking room last night and everything in her suitcase reeks.

He better not search her suitcase. What if he searches her

suitcase? Now she doesn't know what to do with her stash of minis. She can't just put them back into the liquor drawer. How would it look if the carts came back with *more* than they had going out? It just seems wrong to throw them away.

What a way to waste that last cigarette.

Back in the aisle, she picks up, she refills coffees, she checks seat belts and seat backs and the space in front of everyone's feet, and they finally land.

When the last passenger deplanes, Dick says, "KC," and beckons her with his index finger.

She meets him in the first-class galley.

"It was touch and go there for a bit," he says while tapping his pencil against his clipboard. "But overall. Good job." He pats her on the back.

She's so happy and relieved that she follows him right off the plane.

He turns around and says, "Aren't you going to tidy the aircraft?"

Instead of screaming, she cleans up after the slobs of Oregon. After a one-hour hop to any city in Oregon, the plane will inevitably look like it came off a fourteen-hour haul from China—cups and cans and napkins and newspapers litter every row while non-airline-generated refuse from smoothies to Cracker Jacks to gum are ground into the carpet throughout.

Miraculously, KC makes it to her room at the Renaissance Nashville by ten till eight. She fills the coffeemaker to boil hot water for the Cup O Noodles she got from the vending machine and then sits cross-legged on one of the two queen-sized beds.

By the time she finishes her chile chicken noodles, it's a few minutes past eight. She chews on her fingers in anticipation as she waits for her phone to ring. As the clock ticks and the phone remains silent, her anger starts to build. She sits frozen on the bed, afraid that if she so much as moves, her emotions will spill over her edges. She stares at the Impressionist-style painting of the Grand Ole Opry that hangs above the dresser. She considers her reflection in the gray television screen. Her cheeks look a little more full, not less full as she had hoped.

There is a no-smoking tent on the desk, a red circle with a line through a cigarette. She can practically smell the delicious smoke wafting from the cartoon cancer stick. Suddenly, she thinks of something more constructive to do with her time. She will make room 314 a smoking room.

She fumbles through her purse for the pack of Marlboro Lights that she bought in a weak moment as she passed the hotel gift shop. She still hasn't opened the pack, but now she pours all of her attention into packing it against the heel of her hand, carefully peeling the cellophane wrapper away from the box.

She begins feeling good with just the flick of the lighter. She focuses on the flame, gently drawing it into the cigarette and tasting the fresh tobacco of her first drag.

Five cigarettes later KC's phone rings. She doesn't want to answer it. She wants to reject her dad before he can reject her. But she has already puffed her willpower away.

"Kristina?" he says when she picks up. She hasn't been called Kristina since she was ten years old.

He apologizes and says he messed up the time change. "Hawaii doesn't do daylight savings," he says, even though the time changed months ago.

There were plenty of things she had thought of telling him on her way to the hotel, but now her mind is all over the place. So with nothing better, she exhales and asks, "How's the weather out there?"

"Perfect," he says. "You wouldn't believe how great it is here, honey."

She is about to tell him she's actually been there, but he catches her off guard and says, "You should come visit."

"Oh, well, yeah," she says, her smile spreading all the way across the room. "I guess I could do that. I hadn't thought about it, but I do have the flight bennies." For a minute, she is a little girl again, riding on his shoulders through Wildflower Park.

"You'll love it here," he says.

"I'm sure I will." She imagines him teaching her to sail, grilling hot dogs for her by the beach, and showing her off to his friends. She sits up straight and tosses her cigarette in a cup of water.

"You'll see why I came out here."

Her stomach drops to the floor. Why he went out there? As if it's nothing. As if she hasn't been trying to figure that out for her entire life. She would love for him to explain why he went, why he didn't tell her he was leaving. Why he moved to paradise and left her stranded in Tucson and Phoenix and Vegas. Why it's been ten years. Ten years. Why she had to track him down on Classmates.com like a stalker.

He says something about the rat race, about "slow down, this isn't the mainland" and laughs like he made it up. But she already knows that one. She's seen the bumper stickers.

Then she hears a baby crying in the background. A baby? The big-titted bimbo was younger than him, but a baby? Maybe there is a new bimbo bouncing a new even more perfect little baby on her young, shapely hip. For a second she feels sorry for any potential half-siblings lost in the wake, then a bittersweet satisfaction spreads through her. Maybe his second family wasn't better after all, maybe even the oh-so-irresistible bimbo's kids weren't good enough to stand by.

"How's your mom?" he asks. "Still tending bar?"

KC betrays her cool by letting out a sigh. She wishes she could tell him everything so that even though he's an asshole he would comfort her or come for her. But she feels an even stronger need to protect her mom, hide her mom's vulnerability from the man who broke them both.

"Mom's great. She's in management now," she says, although that wasn't even true before she got sick.

"Remarried?"

"Oh no," she says and laughs a forced ha, ha. "She never wanted to do *that* again. There is this guy Rocco who proposed a few times though." Even KC doesn't know where that came from.

Her phone beeps. It's Raj. She can't imagine what the hell he could want now.

"It's my boyfriend and we've been playing phone tag," she says.

"Oh, okay. Well, talk to you soon, Punkin."

Punkin? She wants to say fuck you, fuck you, fuck you for thinking I'm still the girl you used to call your punkin. But if she said that, he'd be gone again.

She clicks over to Raj, but it's too late. He's already hung up. She waits for the message, but he doesn't leave one. It's too bad. She wanted to tell him to get lost. She moved on a long time ago.

9

Room 612

I finally work up the nerve to knock on room 612 at the Richelieu. Tien opens the door. He stands there saying nothing, and it hits me that my presence here is completely indefensible. And worse, I have no plan, no cute opening line. In the movies, lovers don't hesitate or worry about consequences. They tear each other's clothes off in a moment of raging lust. They roll around in the surf or slather each other in clay.

All the way here, I anticipated that kind of instinctual connection. Instead, I have no idea what to say or do. I wish he would take the lead.

Finally, he says, "Come in," and waves me into the room. It looks just like the room we were in last time—pink brocade wallpaper, clashing Kinkade-inspired prints, shiny floral bedspread, and a bay window overlooking the traffic of Van Ness.

I walk toward the bed, mainly because it takes up most of the room. He stays by the door. Light flashes from the TV, but the sound is muted.

"Would you like something to drink?" he asks. Because he's a flight attendant, not James Bond, he pulls a bottle of water out of his suitcase rather than pouring me a martini.

"That's okay." I catch a glance of myself in the mirror. My arms are crossed and I look uncomfortable, uptight even. I drop my arms and suddenly hate being here. Everything about this feels unnatural. It would be different if I was on a layover and staying in a nearby room, but to drive all the way into the city and show up at his door is a blatant statement of availability. He has all the power that I had back when I was pretending to resist.

I wish he would come over and put his arms around me and end the formality, the pressure. Show me that he wants me, that I'm not crazy for being here.

"Why don't you sit down," he says, even though he's still standing, making me feel like he's brought me into his office for a job interview. Only, his suitcase is on the armchair and there's nowhere to sit but the bed, so I say, "I thought we were going to dinner."

He laughs. "Let's go then." He grabs a sweater and pulls it on over his T-shirt. While his eyes are covered by the sweater, I catch a glimpse of his lean, Bruce Lee body flexing and pulling.

He slips on a pair of brown shoes.

It's sprinkling as we walk to Miss Saigon, where he's been a regular for years. He introduces me to the waitress, Cindy, and her father, the owner. It seems bold for him to be inviting me into his world like this, but clearly he wouldn't be doing it if we lived in the same town. Though it is sparsely decorated with Formica tables and padded aluminum chairs, the room sparkles with palm trees wrapped in white Christmas lights. Cindy shows us to a table in the corner facing a red-and-gold altar that has been stacked with chicken thighs, gold-wrapped candies, and a cup of creamy coffee.

"For their ancestors," says Tien. "From my first layover in San Francisco, this city felt like home," he says.

All around us, people are speaking Vietnamese.

I flip through the menu, which is printed on translucent silky paper. "When was the last time you went back to Vietnam?" I ask.

He shakes his head. "I haven't."

"Isn't the rest of your family still there?"

"We couldn't go for the longest time because of the embargo. Then with the kids, we just keep putting it off until they're a little older. You'll probably get there before I will."

Our conversation quickly grows easy, and just like before, the anxiety I carry from city to city dissolves, and I am flooded with a warm sense of home.

He tells me about getting married at twenty-five. "Too young," he says.

Twenty-five sounds old to me.

I imagine the suburban Illinois home and neighborhood he'll go home to tomorrow and mow the lawn. He says he's ashamed to admit that he drives a Camry, an automatic. "I'm jealous you have a stick shift," he says as if it were proof my life is much more exciting than his.

Cindy sets a plate of spring rolls in front of us. Tien carefully squeezes fish sauce and red-hot paste into tiny bowls for dipping.

I dip my spring roll and bring it to my lips for my first Vietnamese meal. The rice paper is cold and smooth but filled with crunchy cucumber and lettuce and mint. The sauce is spicy, sweet, and tangy at the same time.

We are given a big bowl of steaming soup to split. Pho, which he pronounces like a question—*fuh?* He smiles at me, and our hands brush as we reach for the soup. Cindy brings a jar of peppers. "From the back," she says and nods at Tien. "They're too hot for our regular customers."

I watch him slowly open the jar and spoon several tiny red peppers into his bowl. His sleeves are pushed up, drawing attention to the ring on his finger, a simple band. White gold? Platinum?

"You like?" he asks, looking up from his soup.

"Very much." I breathe in the steaming scent of green onions and cilantro, relieved that I'm not in Bakersfield staring down a build-your-own-burger condiment tray at the Boll Weevil.

"The trick is to let it simmer for hours," he says.

I watch him lift a spoon to his lips and blow softly to cool it.

As he refills our water glasses from a pitcher, I notice how slow and deliberate his movements are. He brings a glass to his lips. He winds the noodles around his chopsticks, savors each sip of his soup. His legs are crossed elegantly, and he looks so grown-up. I realize this is the first time I've been out with a *man*.

For dessert, we are given a plate of mandarin oranges. He skillfully peels each one into a continuous long spiral. He licks a sticky finger. I am enjoying the elaborate prelude, but we both know why I'm here.

When we are finished, he folds his napkin and sets it on the table. He neatly stacks our dishes and wipes the table to make things easier for the busboy.

"Next time I'll show you the really hot dish," he says.

"I can't handle spicy."

He laughs. When he stops, his eyes are fixed on me. I imagine their intensity meaning that he needs to see me naked. A tornado of warmth twists through my core.

After dinner we stand on the street in front of his hotel. I'm not sure if we're saying goodbye or not.

"Want to come up?" he asks.

I can't say yes, but I don't want to say no.

"Come up," he says. "You can keep your shoes on again if it makes you feel better."

I won't keep my shoes on.

10

Lucky Break

Determined to get drunk enough to forget her dad's call, KC walks up and down Lower Broadway, one of Nashville's main tourist attractions. She walks along the neon-lit stretch of at least a dozen bars, all with live music, and picks the one advertising a mechanical bull.

It's only 8:30 and the bar is not exactly rocking yet. Only half of the twenty or so tables are occupied, and in a deserted back corner the bull sits idle, its head hanging down as if in despair.

Despite the small audience, an enthusiastic bluegrass band is up on a small stage in the corner wailing away on their steel guitars, fiddles, and banjos. From what she understands, Nashville is a lot like Vegas—everyone is hoping to make it big. But here the end goal is fame, not money.

KC slowly nurses a Jack and Coke and looks around at the mix of clientele. Some look like locals with well-worn Stetsons and scuffed boots. Others sport shiny new cowboy gear, most likely purchased at one of the half-dozen neighboring souvenir shops with signs advertising buy-one-get-one deals. She wonders how many of them are aspiring musicians.

A man with a graying goatee and a blue University of Kentucky ball cap comes over to her.

"You here for the convention?" he asks.

She shakes her head.

"I'm meetin' a lady I work with, but she's running late." He pushes a drink toward her. "Cap'n and Coke," he says. "The ice'll be melted by the time she shows up."

"Oh, no thanks," says KC. "I was just leaving." She's not about to get stuck talking to some lonely guy who would chat up any strange person in a bar.

He looks down and says he's sorry to have disturbed her.

"What convention are you here for?" she asks. She feels bad for him. Being away from home can be hard.

"Buildin' convention. Again, sorry to have bothered you, ma'am." He turns and walks away. She notices that he forgot his friend's drink.

"Sir?" KC says three times, but he doesn't turn around.

Eventually the bluegrass band finishes their set and two guys, both too skinny to be wearing the ultra-tight jeans and oversized belt buckles that seem all too popular in Nashville, strap on acoustic guitars and start playing Eagles covers.

KC still sits with the donated drink in front of her, too self-conscious to order another and look like she's double-fisting. She sees the builder guy talking to the bartender and looking at his watch. She feels bad that she brushed him off and now his friend has clearly ditched him. At this point, she is convinced there are no strings attached. When he looks her way, she waves and mouths the words "Thank you" and takes a sip of the free drink, a lucky break. He nods back. To think she was worried he was trying to hit on her when he was probably just being nice. She was rude, and now she feels even more lonely than before.

She's not sure how much time has passed when she decides to go home. She's starting to feel a little tipsy and completely exhausted and the layover is short anyway. She should definitely get some rest.

She stumbles as she leaves the bar and realizes she must be a little more buzzed than she thought. Her legs are heavy and don't want to move, so she takes extra-big, long strides and it's fun and funny so she laughs, but she doesn't know which direction she's going. Isn't this the way she got here, but it can't be because she doesn't remember the man on the corner with the desk selling hot dogs and the look-alike Minnie Pearl in her gingham dress and straw hat saying "Howwwdeeee!" Music is blasting from every door and it's country and it's rock and it's rap and it's all merging together in the street and becoming an indecipherable mess of noise. She spins around and the neon signs of wagon wheels and cowboy boots and flying pigs start to move and turn and get closer and closer to her and she feels so tired and heavy and can't figure out which direction to go for her hotel. It's just up a street by that tall building or was it that one, or oh God maybe that one with the pointy top.

The builder man from the bar comes up behind her. He laughs and puts his arm around her to steady her and says something about not falling down and about being a bad girl and drinking too much, but she thinks she only had two drinks or maybe she had three, it's hard to remember but it was hardly anything.

He tells her he knows how to find her hotel and that it's not far which is good because she really needs to pee but it just feels so far. Only one block, he says, but that's too far and she feels so sick and he puts his hands on her shoulders for a massage which she doesn't like and she doesn't like him like that and he's thinking she does because she was probably too nice and so stupid to get so drunk and how did she get so drunk so fast? Something is wrong. She knows something is wrong and she has to be sick so she runs through the door with the flying pigs and the builder man from the bar says don't go and she sees a woman with a big white cowboy hat coming at her with a tin bucket and she's saying tips for the band tips for the band and KC says help me and the woman can see something is wrong. She calls her honey and there is commotion and the bartender and the woman with the tips for the band are holding her up by the elbows.

The phone is ringing. By the time KC wakes up and finds the phone it stops. She rubs her eyes and looks around the hotel room. She has no idea how she got there. Her phone starts ringing again, and when she answers, it's the crew desk. Her flight is ready to board and they want to know where she is.

The only thing she can think to say is, "I'm lost."

11

Flying Circus

The clock says 5:30 A.M. when I check out of the New York Hilton. A bellboy offers to carry my bags. With nothing for a tip, I roll my suitcase to the edge of the curb, drop the handle, and sit down on the bag. Five months into this job and I've yet to log eight consecutive hours of sleep.

The hotel doors slide open with an electronic swoosh, and a sixty-something flight attendant jogs outside. A tornado of shopping bags swirls around her. When she looks at me, I have to look away. She's Michael Jackson—skin too tight, nose too plastic. I try not to stare. I've never met her, but since we're in matching navy blue uniforms, for now we're family.

In third grade, I read a book about circuses and for years I wanted to join one. Not because I was double-jointed or a natural for showbiz, but because I dreamed of belonging to a group of wanderers who grew into a family as they moved farther and farther from home. Today, United Airlines is my surrogate circus.

"Oh God. I didn't get enough sleep last night," she says with the voice of a seasoned smoker. "I'm a mess."

She looks a mess with her frizzy blond hair only half re-strained by a once-white now-gray scrunchie. But I'm probably worse. My contacts feel like acid film, and I'm thinking so slowly I can't even remember if I brushed my teeth. I cup my hand around my mouth with a little blow and sniff. It doesn't work, it never does. Just to be safe, I pop a breath mint.

She slips on a pair of Chanel sunglasses, their big gold double Cs reflecting against the overhead lights of the porte cochere. I wonder if they're real or if she bought them for three bucks on a trip to Shanghai. I'm not sure which I think is cooler.

"Did you have a good layover?" I ask.

She nods as she fumbles through her black purse, which could easily double as a diaper bag.

This is my first trip to New York. I didn't have time to explore, so now I soak in what I can of Manhattan from the door of our hotel.

"I'm headed home to San Francisco. How about you?" I say.

"What?" She looks up. "Oh yeah, me, too. I'm based in L.A. but headed to San Fran first. I guess we're working together. I'm Val." She extends her hand but realizes she's holding a hairbrush and just shrugs while pulling her hair out of the scrunchie.

"I'm Emily. Nice to meet you." I pretend to be looking for our van so she has a modicum of privacy to perform her toilette. She brushes, she teases, she sprays. The offensive scrunchie goes into the diaper bag, and with one reassuring look at her compact, Val is satisfied. Her look is a bit *Dynasty*, but judging by the rock on her finger, it's working for her.

I have finally healed the white tan line that clung to my ring finger for months.

"Do you have a mint or gum or something?" Val asks.

"Sure." Maybe she forgot to brush her teeth, too.

Our van pulls up, and the driver leans over to the passenger side, manually rolls down the window, and tells us to hurry up.

We squeeze in next to an American Airlines crew that must have come from a nearby hotel. I stare out the window to watch the few store owners who are already rolling up their metal-grated doors and the early office workers speed-walking in suits and carrying steaming cups of coffee. The city still shimmers with lights even as it reflects the pink-and-orange colors of breaking dawn.

As Val tweezes her eyebrows only to draw them in again, we roll up to JFK, where I revel in the roar of airplanes taking off, and the crowds of eager travelers rushing to ticket counters, security lines, and fast-food restaurants. My earliest childhood memory is of the airport. I must have been really little, but I can just barely remember my real mom taking me to the airport to meet my dad after a business trip.

We sat next to each other in the cafeteria eating pudding. She drank coffee and I had hot chocolate. She bought me a windup PSA 737 that I zoomed along the carpet while an identical full-sized airplane with matching smiley-faced nose pulled up to the gate. My mom held my hand as we leaned against the glass and watched the fuel trucks and luggage cars whiz by.

She seemed happy there. My dad admitted as much, though he probably doesn't remember indulging me in the conversation. He once told me that he met my mom when she worked at a bank near LAX. He said she had worshiped the stewardesses who came to cash their paychecks the way some people fawn over movie stars. She liked her freedom better than she liked us, he said. She deserted us, and my dad moved me home to Bakersfield. Or we moved to Bakersfield and she refused to come with us. Something like that.

"Omelet or fruit plate? Omelet or fruit plate? Omelet or fruit plate?" Val sweeps through each row without managing to look at a single passenger.

I can't keep up as I follow with the beverage cart.

I realize we must be getting low on fruit plates when Val mixes up her pattern. "Would you like the grilled omelet with sautéed mushrooms, cheddar cheese, and a breakfast sausage, or the fruit plate?" she asks. The words *fruit plate* are all but indiscernible. It borders on a cough. They don't teach this advanced meal-conservation technique in training. Like most things about flying, it's something you learn on the job.

"Uh, the omelet I guess," the lady in 23F says. Maybe it worked, or maybe she just likes lard-infused eggs.

I make a few Bloody Marys, a dozen coffees, and a few more OJs. By the time I'm two-thirds through the cabin, my legs are exhausted from the normally benign motion of squatting to find the right soda can in the bottom bins.

"What do you mean you've run out of omelets?" spits a man wearing a wrinkled button-down and a belt with a DIY hole he probably added with a screwdriver. "You just told someone you were getting low on fruit plates."

"I'm sorry, sir. I was mistaken," says Val.

"No, you don't get it. I want an omelet. And you're gonna find me an omelet." He stares straight into her face as if attempting a Jedi mind trick.

"Well, I don't see an IHOP up here, and take a good look at me, sir. Do I look young enough to still be producing eggs myself?" It seems thirty years of seniority has given her enough job security to sass passengers without fearing a write-up or suspension.

The man stands up, slamming his thighs into his lowered tray table and jerking the lady in front of him into her coffee.

"No, you're right. I apologize for the tone, but you're going to have to sit down," says Val.

When he does sit back down, she kneels to his level and puts her hand on his shoulder. With a soothing voice loud enough for everyone around to hear, she says, "I really do understand you're upset. But sir, I told you we ran out of omelets, not jet fuel."

I like Val.

"Well, that was hard work," she says sarcastically when we're done. She has raced through the service and now she has nearly four hours to kill before we land.

"Should I go do coffees?" I ask.

She smiles and says, "Not yet, sugar. Let 'em rest for a minute."

Like the girls my mom once envied, Val is a sixties stewardess. I can just see her taking a last-minute drag from her Virginia Slims in the galley before shaking martinis and carving prime rib in the aisle. Although she preceded the service downslide, she has clearly embraced it.

She looks at me, contemplating something. "Look," she says. "You gotta relax. I love your attitude. And maybe I could stand to be a bit more, um, accommodating. But you—don't let them walk all over you. Pretty soon you'll be thanking passengers for handing you trash and apologizing when they hit you in the head with their suitcases."

I pull down the jumpseat to get off my feet for a few minutes. I wonder if I'll still be up here when I'm Val's age. I ask her how long she's been flying.

"Forever," she says and points her index finger at me. "But don't you dare call me a senior mama. I've got a long way to go before I'm Iris."

I've yet to see Iris, but she is a legend. Number One, the senior-most flight attendant we've got. To put that into perspective, I currently rank 25,674 on the flight attendant seniority list. Iris is eighty-two years old and got hired by United in 1943, before planes were pressurized, when it took all day to get from Seattle to San Francisco because under ten thousand feet, they had to dodge the mountains. She's been up here ever since, feebly pushing that beverage cart down the aisle like it's her crippled husband's wheelchair. I've heard that every year at recurrent training, someone tries to revive Annie the CPR doll by tapping her and saying, "Iris, Iris, are you okay?"

"You'll get the hang of it," says Val. "You just have to think,

unless we start blowing slides or donning life vests"—she crosses
herself—"this isn't rocket science. We have some food, we pass it
out. They get what they want, great. If not, tough luck."

A little boy comes running into the galley, a tiny sweatshirt
swinging from around his waist.

"Wait, wait, wait," says Val as she grabs his shoulders before
he can reach the lav. She spins him around and asks after his
mother, using her eyes to point to the boy's bare feet.

He claps his arms against his sides, tilts his chin up, and yells,
"Moooooooooooooom."

A girl about my age anachronistically dressed in a pink, pearl-
trimmed sweater set and sporting a soccer-mom bob runs back
from midcabin. When she sees there is no emergency, she says,
"Hunter Slayton, what did I tell you about yelling?"

Val pushes the boy to his mother and says, "Put some shoes
on him. That isn't water on the bathroom floor."

The mother nods and marches her son back to his seat.

"You're good with kids," I tell Val.

"Yeah, right. My dogs are my kids."

A few minutes later, I get up to brew some coffee and she
whips out her photo album to show me shots of her two yellow
Labs running through waves, standing up to look out the window, and then lying next to the toilet, as if they'd had a long
night.

We all have travel-sized albums, just big enough to show a
few pictures of our "real" life. My pictures? Shots of KC and our
messy apartment by the airport.

Val squats down and starts rifling through the liquor drawer.
"You know, if I'd had a kid when I was married, it'd be about
your age." She continues searching until she's pulled out six
Johnnie Walker Black Labels and then throws them into the
waiting diaper bag behind the last row of seats. "What's your
poison?"

We can be fired if we take anything off the airplane—half-eaten leftovers or a half-empty water bottle. It's all company property.

I shake my head.

"Suit yourself. So what's your story anyway?"

"My story?"

"Got anything juicy for jumpseat therapy?"

I try to buy her off with a small tidbit. "I got a tattoo last week."

"Hmm. Where?"

"My lower back." KC talked me into it.

She makes a *pshhh* sound. Not impressed. Personally, I thought it was pretty wild. Not as wild as KC's four-inch palm tree, but wild.

"It's forever though. What if I hate it someday? It was a pretty crazy thing to do."

"Oh honey, it's not permanent. I got one in the same place and it fell into the great divide years ago."

A man in a business suit clears his throat and steps into the galley. He looks to Val and says he *really* needs to go to the bathroom.

"The seat belt sign is on, so I'm not allowed to give you permission." She winks. "Interpret that as you will."

He rubs his head and mutters something that includes *god* and *damn* before saying, "But I *really* have to go. I'll be really quick."

"Sir, I can't explicitly give you permission. Interpret . . . that . . . as . . . you . . . will," she says, enunciating her words carefully.

He does a literal about-face and heads back to his seat.

Val rolls her eyes. She asks me if I'm seeing anybody.

"Kind of?" I say, adding a high-pitched question mark at the end. This is to give her an opportunity to shake her head and say she doesn't want to know.

"Oh, do tell."

I'd like to say, "I know, I know, it's terrible." But it isn't terrible. It's wonderful.

So wonderful that I'm still trying to convince myself I can walk away from it if I wanted to, a junkie's excuse I've been using from the beginning. That first night after dinner at Miss Saigon, I gave myself permission to follow him back to his hotel. After all, I could leave anytime. We tried to act natural as we strolled through the lobby of the Richelieu, both fully aware of what would happen when we were alone. I looked at my watch and considered making up an excuse.

But when he opened the door to his room, a current of desire swept through my knees. I let him pull me inside. He pressed his lips to my collarbone, my shoulder. I felt my shirtsleeve slipping off my shoulder.

He was nothing like Carl.

I was different, too. Knowing I wouldn't see him again and having absolutely no expectations, I allowed myself to completely let go.

I felt the heat of his lean, smooth body and threw myself into the moment. Within moments I knew what I'd been missing out on all these years, this hunger, this intensity. Even completely naked, I wasn't the least bit self-conscious.

I wrapped my legs around him and pulled him close. He took his time. I burned with lust.

Now every Friday and Sunday night, Tien opens the door to his hotel room, sees me, and breaks into an enormous smile. I see a whole new me in that look. Not the girl from the passport photo I had taken before reporting to Chicago for training. That girl had limp mousy hair, and wire-rim glasses covered her makeup-less, soul-less eyes. She was a body without a person inside. I have to carry her around with me at all times in case I'm thrown on an international, and every time I flip open to that picture I am reminded of the life this job has breathed into me. I think of the new me and see 747s and shimmering skylines. I feel

Tien sliding his hands along my hips, making me feel curvy and confident, sexy and mature.

I use Val's fruit plate voice and mumble that he's married.

"Just don't tell me he's a pilot."

"Flight attendant."

"That's no biggie."

She sounds like the employee assistance therapist I went to once and only once. After the first night with Tien, fearing I would combust from the guilt, I sought out the good doctor and told her that I'd done something truly horrible and that I was going to hell. She looked up from her notepad and leaned in, possibly anticipating the mouthwatering moment she had been waiting for all day. When I revealed that I'd slept with a married man, she slumped back in apparent disappointment and told me not to beat myself up too much—what I'd done was actually, in her words, "garden variety." I may have feared confessing, but I'd hoped for more disapproval than that. Maybe if she had assigned a few Hail Marys, I would have felt absolved.

I still hope for a path to absolution every time I spill my guts on the jumpseat, but my flying partners inevitably say something like, "Been there, done that, get rid of him," or they look to the door handle as if they want to push me out.

I know how it sounds, but I didn't expect things to go this far. After two months, what should have been just a rebellious rendezvous is starting to feel serious.

A few weeks ago, he had a luxuriously long layover, twenty hours instead of the typical eleven or twelve. We let ourselves pretend we were real. We sampled wine at a local tasting room, shared a chocolate sundae at Ghirardelli Square, and then walked across the Golden Gate Bridge, bracing ourselves against the cool, gusty wind. We held hands as we admired the awe-inspiring height of the rust-colored towers, the patience and courage of the people who built it.

Being surrounded by thousands of tourists only added to the romance, because to them, we were just another couple, no doubt with an adorable story about how we met.

"We could say we met at church," I suggested.

"Or online."

"How about a reality show?"

"You know, we could just tell the truth. That you got me drunk and picked me up at a bar."

I nudged him toward the side of the bridge.

"Well, let's see a picture," says Val, as if a married lover is as natural as a new baby or a pair of yellow Labs.

"I don't have one," I tell her. "Things haven't gotten that bad yet." Unfortunately, that's a lie.

A few weeks ago, after we'd had a couple of glasses of Napa wine, I pulled out my camera so that someday when he is gone I would have something to remind me that I know how to live with passion and abandon. Every time we're together, I assume it will be for the last time, that his wife will say or do something wonderful and our time together will end. He must have thought so, too, because he wanted copies. We sat on the armchair in a room at the Richelieu, him on the seat, me leaning toward him from the arm. We held the camera out in front of us and smiled our cheesiest flight attendant smiles, only they were real.

A little while later I took a picture of him looking out the window at the taxis and pedestrians on Van Ness. "You look so handsome," I said.

"I need to get you drunk more often."

He said he would keep the pictures in his company mailbox at O'Hare, but the other day he told me that he was in a daring mood and brought one of them home. The one that was just of him, because, "I know who's behind the camera."

He expected me to find this romantic. I worry that he's getting careless.

"Well then, tell me what he's like," Val says, which almost makes me cry. The chance to speak of him uncensored leaves me dumbstruck.

Not used to such talk, I hardly understand her as she says, "You never know."

"What do you mean?" I ask.

"I'm just saying. It could work out."

"I can't see how."

"It worked out for me." She slips a locket from under her uniform.

"This is my fiancé, Ken." She just looks at the photo instead of showing it to me, so feeling obligated, I go over to take a look.

"Ooh, he's cute," I say. I'd say that no matter what to be polite, but this time I mean it. He looks about my grandpa's age, with a beaming smile like he's just told a hilarious joke and is proud of himself. "When's the wedding?"

She doesn't answer, but instead tells me how they met thirty years ago on the plane, when she was a hot stew and he was a young lawyer. They were both married, but she managed to lay over in his hometown of Eugene almost every Tuesday for twenty-eight years. They had a weekly lunch date but she swears no funny business. They were just friends.

I'd believe her, but I said the same thing yesterday when KC was pestering me about Tien. But twenty-eight years? Could I possibly keep this going for twenty-eight years?

"Then I got divorced, oh, way back," says Val. "And then his wife passed away a couple of years ago. So last summer, we finally got together and it was bliss." She smiles and is lost for a minute.

I smile back at her. If I can just hold on for twenty-eight years. "All the way until February."

"What happened then?" After all that time, could he really have just wanted her because he couldn't have her?

"In February, Ken had a heart attack and died."

She looks straight at me, confronting me, searching for my reaction as if I have some answer for her.

Tears begin to fill her eyes, but then she closes them, takes a breath, and calmly drops the locket back under her dress.

As if we hadn't even been talking, Val pulls down the jump-seat, labels the lav in front of her OCCUPIED so when the light goes out, no one will make her stand up, and opens a dog-eared Danielle Steele paperback.

Only a minute later, she says, "God, I'm bored," and grabs a pot of coffee in one hand and a tray with milk and sugar in the other and heads out into the aisle. Although her hands are clearly full, a man tries to hand her some trash.

She says, "Why don't you stick a broom up my ass and I'll sweep the aisle while I'm at it."

12

Going Home

KC sets a fresh bouquet of orchids on the little rolling stand beside the bed where her mom sleeps. She tiptoes to the window and pulls back the curtains to let natural light into the pale peach room that boasts nothing more than a television, an oxygen tank, and an IV pole for décor.

Through the window, she can see the gleaming skyline of the Strip just beginning to glow against the waning afternoon sun. Only a few miles away, blue lights shimmer on the McCarran runway, and a 737 screams down the runway, lifting off into the promise of an unknown destination.

She hears a cough from behind her and turns. For at least ten years her mom has been waking with a cough. When she was a teenager and up to no good, it came in mighty handy. There was always ample time to turn off the R-rated movie, crack open the science book, shuffle a boy out her bedroom window.

KC's mom lifts her head a bit. "You made it." Her voice is raspy yet cheerful.

There was a time when her mom's voice was achingly beautiful. When KC was a little girl, her mom would pick her up and dance her around the house while singing tunes from *West Side*

Story and *The Sound of Music*. Apparently, she had always wanted to be an actress, but, as she would often say with a sigh, "life got in the way." Every now and then when KC was a kid, she would audition for hotel productions. Once she even got a part in the chorus of a community theater rendition of *Evita*. Unfortunately, she got cut for missing rehearsal. That must have been one disappointment more than she could bear because she soon gave up for good.

"Sorry for waking you," says KC.

"Oh, I'm not sure I was actually asleep."

KC puts the back of her hand to her mother's forehead.

Her mom closes her eyes for a second, but then pushes KC's hand away with a smile. "You know they have high-tech stuff here, don't you? Like thermometers for example."

Since getting sick, her mom has resisted any attempt on KC's part to be the caretaker. "We have nurses for that," she'll say and wave her hand jokingly like an heiress talking about the help.

"Your hair's growing back," KC says, trying to sound positive.

Her mom half laughs, half coughs. She presses a remote, which folds her bed into sitting position. "It's white though. Beg as I might, they won't dye it for me in here." She inhales sharply to recover from speaking.

KC puts her finger to her lips to encourage her mom to rest.

Her mom continues on. "But it came in curly. I always did want curly hair." She gently fluffs what little hair she has as if she had just had it set in hot curlers.

"Funny," says KC. She does not feel up to laughing.

Her mom looks in her direction and sniffs.

KC steps back, afraid her mom can smell the cigarette she smoked in the parking lot, as if once on the scent of betrayal, her mom will then find out what else she's been lying about.

Her mom gives her a look but doesn't comment. The look is as much about envy as it is disapproval. She is always saying the worst thing about lung cancer is not being allowed to smoke.

She'll beg the nurse for one drag and when the request falls on deaf ears, she'll say, "What, are you afraid I'll get cancer?"

KC pulls the woven hospital blanket up to her mother's shoulders to stop her shivering. "How's your right side? Did you ask the doctor about that pain?"

"It's fine."

She checks her mom's catheter bag for output. It looks low. "Are you comfortable? Does it feel like the line might be blocked again?"

"KC. I told you I'm fine."

"Okay, okay," says KC, though she doesn't believe anything is okay.

"You missed *Days,*" her mom says. "It was a good one."

From kindergarten through high school, when KC was off for the summer or a school holiday, watching *Days of Our Lives* was their ritual. They would sit in front of the TV with egg salad sandwiches—lunch for KC and dinner for her mom, who had usually just finished a night of running chips at a casino or pulling pints in a bar. Her mom would catch her up on all she'd missed and they would talk smack about the characters whose lives, her mom loved to point out, were more fucked up than theirs.

Every so often, her mom would surprise her at school and take her out of class for a "doctor's appointment." Sometimes they would stay home and watch *Days,* but other times they would head out into the world—pretend they could afford the Gucci and Pucci on display at casino shops, gorge on discount prime rib and crab legs at buffets, or sneak into hotel pools. It may not have been stable having a mom who acted like a friend, but it was fun.

KC tries to humor her mom, pretend it's the old days and they still care what happens on a silly TV show. "So what's new? How is Bo? Did they find out who J.T.'s real dad is yet?" asks KC.

Her mom looks confused.

"Did Hope say anything?"

"Oh, *Days*. Hmm, I don't remember. I must have fallen asleep. Tell me about your life. It must be more exciting than some old soap opera."

With all the deception, KC's life is actually starting to feel like a soap opera. Unbeknownst to her mom, her dad e-mailed her again and once again mentioned a visit. Someday. She's been too proud to respond, but after that awkward phone call, she was relieved that he got back in touch. She has read and re-read the e-mail so many times that the words now seem senseless. Yet every time she opens it, she hopes to decipher the real meaning between the lines, like a poem hiding a profound and enlightening truth.

The first few reads were thrilling, and all of the old hurts seemed as if they could heal. But then she realized she had ignited a new cycle of betrayal. Going behind her mother's back, keeping secrets from her, communicating with the man who wronged her.

The last time KC brought him up, five years ago, her mom lost it. She yelled, "What? I'm not enough for you?" and then slammed the car door with her own finger still in it. Several curse words were followed by their first trip to the ER together.

"Well," KC says, deciding to distract her mom with her latest trip. "Do you want to hear about Detroit or Charlotte or Nashville?"

"Nashville, obviously. Did you go to Graceland?"

"No, I didn't have time for Graceland. Wait. Isn't that in Memphis?"

"Oh, I don't know. That sounds right."

"Anyway, you'd have liked Nashville. Every single bar and restaurant has live music. Not just country either. It all starts to kind of blend together into noise when you walk down the street, but it's so alive and exciting."

"I hear Nashville's tough. All those people trying to make it."

The nurse pops into the doorway and flips on the light. "Good to see you're awake. And lovely to see you again, my dear." She turns to a cart in the hallway and slides a meal tray from a shelf.

KC is warmed by Fiona's presence and glad she's on shift. She's always calling KC "darling" and "love." They hardly know each other well enough for pet names, but KC lets the endearments soothe her.

Fiona is from Kent, a place known as the garden of England. KC can't understand why anyone from somewhere green and brimming with life would move to Las Vegas where everything is brown and dying.

"How are you feeling?" Fiona asks KC's mom.

Her mom, of course, says, "Fine."

"Last time I was here, she was having a pain in her right side. Down here," says KC, pointing to her own abdomen. "Have you guys done anything to address that?"

Her mom rolls her eyes, and Fiona recommends talking to the doctor when he comes by for rounds.

"What about the catheter? I notice that there's not a lot of output in the bag."

Fiona looks at the bag carefully, noting the seventy-five milliliter mark. "We just cleared it and emptied the bag, so the output looks appropriate. But good job keeping an eye on these things."

"Sorry," says KC, though she suspects Fiona understands her need to stay involved. She can't be the only loved one trying to make up for not being there as often as she should. In fact, she learned this from her mom. She was never as concerned with the state of KC's math scores as she was after working a series of double shifts or spending a few nights at a new boyfriend's place.

Fiona sets a bowl of cream of broccoli soup in front of KC's mom, who makes a face and says, "This again?"

Fiona shakes her head. "Well, madam, we shan't let you leave here without one last helping."

"Leave here?" says KC. "You're finally leaving?" They've been waiting for this for months. She was only supposed to be in the hospital a few weeks, but then there was a complication with the lobectomy and then the infection and then a surgery to fix the first surgery and then another infection and then the pneumonectomy and then the hospital room slowly became home.

Her mom and Fiona exchange glances. "Yes, dear. My luck is finally changing."

"You're going home?"

Her mother smiles.

KC has to stop herself from jumping up and down like a child. Her mommy is coming home.

They'll move back in together and eat egg salad sandwiches and sneak into hotel pools. Maybe someday she can transfer to the Las Vegas base or move her mom to San Francisco.

She feels so much lighter that she almost wants to confess that she's been in contact with her dad. Who knows, maybe her mom would be happy about it. Maybe they would finally talk and smooth things over.

Fiona leaves the room, and KC pours her mom a glass of water.

"I want to hear all about Paris again," says KC's mom.

"You'd love Paris. It's so beautiful this time of year." She just watched the movie *French Kiss*, so she tries to think of some authentic details. "The cheese is incredible. I gorged on it until I felt sick. And you have to watch out for pickpockets, but as long as you're careful you can walk along the Seine and pop into a *boulangerie* for a baguette, and ride to the top of the Eiffel Tower." As she grasps at details, she starts wishing she'd never made up the Paris layover.

"Okay, okay. I know you've been there, done that. Now tell me. Are there any boys? Anyone special?"

There are no boys. No one worth mentioning anyway, but her mom looks so hopeful and excited. The only action in her mom's life happens on television, and KC knows she's the entertainment tonight. So she lies.

She says she met a wonderful guy named Raj who lives nearby, a real gentleman who takes her out to fancy dinners and never lets her split the bill.

Her mom looks happy enough to cry. "Someone to take care of my baby."

KC struggles to describe her deepening relationship with Raj and is relieved when her mom dozes off. She sits quietly, watching her mom breathe just a little bit easier.

It's not like they haven't always known this could happen. Every year of elementary school came chock-full of warnings about cigarettes and secondhand smoke. For a long time, KC was certain her mom would kill her since they always chose the smoking section at Bob's Big Boy. No matter where KC sat, clouds of smoke would drift in her direction. When she complained, her mom would just say, "Smoke follows beauty."

Her mom wakes with a cough. "Sweetheart, can you turn on the radio?"

They listen to the best of the eighties and nineties—Billy Joel and Elton John and the B-52s. Bette Midler sings "Wind Beneath My Wings," but when KC remembers what the song is about, she jumps up to turn the channel.

Her mom stops her. "I like these songs. Every one of them is a memory."

"God, this one is so depressing."

"Sweetheart," her mom says. "I'm not going home."

KC flinches. She can guess what happens next, but she doesn't want to hear it.

Her mom tries to explain, but KC is distracted by the heartbeat thumping in her ears. Unfortunately it's not loud enough to block out the words "hospice" and "comfort care" and "metha-done" and "months, not years."

KC is biting her lip and shaking her head because this can't be happening. She stands up and turns to the window so she doesn't have to look at the truth that is bearing down on her.

Her mom says, "Remember when you got your training wheels off?

"Remember when we tied notes to balloons and set them free in the park?

"Remember when you were scared of the clowns at Circus Circus?"

"Stop it," KC says.

"Remember when we went shopping for your prom dress?

"Remember when I picked you up at the police station when you were at that rich kid's party?"

As KC fights back tears, her mom is still smiling about that time with the cops, the time her daughter got invited to hang out with the charmed kids whose parents were "the entertain-ment," singing or cracking jokes instead of dealing or stripping for tips like the rest of them.

"Remember those impossible Rollerblades when we went to the beach in L.A.?

"Remember when there was a scorpion in the kitchen and you were so damn scared?"

That was nothing. KC has never been as scared as she is now. She doesn't know how to live without her mom.

She tells herself she's strong. That she has always taken care of herself. More and more lately she has been focusing on the times her mom wasn't there. How she let herself into their apartment after school with a key tied around her neck. How she made herself macaroni and cheese while her mom worked nights. But when she broke her wrist playing dodgeball, when she got sick and had to leave school, when she faked sick so she

could leave her dad and his bimbo on their weekend, when her
dad skipped town, no matter how inconvenient it was, her mom
was always there.

And there it is, the familiar thought. If she had been a better
daughter, this might not be happening. She knows she shouldn't
feel that way. Every school counselor she's ever had has told her
it is irrational, but she can't help thinking that if she had been an
easier kid, if she hadn't broken the screen door and she hadn't
needed to get her tonsils out and she hadn't lost the car keys,
they would all be together and happy.

"I'm quitting my job."

"You're not quitting your job."

"I'm quitting and I'm moving home and I'm taking care of
you." She doesn't need the plane tickets anymore. She would
trade her dad's life in a second. Maybe if she stops wondering
about him, her mom will get better. Maybe if she could stop asking for so much, stop trying to make things how they were and
just appreciate what she has, this test will be over.

"No." Her mom shakes her head vigorously, and though the
machine is on silent, KC can see the blips on the heart monitor
getting taller and coming faster.

"Yes."

"I want you to have a better life. You've already seen more
than I could have dreamed of."

If only her mother knew that the glamour she dreamed of
was just normal life in other places. Layovers spent buying
pantyhose in Atlanta and cough syrup in Dallas, getting shoes
repaired in Los Angeles and a filling replaced in Chicago. "I'm
coming home."

"Over my dead body."

Her mom has been using that phrase for decades, but this
time KC begins to cry.

13

You Know the Drill

The crew desk has kept us apart for weeks, so only a few hours after checking out of my hotel in Los Angeles, I decide to surprise Tien at *his* hotel in San Francisco. I am wearing nothing but high heels and black lacy lingerie under my United raincoat.

He opens the door.

I open my coat.

"It's so good to see you," he says over and over as he pulls me onto the bed. For twenty minutes, we lie there holding each other, my coat and shoes still on.

I rest my cheek on his chest. He strokes my hair, and I am at peace. Despite our impossible circumstances, in this moment, life feels uncomplicated.

He traces my body with his hands, resting on the widest part of my hips, making me feel voluptuous, womanly, confident. This is it, this is everything I missed while playing the good daughter, the good wife.

He looks at me with an expression of awe.

Tien moves slowly, leaving no place untouched. He unhooks my bra. Unsnaps a garter. Follows my curves with his lips.

He is willing to invest everything in my pleasure. I wrap my

silk-covered legs around him. Before long we are a tangle of arms
and legs, hips and thighs, slick with sweaty rapture.

Being with him makes me feel like the homecoming queen,
the kind of girl who deserves to be admired and loved, a girl who
would never think to doubt her worth.

When there is nothing left to give, I flop back against the pillow. Even though I don't smoke, I want a cigarette. Something
about the act of taking a drag and blowing out a rebellious swirl
of smoke would perfectly express how I feel—exquisitely de-
pleted, content, and ready to say screw what's right or wrong,
this is what I want.

I leave his hotel at 3:30 A.M. to head to the airport. I drag my
suitcase uphill toward my car. It clacks against each crack in the
sidewalk, alerting the quiet neighborhood to my departure. As I
pass a group of guys my age who are milling around outside
Mel's Drive-In, a muscle-bound guy with a can of Miller Lite in
his hand looks at my uniform and half sings, half yells, "I'm leaving on a jet plane."

Twelve hours later I reach another hotel in Oklahoma City. I
try to sleep even though it's still daytime and I'm four floors above
the pool. Kids are shouting "Marco" . . . "Polo" . . . "Marco" . . .
"Polo" . . . "Marco" . . . "Polo." I fantasize about holding them under water. But I don't mind in the end because their noise means
I'm awake when Tien calls me from home, whispering.

Three months together and I am spending all of my days on
and my days off in hotels. From the beginning I've been trying to
convince myself it's the perfect situation. I can have all of the
fun with none of the responsibility. He is not my husband.
He will not accuse me of neglect when the mayonnaise is on
the wrong shelf or the hospital corners aren't tight enough or
when I buy the brand-name rather than generic raisin cereal.

I can travel to dozens of new cities, free to explore their restaurants and shops and parks all on my own, knowing the whole
time that I'll soon be welcomed home by Tien.

Whenever he opens the door to his room, I smile, and not because I have to. It's no longer part of the uniform. It's part of my life, this happiness. When I walk into the room, I can see the joy in his face. When we make love, I know it will be slow and sensual and magnificent and nothing like Carl's quick pump and grunt. He will brush the hair out of my eyes and put his hands around my face and kiss me like I am the water supply that will bring him to life.

I can relax, slump my shoulders, knowing that even if I cry, he will stay. I bask in his kindness.

As summer fades and the leaves pile into a soft and colorful ground cover, we have gone from exploring the city together to developing routines. We sip our morning coffee in Parisian bistro chairs atop Russian Hill. Every time, I know he'll get an Americano and dip his croissant into it. In the evening, we always end up at Miss Saigon. I pretend we are a genuine couple when Cindy starts waving and bringing soup without asking— shrimp for me, beef and extra-hot peppers for him.

One night he says, "Maybe I'll take you to Vietnam someday when I finally go back."

"That would be lovely," I say, though I only know the country from brief military history units in high school and college.

"It would." He stares off into space. "We could walk along the bay and pick mangos from the trees. We could ride bikes along the river, see the countryside from top to bottom. I've always wanted to do that."

I'm touched that he would even fantasize about taking me there.

For a while he says nothing, continuing to stare into the distance. "I like to imagine Vietnam as it could be now, not how it was when I left. I'm not sure what it would be like to return."

"What was it like when you left?"

He shakes his head.

I don't look away, and I hope he'll take that as encouragement to talk.

Without blinking, he says, "It was war."

I nod as if I understand, which obviously I don't.

"The last thing I saw was my dad racing away from the bay after pushing me into a boat full of strangers."

"To come here?"

He looks down at his bowl as he speaks. "Eventually. First there was the refugee camp in Thailand."

I nervously prepare myself to hear about the scars and the trials that have made the man I am beginning to love. I'd like to be there for him as he has been for me, listening to my fears that Carl will come to find me, the frustrations of waiting for the divorce to go through.

"It's not something you want to hear," he says. But he still looks like he'd like to share more.

Before he can continue, Cindy comes over with a pitcher of water to refill our glasses. Tien sits up straight and is smiling again. "Thank you," he says, with complete composure.

I wonder if she was there, too, or if she is too young and only knows about the past through her parents' memories. She turns to me. "Is there anything else you'd like to order?"

"No, thanks."

She looks to Tien, and he shakes his head.

When she leaves, I give him a moment to continue. He doesn't, so I gently prod. "You were saying?"

He grabs a menu at the side of the table. "Nothing. I was just thinking about whether or not we should have ordered an appetizer."

I want to know more about his past. And I also want to know more about this future he sees, a future that includes us traveling to Vietnam.

He studies the menu.

"Is there anything traditional, something you remember from home that I just have to try?"

He shakes his head and sets down the menu. "I think you're

starting to become a regular here. You probably know their se-
lections as well as I do."

I nod, enjoying the fact that I'm so comfortable in his world.

"Maybe we need to branch out. Maybe we should try a new
place next time."

I sense that his reluctance to let me in is about more than his
marital status. "You don't talk about Vietnam much," I say.

"No."

"You want to go back though?"

He sighs. "I've been meaning to. You know, when my dad
died a few years ago, I couldn't even go to the funeral because of
the travel embargo." He looks away, and I wonder if he's holding
back tears.

I think of my own dad, and for all his ills, I would be devas-
tated if he died. Especially if we hadn't seen each other in decades. We weren't always so cold with each other. Before he met
Nancy, who related more easily to girls and mostly took over
raising me, he would push aside his discomfort and play Barbie
or clumsily attempt to put my hair in braids and ponytails.

I reach out and put my hand on Tien's. "I'm sorry."

"Don't be," he says. "It's just the way it is."

"You should definitely go," I say, conscious of sounding too
upbeat. I meant to say *we* should go, but I don't have the courage.

Over the next few weeks, he continues to talk about the future
as if we have one together. He sees us walking side by side
through airport terminals, wheeling our matching suitcases
around the country, eating dinner in Omaha, waking up in Albany. He calls me *honey* and *babe* and plans which flowers we'll
plant in a garden we'll someday tend together, considers ingredients in Asian meals he will teach me to cook, all of this as if he
weren't actually married and on his way home to her.

Our conversation is filled with delusion.

"Where else do you want to go on vacation?" he asks one evening, ready to plan out an imaginary jaunt. "Buenos Aires? Cape Town? Casablanca?"

"Why not all of them?" I mean this half sarcastically, knowing we will never go.

He grins widely and wraps his arms around me. "I love it. Your sense of adventure is infectious. You inspire me to travel again."

It occurs to me that I am his weekly escape, his glimpse at freedom. He doesn't realize that he is my sanctuary, the safe place I belong between trips.

"It's not that I don't like my life," he says. "I'm proud of it. Stability, it's what I wanted."

"But?"

"I had nearly forgotten there was more to me."

I like that I, too, bring things out in him. It is through his eyes that I'm starting to see myself as courageous and strong. "How about Venice?" I say.

"That would be nice. We could look out over the city from the Campanile and cruise the canals in a gondola. Or we could go to London and watch the changing of the guard."

Day after day, he pretends to be free, and I pretend I belong to him.

Lately, I am having a harder and harder time accepting that I don't. I start to envy the things we can't do, the regular stuff of life like paying taxes and making breakfast. I'm getting sick of knowing none of it will ever happen.

One day I say, "I think I'll move to Europe."

"You should. You'd like it there." He believes I can do anything I want to since I'm unfettered, full of options.

"Wouldn't you miss me?" I ask.

"Of course, but you know my situation."

I hate that he refers to his family as his *situation*. I hate that we talk about forever when we don't even believe in tomorrow.

Eventually I start wondering if he could be having a midlife crisis and I'm the Corvette he can ill afford. "Do I make you feel young?" I ask one day.

He laughs. "No. You make me feel old!"

"Old? That can't be good."

"It's not bad. It's just that compared to you I'm, I don't know. I'm crickety."

"Crickety?" I laugh.

"One of these days you're going to realize it, and that will spell the end of Tien."

I shake my head. "That's not going to happen."

"You need someone who can keep up with you. I'm going to be forty soon."

"In four years!"

"Still, I've got a lot of younger competition out there."

"You're right. I meet planeloads of incredible prospects every day."

"You do?" he asks, perhaps worried for a second. But then he starts to laugh.

The routine continues. Week after week it's the same. He falls asleep in his contacts so he can see me the moment he opens his eyes. I keep my eyes open to hold on to one more minute where I feel like the whole world is in our hotel room.

Then the alarm goes off and he gets up to take a shower. I lie alone in the bed reaching my arm out to him. "Don't go."

"Stay in the room awhile. I'll tell the front desk." He closes the bathroom door.

I hear the water blast from the shower, then the blow dryer. He leaves a stripe of toothpaste on my toothbrush and puts a glass of water on the nightstand. On his way out, he starts the coffeemaker and sets out one sugar and one packet of creamer. I tell myself it's nice that someone knows how I like my coffee, even if it's the kind from a hotel packet.

"I love you," I say.

"Je t'aime," he says. He grew up speaking French as a second

language in Vietnam. But I know he's also refusing to say it in English.

I log another month as his mistress and one morning, somewhere in the air between Kansas City and Chicago, I go into the lav and don't recognize my face. I know people are always saying that, but now that I've done something shitty enough, I find out it's true—my eyes seem grayer, as if some of the blue has drained out. When I'm with him, the happiness is all that matters. When I'm alone, the guilt is enough to drown me.

I use the bathroom and when I try to retighten my belt, I notice I have to hook it four notches farther out than before. I start to freak out. But it's not a baby. It's what we call a jet baby. Gas. We expand and contract in the air just like a bag of chips. I think of a real baby and stare into the lavatory mirror at the woman I don't recognize and tell her it has to end.

Back in the aisle, a man asks for a cup of coffee and when I bring it, he asks, "Is this your regular route?"

Amateur airplane men ask this all the time. It's like going up to a girl in a bar and saying, "Do you come here often?"

I glare at him.

"Well, what is your route?" he asks.

I pull a *Hemispheres* magazine out of the seat-back pocket and open to the route map with its hundreds and hundreds of dots. "Pretty much any city with an airport."

I am sick of men. I don't need a man. Like Houdini, I will slip out of this entanglement without a word.

Then when I am in Chicago running to my connecting flight, I see Tien outside of my gate pretending to use the pay phone.

It's his day off but he checked my schedule and came in to give me a Tupperware container of his homemade noodle soup for my layover in Cincinnati. He tells me he loves me, in English. I forget to tell him it's over.

But it's okay. Now that I am sure I have the strength to quit anytime, it doesn't seem so dangerous.

I go to the Richelieu a few days later. When the doorman ushers me into the lobby, just the Pine-Sol scent of the familiar hotel makes me feel like I'm home.

I fly to Boston, where I am supposed to connect to D.C., but I'm coming down with a cold, so my ears block up on descent. Knives jam into my eardrums until I become a human altimeter, registering each foot of altitude loss with a corresponding increase in pain. I tell a supervisor in Boston, and knowing that ruptured eardrums are a job hazard, United medical grounds me. I am stuck in a hotel for five days, too sick to leave my room. I blow into tissues and guzzle cough syrup as I look out the window and watch snow fall. Bundled-up shoppers scurry by, passing rows of trees that are lit up for Christmas, which is just a few days after my birthday. I won't go home for either. All junior flight attendants are on call on Christmas, and I'm convinced I will end up working six legs to Des Moines.

I order the same roast beef sandwich I've ordered every night because it's the only affordable item on the room service menu. I've fallen in love with the mini bottles of ketchup and mayonnaise and especially the teeny, tiny, ten-drop bottle of Tabasco. By the fifth night, I look forward to seeing the four-and-a-half-foot-tall Roseanna, who has been delivering my meals. She's the only person I have been in contact with here and even though she only stops by at dinnertime, I feel like she's been taking care of me while I'm sick. One evening, the familiar knock on the door is accompanied, instead, by a male voice saying "room service," and I feel unbearably alone.

Tien calls from an unfamiliar number. He says it's his home phone, which seems dangerous to me. He must trust me not to call him there. I suppose I should be flattered.

He tells me he won't make it to San Francisco on Friday

because he has to take his younger daughter to the doctor. She caught a cold and it turned into bronchitis.

It is probably my fault. I really am part of the family now.

Six days later I feel better. Medical clears me to fly home, and I'm so happy to leave that lonely hotel room that I could kiss the polished concrete floor of the airport. But I don't. I'm in uniform and people might think I just survived a crash.

Midflight, 12D says, "Is this your regular route?"

Before I can roll my eyes, I notice he's cute, even if he has that too-trendy, pushed-forward Caesar haircut. I know better than to go out with someone from the plane, but I think this guy may be cute enough to help me forget Tien.

I meet him for a drink the next night at the Hotel Monaco in Union Square. When he snaps his fingers at the waitress, I consider leaving. He picked me up on the plane, so he can't have forgotten I work in the service industry. I should have known he'd be a jerk. He was sitting in business class, home of the middle-management types who think they have something to prove to the classes above and beneath them.

He complains about the dot-com bust and how the entire computer industry is in freefall. He says he'll be lucky to keep his job even though he went to Georgetown.

I tell him I went to Cal State Bakersfield. He says, "So, what—you quit? You just didn't like it?"

I graduated. So I'm smart enough to know even a married man is better than him.

On the way home, I drive out of the way to pass the Richelieu. When I get stopped at a red light, I look up at the glowing bay windows and wonder about the flight attendants in those rooms tonight.

—

Tien comes back just in time to celebrate my birthday. I enter the familiar hotel room with its floral quilted bedspread and nicked cherry bureaus. He says he needs a minute to get ready and goes into the bathroom.

I flip through a case of CDs on the nightstand and find my dad's music—Rod Stewart, the Carpenters, Simon and Garfunkel.

I tell myself it's over.

A minute later, he comes out singing "Happy Birthday" over a full-size chocolate cake, complete with twenty-four candles and my name in cursive sugar.

We spend the evening wandering around San Francisco, arm in arm to keep warm in the winter wind. We climb up the hill to Coit Tower and soak in the twinkling views of the Golden Gate and Bay Bridges, the network of piers lining the city, the wealthy enclaves of Belvedere and Tiburon across the bay.

"Look down," he says and points at the ground directly in front of us. A red laser-pen beams the words BON ANNIVERSAIRE, or Happy Birthday in French.

"You've been carrying that around all night?" I ask.

"I know. Too silly, right?" he says, slipping the toy back into his pocket.

"Not at all." He puts his arm around me, and for the first time, I am not anticipating the end. I truly believe that we could go on like this forever.

When I return home, it's Christmas Eve. I hope for a late check-in to New York with a layover long enough to ice-skate at Rockefeller Center, but I prepare myself for a 3 A.M. assignment to Cedar Rapids. KC and I are both on call, but miraculously, our phones never ring. We go to the movies and watch *Dude, Where's My Car?*, a horrible movie made wonderful by the fact that we are receiving double pay for "working" Christmas.

We reminisce about how much fun we had in training and

laugh at our naïve expectations for the life we'd share together once we got to San Francisco. We'd imagined flying to foreign countries together and decorating the apartment with souvenirs, hosting dinner parties, and knowing all the same people. In reality, our paths haven't crossed in more than a month. On top of the trips and my nights with Tien, KC has been spending more and more time in Vegas lately, even risking quick day trips when she doesn't expect to be called to work a flight. I suspect she's seeing someone.

I confess that I have still been seeing Tien and that he's really very loving.

"He should be loving," she says. "He's a father and a husband."

I'm smart enough to know he won't call on a major holiday.

Or for several days after.

When he finally does call, I don't get to the phone in time. I notice he called from his home phone again. I save it in my speed dial, but I'm too afraid to use it. I call him back, on his cell.

He answers and says he's walking around the house tidying up. I can almost see him with the phone pressed to his shoulder as he carries a basket of laundry.

"I picked up an extra San Francisco trip tonight so we can make up for all the Christmas spending."

I get stuck on the word *we*.

"I'll see you tonight," he says.

I try to resist asking him if he misses me. Then I ask anyway.

He asks me to hold on for a second. There is a rustling that suggests he has set down the phone. From a distance, I hear him say, "Go fish."

Tiny laughter responds in the background. It jolts through my eardrum and zigzags right to my stomach. His *situation*. It's real.

"Do you have hammerhead?" he asks. The tiny voice in the background responds, "Go fish."

14

View from Outside

KC plops down on their hideous denim sofa and whips out a cigarette. She slides it between her lips and reaches for her lighter.

Predictably, Emily glares at her.

"I know, I know," mumbles KC, cigarette dangling from the corner of her mouth. "No smoking in the house. As if that's the big crime here tonight."

This party was not supposed to be such a drag. All of her roommates are home for the first time since they started flying, so she wanted to make it memorable. She keeps thinking that under the right circumstances, they can become each other's stand-in family. There is no reason to wait helplessly for the future to come to her. She knows that her trips home to Vegas will stop, and she's determined to be ready long before that day comes.

KC knocked on all the neighbors' doors and asked them to let her know if things got too loud before calling the police. She bought chips and salsa and made seven-layer bean dip and defrosted jalapeño poppers, and she even bought a cute checkered tablecloth, all to make this place feel homey.

She knew the only way she would get Emily to stick around

and skip the Richelieu was to invite Tien, too. "The more the merrier," she had said. Now that he's here, KC feels like she welcomed an intruder into their home.

She watches Emily lean in and whisper in Tien's ear, bring him a drink, all cozy as if they are the ones who were married. At first KC had encouraged the whole screwed-up thing, the foolish one-night-deal that was supposed to break Emily out of her turtleneck-wearing shell. It was actually pretty fun to watch two seemingly respectable people turn to the dark side. The smile here, the sigh there, the hands accidentally brushing on purpose.

KC is thrown by how quickly and easily it turned into something else. She wonders if his wife is better off not knowing, or if someone should tell her the truth. Maybe if someone had told her mom right when it started, they would have had a fighting chance.

KC lights up in the living room and takes her time walking to the balcony.

It's drizzling out, so she stands under the eave, close to the sliding glass door.

Through it, she can't help but watch Emily fix the collar on Tien's shirt. It irks her that they look so comfortable together. She wonders if that's how it started with her dad and the bimbo, if he went to parties with her and without his wedding ring, if he laughed at her friends' jokes like he was just any guy, a guy whose wife and daughter weren't sitting at home waiting for him to return from another late night at work.

Somehow KC always assumed it would be *her* fate to become a home wrecker. At least she could rationalize it away as revenge. Emily doesn't have that excuse. Can't she see that she's killing his children?

KC imagines them at home playing video games or reading Judy Blume books. In their childish contentment, they don't even realize what's coming.

KC does.

She can still smell the scent of Salisbury steak filling their old apartment, see her mom in the dining room, clearing their plates, their napkins and silverware, the salt and pepper, everything but her dad's untouched meal. She thoughtfully covered his with the lid from a pot, keeping it warm until he came home.

"Your daddy has to work real hard at this new job," she said with a look KC confused with pride.

It was past her bedtime when her dad walked in. She had long since changed into her Barbie and the Rockers nightgown. She pretended to be asleep when he came in and kissed her on the cheek, but then she got up and watched her parents from the door to her room.

Her mom was still wearing an apron as if she'd just finished cooking, even though it had been hours. "I made your favorite," she said.

He said he'd had a late lunch and wasn't hungry, but he sat down anyway.

She sat across from him with hands clasped together atop the table. A ceiling fan whirred above them, its chain rhythmically clinking against the light with each revolution.

"It must be exhausting working so late," said KC's mom. "Luckily you have a wife that cares enough to keep your food warm."

KC felt reassured by that kind gesture.

They didn't say anything else for the remainder of the meal. KC could hear her dad's silverware scraping against his plate as he cut his meat.

As her dad forked the last bite into his mouth and began folding his napkin, her mom drummed her fingers on the table, the click of her fingernails growing louder by the second. "I was working on the credit card bill today and I found something interesting."

Her dad set down his fork.

KC felt something in the air that she could not describe at ten years old. But it was intimately familiar. She braced herself for another fight about money, the never-ending source of anger.

Her mom stood up. "It's for her, isn't it?"

KC assumed she must be the *her* in question. She felt uneasy about being the source of their fight but also thrilled that her dad bought her something, clearly an expensive something.

Before KC could find out what the surprise was, her mom was pointing her finger and raising her voice as she said that she knew it, that everyone knew it, that KC probably even knew it.

Then her mom said the words KC would spend years hating her for. Her arms flailed and her voice cracked as she screamed, "Just leave then, if that's what you want."

Her dad simply nodded and walked out the door. He didn't even take a toothbrush or a pair of underwear.

It was years before KC realized that was because he already had a place to go.

15

Houston, We Have a Problem

For the first time, I am glad to see KC passed out on the couch with a pillow over her face and a bucket on the floor beside her. She's been acting strangely all night. She laughed at everything Tien said and tossed her hair and touched his shoulder. It almost seemed like she was flirting with him.

I take Tien to the room I share with KC and feel ridiculous watching him climb the ladder to my bunk bed. I hoped that bringing him here would suddenly zip my two worlds together. I hoped it would make him seem more real to me, more like an actual boyfriend than the married man I have to hide. It hasn't gone particularly well so far.

KC said we seemed happy together, but then she said something about me being a big-titted bimbo. I would have been offended, but I don't have particularly big breasts, so I have no idea what she meant. But that's nothing new, she often lets the alcohol talk for her.

She said, "This is exactly how it starts," poured a shot of vodka, downed it, and slammed the glass on the counter.

Tien climbs into my bed nonchalantly like he sleeps in a bunk all the time. He makes a remark about me keeping things neat, and I realize with embarrassment that I'm still folding perfect hospital corners for Carl.

I am so happy to be caught in this current of warmth and acceptance that even the obstacles of this relationship don't seem so bad. I curl up to him and without reservation, I tell him just how I'm feeling. "This is the perfect moment."

"Are you drunk?" he asks.

"Not really, why? Is my shirt on backwards or something?" I look down at my clothes.

"No. But that would be something to see."

"So, why do I seem drunk?"

"Not drunk. Happy. Lately you've seemed so, I don't know, conflicted, like you're going to end this. I like seeing you carefree and happy again."

For the moment, I really am carefree and happy. I only wish it could last. "I wish you could stay."

"Come to Boston with me tomorrow so we can have one more night."

I fear he is placating me and I don't want to seem too clingy. "Thanks, but maybe you should get some sleep there so you won't have to go home and explain the red eyes and dark circles again."

"I'm not worried about that."

"Aren't you afraid she's going to find out?"

"I don't know. But it's funny you should ask. Last time I met you at the airport on my day off, she said, 'You must be going to see your girlfriend.'"

I sit up.

"Yeah, that's what I thought too. My stomach dropped, but then I noticed she was laughing."

"What did you say?" I grab his arm.

"I laughed, too, and said, 'Yep.' And then she asked if you were pretty. I just kept up with the joke and said you were beautiful."

"You didn't."

"But the thing is, once I was in the clear, I almost wished she did know."

I'm not sure how to feel about that. Does he want her to know so they can rebuild? Or so they can break up? Either way, the thought of her finding out scares me.

I often wonder what she's like. I may be ruining her life, but at the same time, I envy her. They are already there. They've figured it all out and don't have to fear what's next. They literally have a picket fence in front of their house, with roses and everything.

Maybe she's mean or enormously fat. I think about what she might do in her spare time—knit? Jog? Paint? And what she would cook for dinner—Pho? Boeuf Bourguignon? Hot Pockets? I wonder what about me is better or more lovable than her. Maybe they only got married because they had a one-night stand and she got pregnant.

He lies down on his back, and I curl into the nook of his shoulder. "Tien? Do you love your wife?"

I call her *your wife* because he always calls her *her* or *my wife*. I still don't know her name.

He stares up at the ceiling. I roll off of him so I can see his face. He looks back at me with disbelief, even though to me the curiosity seems to be expected.

He whispers, "Why do you ask me that?"

I shrug my shoulders.

He sighs. "Yes," he says. "I love my wife. I do."

I realize the uselessness of my question. Yes or no makes him seem equally deceitful and could both be taken as a lie.

"As much as you love me?"

"EmLee, it's just. Well." He sits up and looks at me seriously. "You date and it's great. You get engaged and it's great. You get married and it's work."

He says this matter-of-factly as if he's giving me a life lesson from his bank of wisdom, only it doesn't seem like he knows much about working hard.

"Were you ever in love like this?" I look into his eyes and wait for him to say no, to tell me he's never experienced anything like the true love that we share. That everything in his life was leading him here, to me, where he belongs.

He looks away from me and toward the window as he says, "Yes, very much so. We were very much in love."

This depresses me. I don't know how someone could ever let go of something like this. If Tien were mine, I would do anything to make it work.

Somehow, I find myself moved by their circumstances. "Tien, you have to fight for her and get it back." I hear myself say this and am surprised by how much I mean it. I almost want to help him win her over.

He says, "You think?"

The next morning I drop Tien off at the airport just like his wife might. I say, "I love you, Tien."

He replies, "*Je t'aime.*"

I go home and crawl into bed. I lie atop my bunk bed listening to the roar of DC-10s and 747s headed to Shanghai and Sydney and Anywhere But Here. I call the screw desk and volunteer to work on my day off. Evil Debbie doesn't seem so evil when she offers one easy leg to Houston out of appreciation.

Later that evening, a towncar meets me and my crew at Houston Intercontinental Airport. I squeeze into the middle seat and put my feet on the hump. It's drizzling as we roll down the highway toward the downtown Hyatt. My phone rings, and it says TIEN HOME. I wonder why he would be at home when he should be in Boston.

I say, "Hello."

A woman says, "Hello."

I struggle to keep from vomiting at the sound of her voice.

"Who is this?" she asks.

"You must have the wrong number," I say to the woman who could only be Tien's wife. I hang up and rest my arms on my knees to slow the dizziness. The driver turns up the radio, so along with the faint patter of rain, we hear Randy Travis singing "Forever and Ever, Amen." I look around the car for escape. My flying partners face forward in silence, their heads floating back and forth in sync with every tap and release of the brakes. The tranquility around me amplifies the hysteria growing inside me until I want to open the door and fling myself onto the highway.

The phone rings again. TIEN HOME.

I send it to voice mail then listen for the message, but she doesn't leave one. I record silence over my greeting, in case she calls again. Maybe she'll think she dialed wrong the first time. Or maybe it will create even more suspicion.

I check into the hotel and call him. He's in Boston as scheduled.

I tell him to sit down. Despite the circumstances, I feel cool for having an opportunity to use this line.

"I'm sitting."

"Your wife called," I say and expect to hear a gasp.

Only he says he knows, no big deal, he played it off. "You scared me. I thought you were going to say you were pregnant and the shit had really hit the fan."

A crude reminder that we'll never have children together.

He says she was going through the phone bill, but now she thinks he was just trying to swap flights with me. A lot of flights.

His calm infuriates me. Partly because I want him to share my fear. Partly because I thought he would have to choose.

"That doesn't make sense, Tien." He must think his wife is stupid. This makes me mad on her behalf. Like the first time he touched my breasts and said, "Wow, you really are twenty-three." I thought, *Yeah, for now.* Even if his wife is fifteen years older than me and has had two kids, I am certain her breasts are fine and that he should be grateful for them.

"It doesn't?"

"She isn't stupid. She isn't poring over the numbers on a cell phone bill on a Friday night and calling you on a layover, which she never does, for the fun of it. Something had to make her suspect."

I tell him to confess.

He says, "I guess I need to lay low for a little while."

"Lay low?" I am yelling at him now. "What do you mean, 'lay low'?"

He says, "This isn't a true-false test. I can't just go with my first impulse and pencil in an answer."

I want him to want me. I want my anger and fear to drip to the floor like liquid steel and allow me to say, "Pick me, Tien, pick me." But I'm scared. Never before have my actions risked such consequences.

"You have to fix this. We can't keep seeing each other."

"Relax," he says.

"This is over. It has to be over. I'm going to hang up now."

"Wait," he says.

I hang up before he can say something that he probably doesn't even mean. As soon as I do, I wish he would call me back.

The next morning I am alone with the driver in an eleven-person van. I am crying and he is staring. I tell him I just found out my boyfriend is married.

Every time the phone rings, I hope it's him. But it's always her. TIEN HOME. I know it isn't him because I checked his schedule and he's in midair. She calls me and calls me and calls me and calls me. And he doesn't.

I can't help but wonder what is happening at his house. Maybe he is leaving or maybe she has thrown him out. The longer I don't hear from him, the more I wonder what would have happened if I hadn't pushed him away.

On Friday night, the crew desk can't find anything for me, so I am home. And he is only a few miles away at the Richelieu. I imagine what he might be doing—eating at Miss Saigon, considering a divorce, getting to know another girl. Over and over I look at the phone, but I don't pick up to dial. I convince myself he's doing the same thing across town.

Two Fridays later, I decide I need closure, the perfect excuse. I go to the Richelieu. Just to say goodbye. He opens the door. He doesn't throw his arms around me or press me against the wall or tell me he can't live without me. He just stands there with his hands in his pockets.

Then he moves around the room, tidying up as if he's about to check out. I love that he always cleans up before he leaves so the housekeeper doesn't have to work too hard.

I want to grab on to his pant leg and say, "Pick me." But I stay by the door, too nervous to talk. I finally say, "I don't know why I came."

He looks right past me and says, "I don't know, either."

It hurts to feel such coldness coming from him. "It's probably a very bad idea for me to be here. Maybe I should go."

He agrees.

I realize I was expecting him to convince me to stay.

I say, "Okay then, I'm going to go."

He sighs and says okay.

But then he rubs his neck and says, "Why don't we get dinner and talk."

I can hardly look at Cindy, the waitress who waves and brings my shrimp soup and his fiery peppers as if we're still a legitimate couple.

He stares down at his bowl as he stirs his soup, playing with the bits of Thai basil and mint, releasing new puffs of steam into the air between us.

He tells me she knows the truth, and I sense that he is angry with me for causing this.

When he looks up, I notice the blackness hanging below his bloodshot eyes, the shadows underscoring his high cheekbones.

Maybe he just needs more time.

I say nothing for the rest of my meal. I slurp and chew and sniff and add nothing else to the score of the restaurant buzzing around us.

When we reach the door of the Richelieu, he invites me up. For closure.

His cell phone rings, and he turns on the TV as he answers.

Seventh Heaven is on, a show about a pastor and his perfect, loving family. Perfect. I sit down on the bed and pretend to watch.

Tien paces the room. "I know you can't trust me . . . no, you have no way of knowing . . . but I can tell you I haven't."

I feel sick to my stomach to see him so deceitful, so good at being deceitful.

I focus on the driver's ed scene unfolding on TV and try not to listen to his conversation. My phone rings—*shit*—I run over to my purse and silence it.

"Just the TV," he tells her. Then he switches to Vietnamese and I am lost.

I wish I could hear her voice through the phone. This is the closest I've been to the other half of my relationship.

I wonder how they are handling the "Emily mess." Does she give him the cold shoulder? Does she keep him up all night with

questions, torturing herself over every nuance of our relationship? Maybe he tells her I meant nothing, that it was just sex.
Maybe it was.

"What are we doing?" I ask when he hangs up.

He sits down on the arm of the chair and says, "I don't know.
What are we doing?"

Anger bubbles in my stomach. I stand up and say, "I hate it
when you do that. You never give me answers. You just ask me
the same questions as if it's up to me, but it's not."

"I'm sorry," he says, standing up slowly.

"See? You're doing it again. You're not saying anything."

"I guess I don't know what to say. I don't know what to do
from here."

"Do you love me?"

"I'm like a shrub, planted, roots in the ground. You're a beautiful butterfly flying around the shrub. The shrub loves the butterfly, but it cannot move to follow her. It is in one place. Someday
the butterfly will fly away."

"What are you saying? That I should fly away and never fucking talk to you again?"

He takes a step back and raises his eyebrows as if he's my
grandma and can't handle a cuss word.

He goes to the window and looks out. "I don't know what to
tell you. It's just, well, it's—"

"What? It's complicated?"

"No, it's not complicated. It's simple. But it's impossible."

"I just want the truth."

"No you don't. The truth isn't what you want to hear."

"What do I want to hear?"

"You want me to lie and tell you I can give you what you
want, that there is some easy way for this to become the rela-

tionship you deserve. But I can't tell that lie. God, EmLee. *I want to tell you that I'm someone I'm not, that I'm a free man, that I can leave everything for you."*

"But you won't."

All he can say is that he doesn't know what to do, he doesn't know what he wants, he doesn't know right from left or up from down.

As the night wears on, he says he loves his wife. He loves his kids. His conviction grows stronger, and in the morning, he picks her.

In the morning, I call her back.

When she answers, I say, "Mrs. Nguyen?" because I still don't know her first name.

"Yes," she says hesitantly, probably assuming I'm a telemarketer.

I say, "My name is Emily."

Before I can go on, she sighs and says, "I've heard the name."

I tell her I'm sorry, so, so sorry.

"I love my husband," she says curtly as if I've challenged that fact. "I can't share him."

I am on the verge of tears, and she sounds so calm, so serious. "Neither can I."

"Promise you will have no more contact with my husband. I want to accept what has happened and fix our marriage, but I can't unless I know it's over."

I feel a wave of dread as this grown woman suggests her future is up to me. I know it isn't, but despite the seriousness of her voice, she has shown a chasm of vulnerability so deep it exposes the gravity of my crime.

"Tell me, EmLee." She says my name just the way he does. "The twelve years I have spent with my husband, the family we have made. Is my whole life a fluke? Not meant to be?"

I know I cannot answer her question, but the sincerity in her voice tells me it is not rhetorical. I could say something like "only time will tell," but coming from me, it would sound like a challenge.

She says they have been working opposite schedules for a decade and they haven't slept without a kid in their bed for years. "Maybe what happened with you and my husband can be a wake-up call." She emphasizes the words *my husband* every time she uses them.

I almost say I'm glad I could help, no sweat. But I'm sweating.

Up against her composure and maturity, it seems so obvious to me now, that she is the one he was meant for, that I was just a fun young distraction.

I tell her I saw him but that he loves *her*, he wants *her*, and that it's not just the kids or the history.

She sighs again.

I apologize again.

"These things happen," she says. "In a way, I'm surprised it didn't happen sooner. *If* it didn't happen sooner."

Is she calling me one of many? Or is she worried that I am one of many?

I tell her he said he hasn't done this before and I believe him.

She laughs.

I feel myself turn red. Could there have been other women? Was I really nothing more than another fling?

She says I sound like a nice girl and that she feels sorry for me and tells me to stop crying and promises things will get better for me. She says she knows I'm new and that it's hard to be a new flight attendant. She tells me stories of their trials with United Airlines over the last ten years, like the time Tien flew three legs across the country, sped across Chicago, and then ran through the hospital, only to arrive covered in sweat, out of breath, and twenty minutes late to the birth of their younger daughter. But, she says, the sacrifice is worth it because the kids are with him on weekdays and her on weekends, and they rarely have to be in day care. She won't put her kids in an institution. She'll do anything to protect her kids.

For a second, I think she says that as a threat, but I can tell by her tone that she is just being honest.

KC has been telling me that I was with Tien because I need a father. I told her she was talking psycho-pop bullshit, but when I talk to his wife, there is no sex to fuzz things up and inside my head I say, as clear as anything, "I wish this woman were my mom."

16

I See Paris, I See France

As KC sweeps through the aisles, at least fifty passengers have tried to speak to her in French. Unfortunately, she will have to get off for a crew change in New York before her plane continues to Paris, but being this close to Parisian sophistication reminds her that, like it or not, her life is becoming as worldly as her mom hoped. Before long she'll be standing on Point Zero in front of Notre Dame, then she'll be standing at the Louvre in front of all that famous art while smartly dressed Europeans discuss movements and themes. Just the thought gives her a galvanizing surge of legitimacy.

A call bell rings, and when she looks out into the aisle, she sees the blond rocker guy in 27H looking back at her and motioning with his finger. She noticed him the first time she passed his seat about three hours ago, but she hasn't had the nerve to stray away from official business, i.e., "*Café ou thé? Poulet ou de boéuf?*"

Not that he's French. That was obvious from the start with his torn jeans and ironic hipster T-shirt that says IRONIC HIPSTER T-SHIRT. His hair is disheveled but with just enough gel to reveal the effort that went into this pretense of looking poor. KC has spent too much time being poor to appreciate the look, but there is something about his cocky air that draws her to him, something about the way he's been sitting there with his legs splayed, tapping his left foot in the aisle as if he owns it.

"*Bonjour*," she says when she reaches his seat.

"*Oui, oui*," he says with a playful, crooked smile that reveals a small gap between his front teeth.

"What can I get for you?" She smooths her skirt as she bends a few inches closer to his height.

"You know those warm cookies you usually serve up front?"

"Yes."

He puts his hands together as if in prayer and says, "Pretty please?"

KC shakes her head with a smile that obviously means yes. She can tell he's the kind of guy who can get whatever he wants just by asking.

"I'll see what I can do," she says.

He tips an imaginary hat in appreciation.

The plane lurches abruptly and KC catches her balance by grabbing his seat. A second jolt sends her pitching forward. He reaches up to steady her and brushes her breast in the process.

He exaggerates a look of shock and they both laugh.

"You might as well give me your phone number seeing as I've already been to second base."

She looks at him like he's crazy, but he holds her eye and just keeps smiling back with that adorable gap between his teeth as if he knows she's going to give in.

"I don't even know your name," she says.

"Jake." He holds out his hand. When she goes to shake it, he takes her hand and kisses it lightly.

She whips out a pen from the Holiday Inn and writes her number on a napkin.

A week later she's strolling through Boston Common when he calls.

"Hey babe, it's Jake."

She covers the mouthpiece as if he could hear her smiling through the phone.

He tells her he's still on the road, too, in Texas this time.

"Let me guess," she says. "You're a bull rider."

"I wish."

"A rodeo clown?"

"Ha! No."

KC looks around the park. The pond is frozen and people in brightly colored scarves are ice-skating. The windows of federal-style row homes of Beacon Hill sparkle with light. It's freezing outside, but the neighborhood looks homey and warm.

"I love the seasons," she says.

"Is it cold there?" he asks.

She sighs. "It seems like seasons make it easier to get into the holidays and really spend time together as a family. I missed that growing up in the desert."

"You're lucky. My family went overboard with all that. Trust me, it would make you want to vomit."

KC doubts that. "So if you're not a bull rider what do you do?"

"I'm in a band."

"I mean for work."

"I'm in a band."

"Yeah, right!" The idea that someone she knows could really make it as a musician or an actor or an athlete is astonishing. She thought she had hit it big simply because she won't spend her life working in a bar like her mom did.

"Cross my heart," he says. He tells her he's almost always on the road, but when he's not he lives in L.A.

"So you make a living from your music?"

"More or less."

"I'm impressed."

"Wanna come visit me?" he asks. Then before she can respond, he says, "Please come visit. It gets lonely being on the road all the time."

She doubts it ever gets lonely for a guy in a band.

"I don't even know you," she says.

"You will."

Two weeks later, KC agrees to meet Jake when he's in Vegas for a show. She has to fly down anyway, but this time, everything about the flight from SFO feels different. She knows the gate agents at the airports on both ends by name, she knows that on a Sunday every flight in will be empty and every flight out will be full, but this time she's not going home, she is taking an airplane to a date. This makes her feel extraordinarily successful.

Her taxi whizzes down the Strip in the direction of the light beaming into space from the Luxor. She is more nervous than she expected to be.

In just a few minutes she'll see Jake for the first time since they met. If this doesn't go well, all of the hour-long phone calls over the last few weeks could be another set of memories to repress.

What if he's not as cute as she remembers? Or worse, what if she's not as pretty as he remembers? She probably shouldn't be meeting him in a casino since she's painfully broke. In Charlotte last week, she got a run in her hose and had to borrow money from a flying partner to buy a new pair.

She focuses on the flashing marquees promoting never-ending entertainment—Siegfried and Roy, Cirque du Soleil, Danny Gans. The cab driver pulls into the porte cochere under the giant sphinx. He pops the trunk. KC takes a deep breath.

As the taxi pulls away, she questions her judgment. Flying to see a passenger she barely knows is just too stupid, even for her.

"I'm here," she says when he picks up his phone.

"I'm at the craps table. When you come in, head toward the pharaohs."

The hotel doors slide open, letting out a blast of air-conditioned air. She notices the check-in desk and long line of arriving guests and is reminded that this isn't just a casino. She is meeting a near-stranger in a hotel. She suddenly feels cheap.

In spite of her nerves, KC steps onto the shiny tile floor and presses forward. She passes between two sandstone pharaohs and is immediately accosted by the melodic clamor of spinning slot machines and the clang of coins being spit out.

After a few visual sweeps of the room, she sees Jake jogging her way, waving. Once again he's able to pull off that indie rock look with another ironically cheap T-shirt and pre-stained Diesel jeans.

"Holy shit," he says. "You're more gorgeous than I remembered." He picks her up and spins her around.

From a nearby slot machine, a digitized audience calls out "Wheel . . . of . . . Fortune!"

Jake bends his arm for her to take hold of, and she decides her New Year is shaping up to be better than expected.

A rowdy crowd is gathered around a roulette table and Jake says they should get in on the action. He pushes his way to the edge of the table. The ball is already spinning along the sides of the wheel and just as the dealer lifts her hand to motion to stop betting, Jake whips out his wallet and throws a hundred-dollar bill on red.

KC squeezes his arm and wills the bouncing ball to drop into a red slot, not a black. When it finally settles, it's on the double zero, neither black nor red.

"Damn. So much for fifty-fifty," says Jake.

"I'm sorry," says KC, giving him a little pout.

He shrugs his shoulders and hands the dealer a wad of cash in exchange for a pile of chips. KC tries to count them without being too obvious, but it seems like he has about fifteen hundred dollars on the table. That's about as much as she makes in a month, and it makes her nervous to see it sitting there waiting to be gambled away.

"You should play," says Jake.

"Oh, I don't really know how," she lies. "I'll watch for a little while first." Her mom worked a roulette table for a few months, and blackjack and Texas hold 'em. She only got out of dealing when she started to like playing too much.

Jake takes a few more spins, expertly spreading chips over corners and rows and numbers and colors. He doubles and triples up on what must be lucky numbers and KC's stomach twists in knots watching him part with so much money.

He rubs his hands together as the ball bounce, and yells, "Wooow!" when he hits a number and gets thirty-six times what he put down. Though she hasn't been counting, KC's pretty sure he's still down.

Again, he tries to get her into the game. "Just put down a couple hundred, so there's no worries."

She doesn't want to tell him that for her, losing a couple of hundred dollars would mean choosing between rent, gas, or groceries. So he doesn't think she's a total loser, she goes to the ATM and gets a cash advance on her credit card for a hundred dollars. She knows she's in trouble when, instead of five twenties, the machine spits out a hundred-dollar bill.

She hands it to the dealer, who folds it into a slot in the table and gives her a stack of five-dollar chips. She spreads them out over the table, and slides fifteen dollars' worth into her pocket as a safety measure.

She closes her eyes while the ball spins, and when she finally hears cheers and sighs, she opens them to see the dealer sweeping the chips off the table. KC's mouth begins to water like she's about to throw up. But then she notices a couple of her chips still on the table. The dealer builds stack after stack and pushes them toward her.

"I won! I won!" She bounces up and down and Jake kisses her on the forehead. She's not even exactly sure how, but she's up two hundred and fifteen bucks.

"Let's celebrate," he says. After cashing out with the dealer, he leads her to the hotel's steakhouse.

She scoots into a candlelit booth with overstuffed leather seats, but then instead of sitting across from her, he slides in next to her. This too-much, too-soon gesture makes her so uncomfortable she feels her first asthma attack coming on. And it's not just her. People around them are looking at them, probably wondering why the hell they're sitting on the same side of the table. For God's sake, she doesn't even know his last name.

"Think you can stay in town tomorrow night and come to my show?"

She'd definitely like to go to the show no matter how tonight unfolds, but she's still not ready to commit, so she says, "Maybe."

He whips open his menu but closes it again just as quickly. He looks into her eyes and says, "I'm so glad you came."

He looks sincere, but she just can't tell. "So what's your last name anyway? Jake what?"

He says, "Doe," but then looks at her expectantly like she should know the name.

She doesn't.

He laughs. "Like John Doe. I'm just kidding."

"Ha ha," she says, feeling a bit off-kilter. It sounds like the kind of joke a psychopath might make. She feels like standing up, but by sitting on *her* side of the booth, he's blocked her in. "So what is it really?"

"Carington."

"Carington? As in Carnegie, Rockefeller, *Carington*, Carington? As in the Carington Tower, Carington Library?"

"I try not to make a big thing of it."

"Why?"

"I didn't want you to think of me differently."

"You think I would just like you for the money?" As much as she thinks she doesn't care about that stuff, she probably would have been seduced.

"No. I thought you *wouldn't* like me. I hate money." He puts his head in his hands and looks up at her with puppy-dog eyes.

He hates money? That's a strange thing to say. He wouldn't say that if he had to grow up in a studio apartment with a view of a drained swimming pool and a basketball court with cracks in the blacktop. He wouldn't "hate money" if he had to spend his youth eating Tuna Helper made with chunk light because they couldn't afford solid white.

But the news does change her image of him. He's in a small indie band called Hell's Kitsch, so she'd imagined him living in a cold-water bachelor walk-up with dirty dishes in the sink and a table stacked with beeramids of Natty Light. She found the idea of him suffering for his art kind of romantic. Instead he probably drives a Porsche and has a three-thousand-dollar coffeemaker on his granite countertop.

"So that's how you can afford to focus on your music?"

He smiles strangely and she can't tell if she's offended him.

"I'm going to make it on my own, but until we break out, it's not bad to already be living like a rock star. There's nothing like being able to spend every night in a nice hotel, have your food delivered, and your bed turned down."

She considers that idea.

"Well, you obviously get it." He nudges her. "No responsibilities and upkeep at home."

"It is nice to be taken care of."

She starts to imagine what life could be like if things were to work out with Jake. Could answering one call bell really change her life in one swoop? No more PB&J dinners. No more socks with holes. She laughs at herself as her imagination takes over. Maybe if she were to marry him, they would even move to a big house with an attached garage and a walk-in closet. KC has never lived in a house before.

Even more importantly, money can bring more than physical comfort. If they were rich, they wouldn't end up just another couple fighting over bounced checks, waving bills in the air, and throwing lamps at the wall.

She wonders how differently things might have turned out if her parents had had an easier life. Maybe the bimbo would have been a one-time thing. He would have come home with flowers and an apology. She might have yelled until he groveled. He would have held her while she cried, stroked her hair until she forgave him. KC would have woken to find her parents contentedly sipping coffee together, a morning ritual that would continue day after day, year after year, and happily ever after.

If there hadn't been fault lines bigger than the San Andreas, the bimbo would be nothing more than a guilty memory he would look back on with disgust.

After rounds of prime rib, lobster, and martinis, they move to the bar in the center of the casino. She notices an elderly couple staring blankly at adjacent slot machines, silently pulling from a shared bucket of quarters. It reminds her of those long-married couples who go out to breakfast just to read newspapers and ignore each other. She longs for the kind of relationship so stable you can take it for granted.

Jake maneuvers her to a spot with video blackjack embedded in the bar. He stands behind her and assuming she doesn't know how to play, proceeds to teach her. Caringtons probably don't go out with girls who know their way around a Las Vegas card game, so she decides to play dumb.

With his arms around her, he points to the screen and the overturned cards. Her shirt has pulled up a bit, and with his thumb, he caresses the skin between her low-rise jeans and her top. Her confidence swells knowing that a guy of his caliber is into her.

She feels his lips brush against her ear. He whispers, "You have a king and a two. What do you want to do?"

"Hit?"

She wins. If things go well, she can buy a new pair of comfy inflight shoes. If things go really well, she and Jake can live out the easy life together.

"You have thirteen and the dealer is showing an ace. What do you want to do?"

"Hit?"

Damn it. She loses.

The virtual dealer flicks KC a new hand. Jake slips his finger just below the waistband of her jeans.

"You have two aces. What do you want to do?"

"Split? Is that what you called it?"

She wins. He brushes her hair to one side, lightly kisses her neck. "I think you've got the hang of it. Now what do you want to do?"

The obvious choice would be to say, "Go upstairs," but it's so obvious that she doesn't have to. She sets her drink on the counter and turns around into his arms, facing him this time. He steps back, takes her hand, and leads her toward the elevators.

When he opens the door to his room, it's a suite with gold chandeliers and oriental rugs, a completely separate bedroom, and a panoramic view of the Strip.

She walks to the window, taken by the twinkling lights and crowds of tourists. To her left, she can just make out the Eiffel Tower.

If she were on *Days of Our Lives*, it would be time for the camera to move in for her close-up where she would say, "I've arrived."

17

Alone

I fly to Albany and watch locals dig their way out of snow-piled front doors. I fly to Burlington, Vermont, where ice coats the loading/unloading zone, creating a hostile version of Slip 'n Slide. Snow blows through the crack between the jet bridge and the fuselage as I greet. Despite uniform regulations, I wear my winter coat and say, "Good morning," even though it is a bad morning. I find solace in the bonus that morning adds another word to my vocabulary, something to break up the "hi/how are you/welcome aboard" loop. At least United doesn't expect me to be funny.

On Valentine's Day, I fly to Cleveland, where green thickets have become wastelands of brown sticks. I expect reprieve when Evil Debbie goes on sick leave and I am sent to Kauai, but I find something even worse. A planeload of lovers.

I lie in the sun in a bikini on a chaise surrounded by hibiscus and plumeria and an infinity pool that leads to the clear blue ocean. Palm trees rustle peacefully in the breeze, and a tropical soundtrack of ukuleles and steel guitars plays from hidden speakers. I am sweating, tanning, and getting paid nearly two dollars an hour per diem to do it. While almost every flight

attendant in the system is somewhere buried under snow, I have
finally scored the Showcase Showdown dream vacation and I
can't even enjoy it. When I met Tien, I thought he couldn't break
my heart because I already knew how it would end. When he
left, it wouldn't be because he didn't love me.

I am splashed with water when a sheet-white guy tosses his
equally white, bikini-clad girlfriend into the pool. They laugh
and splash each other and I delight in the thought of them
squeezing into scratchy airline seats when they go home the
color of freshly boiled lobsters.

Good or bad, my fourteen-hour Hawaiian sojourn won't be
long enough to cook up a burn of that magnitude. When I went
to set the alarm in my room, it was already set to 4 A.M., probably by someone on yesterday's crew. We're all lucky to be here,
but I know I'm not the only one who feels out of place when
popping in for few hours to a destination where everyone else
spends a week luxuriating in the art of doing nothing.

Himani, a flight attendant I worked with on the flight here,
throws a hotel towel on the chaise next to mine. She lifts up her
sunglasses and says the company just asked for volunteers to
transfer to London and staff a new route to Delhi. "Didn't you
say you were hoping to go there?"

"For a layover," I say, sitting up and lifting my sunglasses to
look at her. "But move to a foreign country?"

She nods quickly. "Why not? I would if I wasn't married." She
waves over the pool attendant to order a piña colada. His name
tag says he's from Brunswick, Georgia, which must require at
least ten hours of flying to reach. Maybe he came here on vacation once and never wanted to leave.

It makes me wonder what it would take to pick up and start
over somewhere so far, geographically and culturally, from home.
I begin to imagine a new life where I'd spend afternoons drinking tea and riding around on double-decker buses.

Then it hits me that if I were still seeing Tien, I wouldn't even consider the move. I may have outgrown Carl, but not my tendency to let life pass me by.

I tell Himani she's right, I'm moving to London. For the first time in a more than a month, I feel the stirrings of excitement.

When I get back to San Francisco, KC surprises me with a Valentine's Day card and a bag of Sweethearts candies. She said she bought them for her mom, but the Vegas flights were full, so she can't go home. Once again she asks me to go downtown with her, and this time I jump at the chance. I want to show her I'm not the same girl she first met. I want to prove I can be fearless and exciting. But this time she just wants to go sightseeing.

When we reach the waterfront, KC points to a crowd of about a dozen people gathered along the sidewalk near Fisherman's Wharf. "What are they looking at?"

I'm not sure because there is nothing unusual in the bay to my right, and to my left there is just a mile of red-and-yellow awnings that shade racks upon racks of T-shirts that say I LEFT MY ♥ IN SAN FRANCISCO.

I shrug my shoulders. I'm hoping to convince her we should put our names in for the London base.

Before I have a chance to bring it up, something in front of us moves. KC jumps into the street screaming. A black SUV swerves out of the way.

"Oh my Lord," she says as she bends over and rests her hands on her knees.

Ahead of us, the crowd bounces up and down in laughter and tosses money toward a man holding tree branches. Ah, the bushman. I've heard he makes sixty grand a year scaring unsuspecting passersby. The man scurries back toward the fence, squats down, and hides behind his branches to wait for his prey.

"He got me good," says KC as she straightens up. She throws a dollar onto his pile.

I love that she'll pay a guy for embarrassing her.

"Let's watch," she says and gets into position so she can see the next person be surprised.

The bushman pops out from his branches a few times and scares a few people into stepping back, but nothing too terribly entertaining. While we wait for another good scare, I tell her about London, adding that I'm certain it will help me get over my heartbreak.

"Maybe you need a change too," I say.

"I don't know."

"We could explore Europe together. It would be spontaneous and exciting and you'd remember it forever."

"I think I'm done with spontaneous and exciting. I'm going for mature these days." She says *ma-toor*, the word high school teachers urge their students to embrace. "Don't let me stop you, though. You should go without me."

"But I would miss living with you." Despite our rarely meshing schedules, I still have this fantasy of being bosom buddies and sharing calamities that we'll laugh about for the rest of our lives. "You have to come."

KC sighs. "Things are going really well with Jake."

She doesn't sound convincing, but I'm not sure why.

A blast of cold wind hits me and I pull my sweater around me. I look out over the dark water of the bay. Occasional whitecaps gently break against the shore. Cars and pedestrians cross the Golden Gate Bridge as an inbound cargo ship stacked six-high with crates passes below. It fascinates me that having crossed an ocean, those containers will now be lifted off the Hanjin freighter and dropped onto trains and big rigs to cross the U.S. The ship probably came all the way from Hong Kong or some other Asian port, its crew cramped on board for a week or more. I imagine a seaman going up to the deck for fresh air, all alone in the middle of the Pacific, looking out at a thousand miles of ocean in every direction. At night, he probably looked up at a sky almost completely white with stars. Maybe every now and then he'd spot a twinkling ship on the horizon and feel a distant camaraderie.

"I'm not sure I could go through with it either. It's just a thought."

"Go," she says. "I wouldn't stay behind because of you."

We both stop and focus our attention on the hidden bush, which hasn't moved in a very long time.

"Emily," says KC.

"What's wrong?"

"My mom's sick," she says and looks toward the water.

I turn to her, concerned.

"It's nothing, just the flu," she says, smiling and brushing the comment away. "I just thought I'd go down and help her out a little."

"Maybe it's good the flights were full. You wouldn't want to catch it and go on sick list. We're still new and seriously can't miss work."

She takes an audible breath and closes her eyes. "Yeah," she says, biting her lip and nodding.

I hear a gasp and turn to see a woman falling. Only a few steps away from me her head slams onto the concrete with a sickening *bam!*

Voices from the bush-watching crowd yell out, "Call nine-one-one . . . She's having a heart attack!"

I stand there in shock staring down at the woman, her gray hair strewn out around her pale face. Within seconds KC is by her side.

KC slaps the woman's chest. "Ma'am, ma'am," she says. "Are you okay? Are you okay?" She presses her fingers to the woman's neck to feel for a pulse, tilts her head back to clear her airway, and before I even know what is happening, she is holding the woman's nose and blowing into her mouth. One-and-two-and-three-and-four-and, KC pumps her chest quickly and forcefully.

I hear a crack and wonder if she broke one of the lady's ribs. If she did, she isn't fazed.

Within a minute we hear sirens and then paramedics are rushing down the sidewalk wheeling a yellow gurney. A plastic bag mask is produced and they start pumping air into the woman's lungs by hand.

An idle paramedic pulls out a clipboard and asks us questions about the woman, but we don't know her. No one around us knows her, so KC decides we should go with her to the hospital so she's not alone.

I can't believe how calm she is under pressure. We're all trained for emergencies. Fire in the cabin—pull, aim, squeeze, sweep. Decompression—sweep nearest mask to face, sit down, and hold on. Hijacking—comply, comply, comply. So I probably could have administered CPR if I needed to, but I'm blown away with KC's cool. She didn't even hesitate.

In the small waiting room of the St. Francis Memorial ER, KC paces back and forth like she works there. Her tennis shoes squeak on the linoleum. "Can you please have the doctor give us an update about Mrs. Albasi soon?" she says forcefully to the man behind the intake desk.

I look around at the handful of people waiting to be seen, a woman jiggling a newborn baby, a man with an ice-filled grocery bag on his knee, a girl about our age with a barf bucket by her feet. "I hate hospitals," I tell KC when she sits down next to me.

She shrugs her shoulders. "I guess I'm comfortable in them."

"If there's ever a medical emergency on my flight, I sure hope you're with me. You're made for this stuff."

"I guess."

I don't know what I'm made for. Apparently not a healthy relationship.

I know she's sick of hearing about Tien, but I need her opinion. "So, do you think he ever even loved me?"

She looks at me and rolls her eyes.

"What?"

She tells me to go off men altogether, be alone for a while. She says I won't be ready for a good man until I don't need anyone at all. I remember an old coworker's dog Viper—my gameplaying coworker only coughed up the pig's ear when he was convinced Viper, who sat perfectly still, didn't want it anymore.

KC says she thinks it's more like paying dues, or fasting for Lent. We just have to suffer for an unspecified length of time before finding happiness. She is certain her time is nearly served.

"The trick is not to need anyone," she says. "I don't."

I try not to take offense, but I wish she needed a friend, even just a little. I sit up straight and decide I can be strong like her. I've spent almost every night of the last eight months in a hotel, I have never flown with anyone I know, I very nearly haven't needed anyone, and this job proves it. Enlightenment is near.

"Seriously," says KC. "Forget about him already. He's taken."

I do not want to become Val, who waited twenty-eight years, but something makes me say, "You never know. They could get a divorce one of these days."

"You don't want that."

"No, you're right." I know she's right. But still.

"Don't be so afraid to be alone. It's not attractive."

I cross my arms and try to entertain myself with the rhythms of the hospital—an orderly wheeling an empty gurney down the hall, a doctor being paged over the loudspeaker—but I can't shake the feeling that KC has no right to be judging me. "You *are* the one who pushed me to him."

She releases a puff of judgmental air. "You were supposed to fuck him, not fall in love with him."

Maybe I'm unsophisticated, but it strikes me as cruel that "fucking" someone should be better than loving them.

KC looks me directly in the eyes. "Maybe it's for the best that she found out."

She says that with a strange determination, almost as if his wife was someone we knew.

"How so? I mean maybe it's the right thing for our relationship to end, but I hate that she had to get hurt."

"Ha! Your relationship." She rolls her eyes.

"Whose side are you on here?"

"If Tien were to leave, I know exactly what would happen."

"What? If he cheated *with* me he'd cheat *on* me?"

"God, it's not all about you. I mean his daughters. They would turn out just like me."

"What's so wrong with you?"

A young Asian woman in green scrubs walks over to us. A stethoscope swings from her neck as she leans down to put her hand on KC's shoulder. "I'm Dr. Pack. Are you Mrs. Albasi's daughter?"

"Well, no. But we brought her in." KC looks up at her eagerly.

The doctor looks confused, but continues anyway. "Mrs. Albasi had a minor heart attack, but she's going to be fine."

KC bursts into tears. The doctor squeezes her shoulder. "I'm sure you were worried, but she's doing great now. Everything's going to be fine."

KC is in Vegas when I pack everything I own into six boxes. It's dark and raining when I drop them next to a pallet in the cargo hangar. A man, soaked through from rain, arrives on a forklift. It beeps as he backs the pallet away.

I wish I could have said goodbye to KC in person.

I try calling her when I get to the terminal, but she doesn't answer. The thought of leaving the country without anyone to say goodbye to depresses me. I decide to try my dad. A move abroad seems as good a time as any to break the silence.

"What a nice surprise," he says. I can't tell whether or not he's being facetious. "I've been meaning to call."

"Me, too." In the background, I can hear one of the refinery's test sirens go off. "Are you still at work?"

"Yeah, just getting caught up on some pump checks."

I take a deep breath and say I'm moving to London.

"London? London, England?" There is a trace of disbelief in his voice, like I'm making this up as a way of avoiding him.

"We have a base there."

"But moving there? You're going to live there?"

"Yes, I'm going to live there." I can still hear the siren wailing in the background. "Should I call you another time?"

"No. It's fine." He lets out a long and forceful breath. "London? So we'll probably never hear from you."

"I'm calling you right now."

"Yes. I appreciate that."

I wonder if he thinks my call means I'm apologizing for the wedding.

"Emily. London's a great place to visit. But it's not the kind of place you want to live."

"How do you know? Have you ever visited?"

"You know I haven't."

I check the departure board at the gate. An hour until boarding.

There is a long pause. Neither of us seems to know what to say. I finally say, "Dad, my flight's boarding soon. I have to go."

"Emily?"

"Yes."

"Just be careful."

I slip into a middle seat in economy on a 747 headed to Heathrow and find out the other women in my row are also moving abroad. They are both divorced. One is moving to Addis Ababa where her new boyfriend has contract work in computers. The other is going to Prague with no plan other than starting fresh.

I love this part of my job. It promises that with every mile I fly, I am moving forward, toward something. Maybe if I move fast enough, I can keep one foot in New York and L.A. and Shanghai and Rome at the same time.

I land at Heathrow and let my passport see the glorious light of day. Since I left training, it has been tucked into my purse like a teenage boy's just-in-case condom. A customs agent in a green suit flips to the middle, takes out an enormous stamp, and with one quick *ca-chunk*, I have a three-year visa to live in England.

The second I step out of the terminal, I am immersed in another world. The light is crisp and white, totally unlike the warm gold of California. Black cabs drive on the wrong side of the road with wide, yellow license plates. Around me, travelers speak every language imaginable. I am passed by men with dreadlocks, turbans, and ball caps, women wearing everything from saris to burkas to low-rise jeans.

I drag my large suitcase and small rollaboard onto the Tube headed for central London and my fourth-floor walk-up flat with a view of the Imperial War Museum. My guidebook tells me it was once the famous insane asylum called Bedlam. The flat is a tiny three-bedroom, the rooms barely larger than the beds, but it's gloriously old with its high ceilings, hardwood floors, and glass doorknobs. A half-size fridge sits under the countertop in the kitchen, right next to a washing machine that doubles as a dryer. Its European coolness inspires me.

Despite having been on a plane all night, I wander aimlessly through the streets of London, feel the cobblestones under my boots as I pass pungent curry houses and pubs with names like the Crown and Cushion or the Slug and Lettuce. I can taste the icy winter air and the tangy exhaust from black cabs and red buses. The thousand-year-old streets feel more solid than those of my youth, the ones surrounding hastily built tract homes, where people came from everywhere and kids planned to move anywhere else the day after high school graduation. After the hills had been bulldozed, the developers brought us pleasant-sounding streets named after trees that were nowhere to be seen—Teakwood Way, Applewood Lane, Redwood Crest.

Later in the afternoon, I meet up with a handful of other American transfers who had nothing to leave behind. In London, they tell me, there is constant distraction, no time for your problems. You can go clubbing twenty-four hours a day, even on a Sunday afternoon.

I follow them to the end of a block-long queue at Turnmills, a three-story mega club with resident deejay Tall Paul.

I wrap my scarf over my mouth and blow into it, jumping up and down to stay warm until the doors open and release a tropical storm of body heat.

I am sucked inside a mob of dancers crammed so tight they merely jostle against each other. Tall people protrude from the mass and use their free hands to toss black inflatable mace balls over the sea of heads. Dozens of these oversized S&M toys bounce about, fracturing the rays of green and red lasers that shine down from above. A riptide pulls me along until I no longer know where I am. I'm offered colorful tablets stamped with smiley faces that promise instant bliss. I don't try one, but I lose myself in the trance tracks anyway, and when I look up, I realize there isn't a familiar face around me. Starting tomorrow I will fly to places like Brussels and Amsterdam and Delhi and Hong Kong and Seoul.

I won't need anyone.

18

In Transit

KC squeezes her way up the crowded aisle of Dulles's ancient "space-age" mobile lounge, a boxy room on wheels that will drive her across the ramp to the D concourse and her flight to Las Vegas. She has never needed to sit down so badly, and yet this morning there is standing-room only.

Rain pounds against the window as they wait to load more passengers.

KC grabs the chrome loop above her head and steadies herself against the tide of oncoming travelers. She looks down at the seated man whose horseshoe of gray hair has just grazed her hip.

"They're building a train," he says to the man next to him.

Three men made eye contact as she scooted into the space around their knees. Not one of them has offered his seat, and though she longs to, she can't ask. If she spoke, her voice would crack and they would sense that she is near collapse, look at her with sympathy, and then her air would begin to leak out. She would crumple to the carpet at their feet.

"They've been saying that for a decade. I'll believe it when I see it," says the pilot just ahead of her. Her face is only a few inches away from the back of his starched white shirt. He turns toward horseshoe guy but catches KC's eye. As if he can see the turmoil inside her, he offers a sympathetic smile.

She tries to smile back, but her face doesn't work.

"If it's a guy, forget 'im," he says. She can't place his accent, somewhere Southern, but he says *him* like *eem*. "You're too good for 'im."

He looks wholesome, like a Dave or a Bill. She has always thought the world runs smoother around guys with regular names like Bill or Dave or Jim, guys who take care of their families and pay their bills and show up ten minutes early. He holds on to the chrome strap with one hand and holds his hat with the other. She notices he is wearing blue-and-silver-striped epaulets. United uses blue and gold, so he belongs to someone else.

She wants to lean forward a little, rest her head on his shoulder.

The mobile lounge dislodges from its dock, scrunches a few feet closer to the ground, and pushes back from the terminal.

"Didn't the tunnel for the train collapse last month or something?" asks the pilot.

She shrugs her shoulders. A while back a supervisor did blame a delay on something like that, but she didn't pay attention to the details. You can never trust a delay excuse.

"Where are you headed?" he asks.

"What?" She cups her hand to her ear. He leans in closer to her, but between the conversations and the pounding rain and the accelerating room, she can hardly hear him. She watches his lips as he speaks.

"I'm on my way to Wichita," he says.

"Wichita's nice," she says. She loves the Monte Cristo sandwiches at the hotel restaurant.

The lounge stops moving. The pilot leans down and squints out the window to see why they've stopped. KC looks, too. Through the rain, she sees a United Express regional prop ambling across the tarmac.

When they straighten back up, they are standing several inches farther apart. KC wishes she could start over, end up even closer than before. Maybe he would hold her hand and walk her to her gate, kiss her on the forehead before she heads down the tunnel she can't bear to face alone.

"You all right?" he asks.

"Oh no, it's fine. I'm just tired."

He nods his head as if he knows exactly what she's dealing with. The bus starts moving again.

"Have a long day ahead?" he asks.

She bites her lip and shakes her head. "I was supposed to work four legs today, but they took me off of it. Just one leg to Vegas."

"What?" he asks. "Did you say you're going to Vegas?"

"Yes," she says a little louder. "I was supposed to have a long day, but now I only have one flight." She holds up her index finger as she says "one flight."

"Sweet," he says. "How'd you manage that?"

The hospice called in the middle of the night. Her mom is resting now, they said. Peaceful. The best you could hope for. Sooner than expected is better than suffering. There would be no suffering.

KC hadn't even been able to tell anyone her mom was sick. She tried to talk to Emily, but the timing was never right. The first time she said anything about it out loud was on the phone to Evil Debbie at the crew desk. And now she wants to turn her burden over to this pilot standing in front of her, not even from her own airline, but still part of her world, someone who gets it.

"My mom died," she says, but the people around her are gulping their coffee and coughing up last night's cigarettes and complaining about the weather so loudly that her words get lost.

Her pilot smiles.

No, she thinks, and shakes her head. *You're not listening.*

"Vegas. How cool," he says. "I hope you don't lose too much."

19

By Any Other Name

It's still dark when I come home to my flat after a red-eye from New York. I don't want to wake my roommates if any of them are home, so I leave the lights off. My foot hits something in the hallway, and I wobble on my high heels.

I reach down to find the obstacle—an overstuffed manila envelope. I take it into the bathroom for light and see that it's covered in red-and-blue air-mail stamps and addressed to Mrs. Carl Cavenaugh.

I flip the envelope over, but I can't find a return address. With no idea what's inside, I stick my finger into the opening and begin to tear the top open. I feel a quick sting as the crisp flap slices my finger.

I pull out a stack of papers and see that every last one of them is imprinted with a seal and signed by a judge from the Superior Court, Kern County, Bakersfield.

There is also a yellow page torn from a legal pad, a note from Carl. "These came to me. Looks like there's no going back. Happy now?"

It's legal. I am twenty-four years old and divorced. I jump up and down on the hardwood floor of the living room, wishing KC was here to help me celebrate. I'm free.

I sleep more soundly than I have in months, and when I wake up in the evening, I call a few recent transfers to celebrate. We meet at a nearby pub, the Elusive Camel. It's the first warm day of spring, and the entire population of London is spilling into parks, riding bikes, walking hand in hand along the river, or drinking in the streets outside pubs. Everyone is cheerful, the weight of winter coats off our backs.

We stand outside of the Camel sloshing our pints, toasting my divorce, and chuckling about our new storybook lives. I feel shiny and free with an expensive new A-line haircut with coppery highlights from Toni & Guy and my hot new low-cut top from Kookai—the chic, self-assured look matches perfectly with my new home in Europe's biggest city.

Before long, the flight attendant I least want to hang out with turns up. No one I know was willing to make the move to the UK, but of course, Straight Kevin the Marine would be here.

He slips his arm around me, as if we're old friends. I shimmy away.

I sip my beer and relax into the moment, watch trains as they clack by on their way to Waterloo Station and farmers at the street market selling parsnips and "tom-ah-toes." The stalls overflow with stacks of fruit and bunches of daffodils, tulips, and bluebells.

I wave at the owner of the liquor store on the corner where I regularly stop for milk or bread. He is also an immigrant, from Pakistan. He likes London and says he isn't one bit surprised that someone from America would immigrate here. I like his jolly energy. He hopes I'll go visit Karachi for him someday soon.

"Hey Em," says Kevin.

I hate when people who barely know me shorten my name to pet status.

"You need one of those shirts," he says as he points to a black

T-shirt hanging from a nearby market stall. The shirt says, GOOD
GIRLS GO TO HEAVEN. BAD GIRLS GO TO LONDON.

"Sure," I say, half flattered and half offended. So now even
Kevin thinks I'm a bad girl. I wonder if he knows about Tien or
if he can just sense that I've changed.

My new friends laughingly call me the divorcée, and I chuckle
with them. It *is* funny to be divorced at my age. It's also pathetic.
At least I have an appointment at the embassy tomorrow to
purge Carl's last name from my passport. I will be a new Emily.
Emily Crane.

I watch in pity as Straight Kevin lights a cigarette for an English girl at a nearby picnic table. I pop inside the pub to buy
myself another Newcastle. While I'm waiting at the weathered
wooden bar, a guy in a sharp black suit saunters over to me with
a cigarette dangling from his lips. Under his jacket he's wearing a
vibrantly pink button-down shirt. I like that the men of Britain
are secure enough in their manhood to wear pink or purple to
work, their cheery attire no doubt brightening gloomy office
spaces. In place of the usual tie, this guy has left open the top
two buttons of his shirt, exposing his tanned chest—a look you
don't often see in England. His light brown hair flops into his
eyes like Hugh Grant's.

He winks at me. I wait for the kind of charming pickup line
you would hear in a romantic comedy, but he plucks the cigarette from his mouth and simply says, "American?"

I nod.

"Honestly, I prefer New York to London. Why would anyone
leave?"

As if all Americans are from New York. I'm fairly certain he
wouldn't prefer Bakersfield.

He was outside earlier and had heard my accent. He says he
travels loads for work and is sick of dreadful London.

"Simon," he says and sticks out his hand.

"Emily Crane," I say, shaking his hand vigorously thanks to

the confidence that surges through me at the sound of my own name.

"You announce yourself like I'm meant to know who you are." He gives me a quick once-over, possibly wondering if we once shared a drunken shag he's since forgotten. For a second, I'm tempted to pretend I'm angry that he doesn't remember me.

"My memory is crap. Remind me, just who is Emily Crane?"

"That's a good question." As stupid as it sounds, I don't know anymore. I used to be the girl who got straight As, who played second-chair clarinet, who married her first high school boy-friend. A girl who wore sensible shoes, drove with her hands at ten and two, and got the vacuum lines straight. I was supposed to find true love and live happily ever after. I am not supposed to be twenty-four and divorced. I am not supposed to have been someone's sordid mistress.

I tell him I'm a flight attendant and new in town.

He motions to the bartender, and with one fluid movement, he has ordered pints for both of us. He slides a five-pound note across the bar with an assertiveness that tells me I'm not sup-posed to offer to pay my share.

"Thank you," I say. I wouldn't normally drink with a stranger, but no one this good-looking has ever offered to buy me a drink.

I channel my inner KC and toss my hair over my shoulder. I don't know if it's the new town, the new look, or the new name, but I feel like I can be more interesting, more fun. Tien saw me that way, after all, even if it was only because he had become so settled.

Simon carries our beers over to a high-top table. I follow.

As he pushes my glass toward me, I notice his watch, a Breit-ling with a face the size of a wall clock. He could hang it around his neck and look like Flavor Flav. Having just started his first beer, he inspects the beer selection listed on a table tent.

"Planning on getting me drunk?" I ask.

He shakes his head. "English lesson for you. I'm planning on getting you pissed."

"So if drunk is pissed, how do you say mad?"

He looks up at me like he doesn't know what I mean. After a second he says, "Oh, cross. Mad is crazy."

"Interesting."

"There's something I've always wondered about, and since you're an air hostess, I'm hoping you can answer it for me."

I know what's coming and can hardly stop myself from rolling my eyes. On the plane, men always ask a flight attendant if it's her regular route, but in a bar, we're asked a different question.

He leans over the table as if he doesn't want anyone else to hear the answer I am about to unveil. "What's the secret to bagging first-class upgrades?"

I laugh. "I thought you were going to ask about the mile-high club."

"Whoa." He sits back and puts his hands up, laughing. "Forward, aren't we?"

"Ha. It's not me. It's a popular topic."

"Well, then?"

"What?"

"Have you? You know?"

"No!"

"Not yet anyway."

"Gross. When you work on the plane it loses its mystique. Plus, it would be like having sex in one of those pay-for-use public toilets at a train station."

He bites his lip and looks like he's considering that option and it's not entirely awful. "Only smaller. You'd have to be a gymnast to make it work."

I think about that. "Well, if you were in the handicapped restroom on a big new plane, like a 777, it would be almost roomy."

He sits back and crosses his arms. "Nice."

"I can't believe I'm having this conversation." I take a gulp of beer.

Undeterred, he says, "Have you ever caught anyone?"

"Well, not red-handed. I've seen plenty of college-aged couples fondling each other under airline blankets, and I had a first-class couple ask permission to go to the lav for just that reason."

"What did you say?"

"Well, I said no. Obviously."

He looks disappointed.

"Of course, there was one couple I almost caught."

"Out with it then."

I hesitate and he gestures with his hand, imploring me to continue.

"One time, the lav next to the business galley had been occupied for a suspiciously long time."

"Yeah?"

"As any flight attendant will tell you, your first suspicion isn't mischief. You immediately feel fear, fear that someone died in there. Believe me, it happens. I've heard plenty of stories about passengers who said they felt sick and then croaked on the toilet. So I knocked and asked if help was needed."

Simon snickers. "Very professional of you."

"A man's voice said no, so I went back to cracking ice in the galley. A few minutes later, a bald guy with a head as shiny as Mr. Clean—"

"Who?"

"Nothing, it's an American commercial. Anyway, Mr. Clean comes out of the lav and as soon as the door closes behind him, the lock slides shut and reads 'occupied.'"

Simon flashes a knowing smile. "Oh, there's no hiding that one."

"Nope. Even though I was finished with the ice, I stuck around for a minute to see who would come out."

"Tell me she was hot."

"Actually, *he* was rather hot. It was a guy who had been sitting across the aisle from Mr. Clean all night."

Simon sets his face in his hands and shakes his head, thoroughly disappointed by the big reveal. "Carry on, then. Upgrades. What 'tis the secret?" he asks.

"It's simple," I whisper, leaning farther toward him. "Fly more."

He looks straight into my eyes and offers a devious smile. "You do know you've placed yourself dangerously close to snogging range?"

I look at him for a second too long, and before I can rebuff his blatant come-on, he pulls back. Puts his hands on his lap and says, "Nope, sorry. I don't kiss girls I've only just met."

I laugh and realize there is a cocky charm about him rather than desperation. He could have any woman in the room and he knows it. Although that should turn me off, I can't help but be flattered.

"I've always found the life of an air hostess to be rather fascinating."

I love that he finds me fascinating, even if I do know that people only feel this way on the ground. Once in the air, they're reading newspapers while I'm doing the safety demo.

Simon tells me he's flown more than a hundred thousand miles on British Airways and Virgin Atlantic and Cathay Pacific and Singapore. He's interested in upgrades because his company lost a fortune in dot-com stocks and has been sticking him in business class ever since. He tells me about partying with diplomats in Cairo and Goa and Ibiza, skydiving over the Australian Outback, and skiing black-diamond runs in Chamonix.

I hang on his words, eager to learn about these glamorous foreign airlines and the far-flung cities they serve. "Have you ever been to Vietnam?" I ask.

"Of course," he says. "It's what we call a burgeoning market."

As I look on in awe, he says, "Saigon is madness. You don't

want to go there. The beaches are breathtaking though. But for a really brilliant holiday, you should go to Cambodia. The temples are exquisite."

He grows more and more animated as he tells stories about his trips, and his energy is infectious. I begin to brag, too. I tell him with all the international flights I've been working, I've developed my palate on leftover first-class meals and can't imagine life without lobster or beef carpaccio or crème fraîche or haricot verts or all the cheese, Manchego and Roquefort and Gouda and Camembert.

I am now so comfortable with traveling that last week I got lost in Paris when I just wandered out of the hotel, got on the Metro, and headed for the Latin Quarter. I spent the day poking around tiny side streets, admiring the bookstalls and crepe stands and college-aged lovers, imagining Marius fighting at the barricades in *Les Misérables*, Cosette nursing him back to health. As I watched the sun set over the Seine, I realized that I'd been so at ease that I hadn't checked the name of my hotel or the station where I got on the Metro. It took an hour and a half to find my way back.

"That was decidedly not brilliant," he says.

"Tell me about it." It was pretty stupid, but I also thought it meant I've gone from small-town girl to intrepid traveler.

"Ah, I'm worse. We'd make a sad pair indeed." He finishes his pint, and when he sets his left hand on the table for a second, I notice something I hadn't before. There is a slight tan line on his ring finger.

I take a gulp of beer.

He orders another one and I ask for one, too.

"So, do you always pick up strange foreign women and threaten to snog them in bars?"

He clutches his heart and says, "Oh, you've caught me." After ordering another beer, he tells me he hasn't actually dated for ages.

That's when I get to the point. "Simon, are you married?"
And the second I ask it, I wish I hadn't. We're only having a conversation and I would hate for a conscience to kick in and end it.

He doesn't say anything, and I just know. This is who I am
now, the kind of girl who sits in bars with married men. It would
be so easy to slide into this new role. I'd have license to do everything other girls can't, the girls who haven't already messed up,
the *good* girls.

Finally he looks straight at me and says, "Technically."

"Technically?" A yes or no is an answer I can respect, but
trying to get off on a technicality? I could never fall for a guy
like that.

He is still looking into my eyes, and when I don't flinch, he
puts his hand on mine.

Simon tells me about his wife, Lana, short for Svetlana.
They've been married less than two years. He uses air quotes and
says she's a "model" from Russia. She was here illegally, working
in a hostess bar.

I shake my head because I don't know what that is.

"You know. Girls get paid when blokes buy them drinks."

I don't know, but I say I do. I'm a bit startled that a cocksure
guy like him would fall for a woman who gets paid to make men
fall for her. Then he flips open his phone and shows me a picture
of her. She's so beautiful with her high cheekbones and full lips,
she would give any guy who dated her the confidence of a professional athlete for the rest of his life. For a second, I am jealous
and wonder what he's doing here with me. At the same time, his
company makes me feel sophisticated and worldly.

"I thought I could rescue her." He paid her bills. She quit
her job. Everything seemed perfect until a few months ago
when she wanted money to visit a sick relative in Moscow. He
didn't hear from her for a while so he flew to Moscow and found
her at home with a husband he never knew she had. Her "real
husband."

"So maybe I'm not even *technically* married." He laughs, but his eyes water.

"Breakups are agony," I say.

"My problem is that I can't seem to let go." He clears his throat and looks to the ceiling.

I tell him I can relate.

He reaches his hand across the table and sets it on mine. It's strange being touched so sweetly by a man in a bar, knowing he is only looking for support.

"D'you miss him?" he asks.

I nod.

"Did your husband leave you for another woman?"

I must look taken aback because he apologizes and admits that when he heard my accent outside, he also overheard that I'd just gotten divorced. He didn't even plan on talking about it, but he just wanted to sit with someone who knows what he's going through.

I don't tell him that I am the Other Woman. Instead, I squeeze his hand and tell him I understand. His face softens. The clenched jaw of the last few minutes is gone, as is the roguish smile from the pickup phase. He suddenly looks earnest.

He tells me that he has to go to a glitzy work party at the Groucho Club, an illustrious private club where he'll be hobnobbing with movie stars and diplomats from around the world.

"D'you like to go? Make me look good in front of my boss?"

How can I say no to that?

20

Rogan Josh or Masala Dosa?

KC has handed out tens of thousands of plates featuring chicken or beef in her day—which both taste exactly the same thanks to the chemically concocted orange marinades—but as she pushes her cart down the aisle asking, "Rogan josh or masala dosa? Rogan josh or masala dosa?" she has no idea what she's offering.

The economy cabin is filled with wealthy Indians who are used to servants. Somehow, despite being crammed ten across into a completely full coach section, they believe they are in first class. Hands fly into the air jockeying for her attention. She can hear things like "hot tea" or "whiskey" being shouted from around the cabin. Ten call bells detonate per second. Virtually every seat's call panel is lit up. There is no way to even see where they're coming from let alone answer them. God forbid someone rings for medical attention.

KC has heard about the chaotic London-to-Delhi flights, but this is her first time experiencing one. Following Emily to London was a split-second decision, but not in the whimsical sense. The week before her twenty-first birthday, she had gone back to Henderson to host the memorial.

She went through the motions she had been imagining for

years, ever since she wished her father dead. She bought a new black dress from JCPenney, picked up some flowers, and raced to the mortuary for the short service. She stared at the urn in disbelief, and when it was her turn to speak, she wanted to scream. Someone had collected the wrong ashes. Her dad was supposed to be in there.

There was a reception afterward at the Wooden Nickel Tavern. Most of the guests were regulars at her mom's bar. There was Paul, the mechanic with the glass eye. KC is still never sure which one to look at. Doug, who by the end of the night always fell asleep at the bar with his hand on his fist like Rodin's *Thinker*. Neil, the aerospace engineer who worked at Honeywell and shot Cuervo while filling out the crossword puzzle, in pen, with no mistakes. And of course Rock 'n' Roll James, a feather Indian, as he called himself. He rode up to the bar on his chopper, dressed head-to-toe in Harley gear as always.

A few years ago, he had fallen in love with KC's mom, but she was into some other loser at the time. One day he couldn't stand it. He walked outside, hopped on his chopper, and sat in the parking lot redlining the engines. Flames shot out of the tailpipes like rockets, and the whole of greater Vegas could probably hear him.

He had spent almost every night at the bar, but somehow her mom never hooked up with him. Eventually, they became friends, family almost. He was one of the few people KC thought they could count on, and it always irked her that her mom wouldn't go for him. Attraction isn't everything.

After the reception, James took KC back to her mom's apartment. She had planned on going there to clean it out, but at the bottom of the concrete staircase that led to the second-floor apartment, she threw up. So she left, telling herself she'd try again that evening. Then she left town.

She called James to apologize, but he said it was okay. If her mom could have, she would have flown the coop, too.

She toyed with the idea of flying to Hawaii, quitting United, and landing on her dad's doorstep like an orphan.

The timing didn't seem right, though, seeing as she still wished he would die instead.

She filled her time chasing Jake around the country while his band played at bars and small festivals and eventually sports arenas when they got picked up to open for the band that opens for the Red Hot Chili Peppers. He thinks she's a blast, partying so hard she can't remember anything the next day, but he doesn't realize forgetting is her sole intention.

Then three months later she got a belated sympathy card from her dad. Hallmark said they were deeply saddened to hear about her loss, but the only thing her dad actually wrote was his name. That's when KC decided to put two oceans between them.

"Rogan josh or masala dosa?" KC asks a woman whose plump midriff announces itself from the opening in her sari.

"I am veggie table," she says.

KC sets the masala dosa on her tray and hopes they don't run out of their only vegetarian option.

It is bright and noisy and absolutely no one in coach is sleeping, which means no one passes up a meal. Without leftovers to sample, she still doesn't know what she has spent the last few hours serving. Most likely they're both just a more exotic version of chemical oranges.

"Rogan josh or masala dosa?" she asks the passengers who are seated around her pressing their call bells. A senior flight attendant named Sue echoes from the next cart. Half of the passengers just wiggle their heads, which according to the Hindi speakers could mean yes or no or either or pretty much anything.

Whenever she can, KC steals moments to press her nose against the window at her door. She's peering down at the sands crossed by Greeks and Silk Road traders and Mongols and Muslims and Crusading Christians, the sprawling desert metropolis of modern Tehran. She is finally seeing the other side of the world.

Turns out it looks a lot like greater Vegas.

KC is tapped on the shoulder and told it's time for her break. She opens the door to what looks like another closet, climbs the stairs, and stoops to enter the small crew rest area hidden inside the tail of the 747. She crawls into the top compartment of a capsule-hotel-style rest bunk, kicks off her high heels, and curls up under a United-issue blanket, ready to let the light chop rock her to sleep for the next hour or so.

She pulls a sleeping mask over her eyes and tries to relax for the first time since her phone rang at 5 A.M. calling her to come in to work. Although she was hoping to hide in bed all day, she's relieved to be headed somewhere new. She keeps thinking that if she gets far enough away, a seam will split open and she will crawl forward into a newer, better world.

It's 1:30 A.M. local time when they land in Delhi—five and a half hours ahead of London and ten and a half ahead of New York, where she spent her last layover. Fortunately, she no longer has a body clock. When you bounce around between time zones often enough, you force yourself awake when you need to and sleep when you get the chance.

A Hong Kong–based crew is waiting to take their plane out. They fly in and out at night because Delhi's heat and humidity are so intense that wide-body jets have trouble taking off in the day. When it's 120 degrees outside, the air is too thin for liftoff.

Even inside the terminal, it's muggy. It smells musty, like wet wood, sweet and exotic. At immigration, rather than scanning her passport, she signs her name into a notebook filled with unlined brown paper and then passes through a lobby packed with

people waiting in this middle-of-the-hemisphere transfer station
where they'll connect to Europe and Asia. Families huddle together and sleep on the floor. Women in sparkling saris slump
over their luggage. Packs of flight attendants from around the
world admire each other's uniforms—the chic red skirt-suits of
Virgin Atlantic, the iconic blue-and-red sarongs of demure Singapore Girls, the elegant Emirates' veils. Maybe some of them
even envy the relative comfort of United's loose polyester.

Outside the airport, they pass a group of stray dogs, their ribs
protruding under nearly hairless skin.

"They come here each night to beg," says Sue, the fifty-
something flight attendant KC watched degenerate into a harried
mess of hot flashes on the way here.

The crew van looks like a cabaret theater with tasseled red
velvet curtains draped along the windows and the sides of the
windshield. The dash is covered in gold figurines of Hindu gods.

KC stares out of her window and into the dark. An occasional streetlight or passing truck illuminates billboards for Aloe
Fresh dish soap, Johnnie Walker, Pepsi, and curry-flavored Prin-
gles. This is the promise of the flight attendant gig. It will quickly
fill the hole inside of her with foreign sounds and smells and
sights. Day by day, an onslaught of new memories will push out
the old.

They reach the tall white Sheraton in the diplomatic district
where just about every foreign airline sends its crews. KC quickly
changes out of her uniform and into the new asymmetrical Cynthia Rowley top and CK jeans she bought at sample sales in New
York to impress Jake. She may only have one designer outfit, but
since she's with a different batch of people every day, she can
look chic on every layover.

By 2:30 A.M. she meets the people she flew in with at the
crew room on the sixth floor. The hotel gets so much airline

business it has a room for crew to socialize in, like an executive lounge without the business equipment and free breakfast.

Sue, who had worked the flight a dozen times before, talked about it the whole way over. The room's motto—nothing counts in India. When KC opens the door, she sees the maxim in action. While at least thirty people look on, Sue plops onto the lap of a guy in a British Airways uniform who must be twenty years her junior.

When you're this far away, the philosophy goes, the weight of home can't reach you. No one needs that to be true as much as KC.

She is hit with the smell of sandalwood smoke wafting from an incense burner on one of the conference room's two board-room tables. A Sikh bartender with his long beard rolled up to his chin and wearing a white uniform stands behind a wooden counter ready to pour drinks and hand out dishes of snack mix. Judging by the mountains of liquor minis and bottles of airline wine strewn about the room, he won't be selling many of his wares.

KC sits on a small sofa in the back of the room. A pair of red-faced pilots from Aeroflot enter the room laughing loudly. They plop down on the matching sofa across from KC's and slam bottles of vodka on the coffee table next to a bowl of fennel seeds.

"Wodka," one of them says with a deep cinematic KGB voice as he pours her a full glass. KC grew up watching movies with Russian villains and American heroes, so it's disorienting to be sharing a drink, a job, and a lifestyle with people she'd been programmed to see as shadowy henchmen.

She decides to try out a joke she just heard. "What is the only thing that separates flight attendants from the lowest form of life on Earth?"

"Tell us," says one of the Russians.

"The cockpit door." It lands with a thud. They either don't get it or don't appreciate it.

Straight Kevin walks into the room wearing a tight-fitting red T-shirt that clings to a body that could have been molded out of clay. He scans the room filled with "air hostesses" from BA and JAL, but in the end, he sits next to her. Closer than he needs to, of course. For all his ills, she finds herself comforted by the presence of someone who knows her. Since her mom died, the art of self-sufficiency feels like backbreaking work.

He samples the wodka. She's careful not to brush against him when she reaches for a handful of snack mix that will hopefully help her stay sober.

While still chewing his snack mix, Kevin asks her how the rock star is.

"Great." KC's pride won't let her admit to any weakness on the couple front. No one needs to know that her boyfriend spends nine out of ten nights surrounded by groupies in Wonderbras and miniskirts, who will take the guys two at a time just because they're in a band.

She can't stop thinking about her extended numerology reading in a *Cosmopolitan* magazine, which she consulted during a momentary lull in the flight. It promised to decode the secrets of her personality. She expected she might be called courageous or tough. If there's one thing she inherited from her mom, it's the ability to take whatever life hands her and pick herself up, try a new approach, have fun. Instead, it said she would live a life of excitement and never let anyone tie her down. So according to this magazine, by picking too many C answers, she is destined for eternal chaos.

She finds it ironic that she can see and do so many exotic things when the seemingly realistic things she dreams of are out of her reach. It may not be cool, or feminist, but she's always wished for a normal life—a three-bedroom house with a little yard. A family. Something people like Jake take for granted.

She got a taste of first-class stability when Jake was playing in Providence, Rhode Island. He took her to his family's summer house in Newport for a little scenic tryst. There she found two surprises. First, it was no house—it was the size of an apartment building. Then, to Jake's dismay, the whole clan was there for the weekend.

KC admired everything Jake was annoyed by—sit-down family meals, plans for future get-togethers, the constant buzz of brothers and sisters and nieces and nephews. Though he complained about the stifling Carington life, she envied how naturally he fit into it. It took all her effort to choose the right silverware, hold a wineglass properly, hit a tennis ball over the net. She had never been so quiet or insecure.

When KC did speak, Jake's mother's response would be the same: "How charming." KC didn't know if she was calling KC's life small like a "charming" cottage, or if she was being outright sarcastic.

Neither interpretation suggested a successful debut.

Sue's BA pilot leaves and she comes over and sits on the arm of the sofa next to Kevin and says, "Hey, KC. Thought I'd come say hi."

On the flight here, every time Sue had the urge to tell KC what to do, it started with "In the sixties . . ." She's part of a sub-set of senior mamas who are determined to let everyone know they were hired in the glamour days of cute uniforms, high ticket prices, and admiring passengers, back when tens of thousands of girls applied for every position and only those with the beauty and poise of Miss America made the cut.

After only knowing Straight Kevin for one flight, Sue leans on his shoulders, her arms around his neck. Every so often you see one of these used-up old ladies throwing herself at undiscerning men, trying to prove she can be courted by more than the AARP.

She may be overtanned and overplucked, but it's obvious Sue

LOVE ME ANYWAY   181

was beautiful back then, back when her eyes were bright and shimmering with expectations rather than filled with disappointments. KC thinks of photos of her mom when she was little. Had she actually been as happy as she looked? Or was she just smiling for the camera, smiling like a flight attendant?

Although Kevin doesn't pull away from Sue, he is openly ogling a threesome of Virgin Atlantic air hostesses who are on their way out.

Sue asks Kevin if he's still with his girlfriend.

"You mean Makiko?" he asks.

"Whoever."

He shoves a handful of snack mix into his mouth and mutters something about her being too clingy.

KC wonders if Jake tells people she's too clingy. She thinks of chicks in St. Louis who are probably pointing their fake ta-tas at Jake right now, hoping to say they're with the band.

Jake, who always looked like he hadn't slept in days, claimed he wasn't even tempted by skanks who would offer themselves to strangers just because they're musicians. KC laughed it off, but how can she be sure?

She told him she loved him, stupidly.

He said it back, but it didn't seem totally sincere.

"You don't have to say it just because I did," she said.

"How could I not?" he asked. "You're perfect for me. You can fly to see me wherever I am."

"Don't you ever get tired of being on the road?"

"No," he said. "This is how I make my living."

More or less, she thought snarkily. It wasn't just his words that worried KC, but the joy in his voice as he said them, like the road wasn't only his living, but his reason for living.

"I thought you of all people would get that."

One of the Aeroflot pilots hands Sue a shot of vodka. She peels herself off of Kevin to drink it and slams it back on the table. They fill her up again. And again.

KC must look surprised because Sue laughs and says, "You think this is bad? I used to put a shower cap over the smoke detector in the lav and smoke grass in there."

"No way," says Kevin. "You did not."

"We all did. It was the sixties."

KC holds back a groan. She takes Sue's developmentally delayed maturity as a warning. Although flying accelerates aging of the body, if not properly monitored, it can suspend the mind in a vat of cryogen. It's easy to fool yourself into thinking you're forever young when you live in a state of constant amusement.

Sue leans toward Kevin, and the plunging neckline of her blouse reveals a deep craggy crease that runs the length of her cleavage. "Mutton dressed as lamb," as her mom would say.

KC wonders how wild she really was back in the days of white gloves, girdle checks, and weigh-ins. She doesn't even want to think of how many men Sue must have slept with if she kept it up for the last four decades. If KC's still flying in her golden years, she promises herself she'll become one of the senior mamas who gush with affection for unaccompanied minors who remind them of their grandkids.

"Hey Kev," says Sue, rubbing the top of his nearly shaved head. "I like the high-and-tight."

He reaches up and touches the back of his neck. "Actually this is long. It's been almost three weeks and they used a number two."

"You know. In the sixties, I flew the Vietnam charters to bring our boys home."

He looks at her like she's out of touch. KC realizes Sue really does have an involuntary tic. Why would she remind twenty-something Kevin of her age?

"Lemme tell you. They were effed up something bad," says Sue.

"No shit," says KC. "My mom dated this vet whose idea of a

Friday night was sticking a half-loaded gun in his mouth and pulling the trigger to find out if it was his night to die."

Kevin looks at KC softly, protectively.

For a second she feels shielded and safe and almost wishes she was the kind of girl who could let herself need someone.

"Don't go thinking that's a military thing though," he says. "The guy who beat the living shit out of my mom didn't serve his country for a single day. Such a pussy. I knocked his teeth out the day I turned thirteen."

There is a moment of silence before Sue breaks in. "Well, I always liked Marines," she says, nudging Kevin. "Still do."

He lifts his glass and they clink their drinks together.

As Sue leans and thrusts in Kevin's direction, he turns and looks at KC, again. She can't help but look back.

She decides to show Sue how it's done in the twenty-first century. Instead of flirting with Kevin, she smiles at the Aeroflot pilots, laughs at everyone's jokes besides Kevin's. It isn't long before he is accidentally brushing her leg as he reaches for his drink and poking her or clapping her shoulder when she says something funny.

The sun starts to rise and through the window, KC gets her first glimpse of New Delhi. Layers of haze hang around the green trees and white concrete buildings of the diplomatic enclave surrounding them.

"I know what we should do," Sue says, as if they were trying to come up with plans together. "We should go to the Taj this morning."

Kevin says he went last week and isn't up for the drive.

Sue sticks her lower lip out in a pout.

"I'll go," says KC. Although spending the day with Sue isn't KC's idea of a good time, she is dying to see more of India than the inside of a hotel.

Kevin looks at his watch. "If you're going to go all the way to Agra and get back in time to eat and get ready for our flight, you'd better leave now."

"Fine," says Sue sadly. Clearly her invitation wasn't for KC, but she tells her to meet in the lobby in fifteen minutes. She has to get her purse and camera.

KC finishes her drink, and when she heads back to her room to get her own purse, Kevin follows her. In the elevator, she backs up against the wall and he stands right in front of her, just inches away. The doors open. He walks beside her down the hall but says nothing. She slides her key into the lock and feels him against her back as she waits for the click. She opens the door and he puts his hands on her shoulders, turns her around, and presses his lips to hers.

But she doesn't feel them. She doesn't feel anything physical or emotional, only a completely cerebral flicker of pride for being the one he wanted.

Kevin puts his hands onto both sides of KC's head, his fingers slide into her hair. He presses his lips against hers again, pulls her hard against him.

She wants to bury her face in his neck, wishes she could let herself cry. But even in India, she knows he cannot help her.

She pushes him away and says stop.

"What?" he asks, looking down as if she were laughing at him.

"I have to meet Sue."

"Well, I'm in four-eighteen if you want to stop by after the trip."

KC turns on her heel, flashes a quick smile, and says she'll think about it.

KC and Sue slide into the back of a taxi. Even at dawn it's well over one hundred degrees, and there is no air-conditioning. To make matters worse, KC had nothing to wear but jeans because she was packed for Chicago when they pulled her out of the pre-flight briefing and sent her to Delhi instead.

Their driver's gums are caked with dried blood from lack of dental care, and what might be his only shirt is torn halfway across his chest. KC immediately notices that his BO smells like curry. It reminds her of a flight attendant who claimed Asians think American funk smells like butter and eggs.

The driver burps almost as often as he slams on the brakes. With no seat belts in the car, Sue and KC lurch forward into the front seats every time there is a reason to slow down.

The road they're on has only three lanes, but six rows of cars squeeze alongside each other. Every driver honks incessantly, especially the young men on mopeds who carry their girlfriends sidesaddle on their laps. *Tuk tuks*, rickshaws, buses, dogs, and cows compete for the road.

"Look, a monkey," says Sue, pointing to a patch of trees in the center of a roundabout.

It swings from one branch to another and then almost disappears behind a dense clump of leaves.

KC has never seen anything like India, and the timing couldn't be better. This taxi may not be an ashram, but India is *the* place to go when you're recovering from a loss. She leans back in her seat and tells herself she didn't make a mistake. The move, the job, the lifestyle, it all might work out after all. She loves taking care of people. By now she should be comfortable with instability.

Once out of the Delhi crowds, they're on open highway. Golden fields and grassy farms are edged with mud hovels and more billboards for whiskey and household cleaning products, and of course Leonardo DiCaprio's new movie.

KC closes her eyes, breathes in the musty air, and pretends she's alone. She feels the promise of freedom. No one in India knows her. Her phone doesn't work and she doesn't have a computer, so no one can reach her with good news or bad.

Looking out at the flood of foreignness all around her, she feels her first real sense of hope.

Sue starts complaining about the crew desk and contract violations and renewed talk about a merger with another airline.

KC stares out the window, tuning her out. She sees an elephant carrying construction material in its trunk as it ambles down the road with a handful of workers.

The driver turns up the radio, providing an indie-pop soundtrack of sitars and warbling sopranos to their journey.

A few hours in, the driver stops at a roadside building in the middle of nowhere. "It is time for my tea," he says in carefully enunciated English. He points to the main building and says "souvenirs" and then points to a smaller outbuilding and says "toilet."

Sue and KC immediately head to the toilet. KC's new CK jeans, wet with sweat, feel as thick as a firefighter's uniform as she swishes down the path. It's just barely summer, and she can't imagine what this place is going to feel like when she comes back at its height.

"My buzz is wearing off," says Sue. "Can you get a hangover if you never go to sleep?"

"Definitely."

"Kevin's pretty great, right?" she says, nudging KC.

KC doesn't know if Sue wants to be reassured or if she's testing to see if she's competition. "He's not so bad, I guess."

KC's heart sinks when she sees that the "toilets" are just holes in the ground. She looks to Sue, who just shrugs.

"When you gotta go, you gotta go," says Sue. She heads over to a hole, looking only mildly intimidated.

KC hesitates. She hasn't done much camping and has never had to squat before.

"It's at least another two hours and they probably won't have our type of toilets either."

After they've both navigated the open plumbing system, Sue pulls out a compact and stands in a corner of the room. KC's not sure if she should wait or not, but she does. She watches Sue squint into the little mirror and line her lips with the pencil. If KC doesn't go see Kevin when they get back, he'll probably just invite Sue.

She can't help but wonder what Sue really wants from her life. And what she already has. Does she have kids somewhere living with their dad or away at college? Is she having a midlife regression or did a grown-up life just pass her by while she was living for the moment?

Sue smears an almost clear lip gloss over the pencil and puckers her lips while examining them in the mirror.

Maybe Sue once faced her own crossroads, and instead of dealing with it, she decided to run.

Whatever it was, it probably happened in the sixties.

KC may only be twenty-one, but she is too tired to keep running.

They wait about a half hour for their driver to finish his tea. They wander the stalls of souvenirs, circling and circling, browsing trinkets they have no intention of buying until it becomes clear that they have been brought there for a reason. They are expected to buy, and the driver is expecting a kickback. KC picks up a white marble elephant, which she might buy for Jake if she had any money. The stall owner urges her to buy it. He doesn't believe her when she tells him she has no money. "You Am-rican," he says. "You rich."

They don't take credit cards and there is only one ATM in downtown Delhi, thirty minutes from their hotel. KC had had to borrow enough rupees for the cab from Sue, who had some left over from her last trip.

"Do you want that?" asks Sue. "I probably have enough, I'll totally get it for you."

Even though KC could afford it if they took a debit card, the gesture makes her feel poor. She doesn't want Sue feeling sorry for her.

"Seriously. It's not like I have anyone else to buy for." Sue looks at KC imploringly. "You should get it."

"You take it?" says the stall owner, already wrapping the elephant.

KC gives in, and Sue looks relieved, like she was desperate to have someone, anyone, to buy for.

And now KC feels sorry for Sue. She can't bear the thought of still having no family at that age.

On the way out, a man in white robes walks a bear that is chained to his stick. The man says if they give him money, he'll make it dance.

Another two hours later, the driver stops the car again. "Taj Mahal," he calls out as if they were on a bus. KC steps out of the car and into the crushing heat that bears down on a parking lot full of beggars, most of them lepers. One completely limbless man lies on a scraggly piece of wood fashioned into a skateboard and uses his chin to propel himself across the blacktop as he asks for money. It pains her to shake her head. She had to borrow the cash to get through the gates, and besides, she's heard that if you give money in India, you'll immediately have dozens of beggars following you. They already have seven following them to the security check.

Finally, they enter the grounds of the Taj Mahal. The sun beats down as they pass through the red sandstone gate and walk along the iconic reflecting pool where family after family poses for photos.

Sue hands her camera to the head of a family of six and points at herself and KC and the Taj Mahal in the background.

She puts her arm around KC and they both smile into the camera as the father lifts his fingers to indicate one, two, three.

Sue jogs over to retrieve her camera and stares at the newborn the man's wife is carrying. She does not smile and coo like someone who is recalling her own children's early years. She stares as if this beautiful giggling baby has emptied her.

KC will not end up this way. She feels her own heart being stripped of pride and anger and filled with a burning need to see her father.

At the base of the gleaming white mausoleum, they are instructed to take off their shoes. KC jumps from foot to foot on the hot sandstone, but when they reach the marble steps, the white stone is cool beneath her feet. She is dazzled by the shining dome and regal minarets, inlaid with inches of semiprecious stones, the views of the Yamuna River.

Without a penny to spend, they try to avoid the tour guide who is telling them about the buildings and the tombs, about the love of Shah Jahan for his wife Mumtaz Mahal. He was so heartbroken by her death that he hired twenty thousand workers to spend twenty-two years building this monument to her.

Sue gasps.

KC knows what she's thinking. "True love."

"I gave up on that decades ago," says Sue.

KC won't give up on love, but at this point, she is more than ready to dump the Cinderella version her mom always seemed to be holding out for, rejecting decent men like Rock 'n' Roll James for the fantasy of a suave savior. They never tell you what makes that Prince Charming so alluring anyway. Looks? Money? Power? Those qualities aren't exactly known to produce a lifetime of love and devotion.

21

Status Quo

Simon hooks his thumbs on his pants pockets and smiles. "Everyone's looking at me."

I scan the Heathrow arrivals lane and see cars and buses pulling over, passengers lifting suitcases off trolleys, airport workers smoking cigarettes. Everyone is pretty much just going about their business. "Why do you think that?" I ask.

He takes a step back and motions toward me, like Vanna White revealing a letter. "I have a BMW *and* an air hostess."

I shake my head and laugh as he opens the trunk, or the boot, and throws my rollaboard inside. I underestimated the effect when I signed up, but being a flight attendant is the grown-up version of cheerleader. After marching band, I'm enjoying the role. I straighten the little blue scarf tied around my neck and press my lips together to bring out the color.

I walk around to the right side of his brand-new black M6. It's the perfect trade. He gets to tell people he pulled an air hostess and I don't have to spend all morning getting home on the Tube, asleep with my mouth hanging open.

He steps up behind me and puts his hand on my shoulder.

How gentlemanly, I think, *he's going to open my door*. I turn around and look up at him, definitely placing myself in kissing range.

"Shall I let you drive?" he asks.

I look down and notice the steering wheel. "Duh," I say and go to the passenger seat on the left.

"That's my girl," he says.

Although we still haven't slept together, we've been seeing each other pretty regularly for the last month or so. It's a glamorous life he's introduced me to—private car services, designer cocktails at private clubs, dinner at places like Momo, the North African–inspired casbah that happens to be the hottest spot in London at the moment.

Our lunches aren't half bad either. Simon works at an investment firm in the Square Mile, a two-thousand-year-old neighborhood that is now more or less the Wall Street of London. His building dates from the nineteenth century, but the inside is strikingly modern. I wouldn't be surprised if it was designed by Philippe Starck. It has a killer cafeteria that overflows with gourmet juices and strawberries and brie and prosciutto and fresh-baked bread and even beer and wine. The only thing it's missing? Cash registers. Everything is free.

I figure I'm not the sleazy meal-ticket type if my date isn't paying either.

As soon as Simon starts the car, I close my eyes and yawn. After just working an eight-hour night flight, I'm not what you'd call a good time. But I think that's part of my allure. I have inadvertently played by "The Rules," not returning calls or e-mails right away, turning down dates, and even better, I leave the country at least once a week. Simon's loving every minute of it.

Although everything about him—the pinstripe suits, the swagger, the ever-present smirk—suggests a confident ladies' man, there is a boyish side to him that hasn't been angling to get laid. If it is intended to be reverse psychology, it's working. At the very least, I have to admit I'm curious about where this could lead.

"You look knackered," he says.

Oh and the accent. I love that he gets knackered and cocks up and wears bespoke suits and smokes fags whilst turning things anti-clockwise.

"How was Singapore?" I ask.

"Mad. Chicago?"

"Same old." Through my window, I watch an obese family of four struggling with their wheel-less oversized suitcases. The father is wearing clean white tennis shoes, Dockers, a tucked-in plaid shirt, and a fanny pack. He looks so obscenely American that even I want to pickpocket him.

"My parents are throwing a little soiree for my granny's eightieth birthday. I was thinking of bringing you along."

That wasn't quite an invitation, so I don't know how to answer.

"My mother would be thrilled to see me dating a girl like you."

"What do you mean?"

He looks at me for a second. "No one's ever told you that you're the kind of girl to bring home to mum?"

I sigh. "They have." I suppose I should be relieved, but I find myself a bit disappointed that after everything I've experienced, I haven't really changed that much. Then again, I am following Lana, who may or may not have been paid to sleep with the customers at her club.

I imagine bringing Tien home to meet my dad and Nancy. Would they throw him out of the house? Disown me? It's a strange thought. Not that I want to go home. I'm having the time of my life here. But it's disconcerting to think that if they knew what I've been doing, I might not be welcomed back.

Simon reaches over to my side, opens the glove box, and pulls out a European-sized ten-pack of Marlboros. "Lana rang this morning," he says, watching my face as he taps a cigarette out of the pack.

"Oh?"

He hits the gas and I am forced back in my seat. Only seconds later we jerk to a stop at a red light. "It was a voice message. She asked for money, but I haven't rung her back."

"Oh," I say with a sympathetic tone this time. I do feel for him and the Lana business. But I don't believe that he didn't call her back.

"Birds. You and your mixed messages," he says.

I don't know if he means me or womankind when he says *you*. If he just means Lana, I wonder if someday he will realize that she is giving him a clear message. I consider pointing out the obvious—that she had only ever been in love with his money and his citizenship. Wouldn't that make it easier? To know why something ended or find out that it wasn't really love anyway?

I think that would help. I know a black-and-white answer is what I was hoping for in Chicago when I poked my head into Tien's company mailbox last night. They're all accessible so that onboard services can slip in tyrannical corporate updates on a weekly basis ("Don't forget you can only wear nude pantyhose, not tan"). Snooping isn't too difficult. I slipped my hand into the file folder and felt a thick envelope. It wasn't just licked closed, but was taped around the edges. I pulled it out and felt my heart rate sprint to the next zone. I was sure I had found something. After staring at it for a few minutes, I gently peeled back the tape, both fearing and hoping I would find letters from another woman. If he was cheating with someone else, or had been all along, I needed to know. Then I would hate him, and it would be easier if I could hate him.

We turn right onto Lambeth Bridge, heading to my side of the river. Simon's phone rings. The ringtone is "Cold as Ice." Without looking down, he grabs the phone and silences it.

I hope he doesn't ask me if I think Lana's just after his money. It's not that he doesn't have anything else going for him. For God's sake, he's racked up a résumé of things going for him—he skydives and scuba dives, plays the guitar and plays tennis, rides a motorbike and uses power tools, speaks French, and has a degree from Cambridge. It's just that *he* believes the money is his best quality, and that affects the way women look at him.

Last time we were out he spent thirty minutes describing his new stereo system. At least three times when I didn't seem enthusiastic enough, he reminded me, "It cost four thousand quid!"

Sometimes I even have to wonder if he was ever in love with Lana or if he just loved how successful he looked with a model-beautiful woman on his arm.

He grew up in the council flats of the East End, a place Americans would call the projects. So it's not like I don't understand why he's proud of his accomplishments. It's just that none of it seems to be coming from a place of passion. It's like he does these things not to experience them but to hang a certificate on the wall.

While I admire some of the bullet points he has amassed, I still don't know who he is. And if he only goes rock climbing so people think he's athletic and daring, that's hardly living. Is it any better than staying in a small town and doing the job your parents expect?

For years, I was embarrassed by having seen so little outside of the farms and factories of my hometown. Lately, as exciting as the jet-set life is, I'm starting to admire something in the realness of the people of Bakersfield, people who don't feel they have anything to prove. Of course, I would never, ever, admit this to my dad.

As we pull up to my building, he pops a breath mint into his mouth. He thrusts the tin box out to offer me one as well. I take one.

My suitcase rumbles behind him as he drags it over the cobblestones outside my flat.

We climb the stairs and slip into my room. It's nothing fancy, not like Simon's loft in the middle of posh Islington, but I love its Englishness—vintage floral wallpaper, high ceilings, and cased windows.

Simon lifts up a small, framed photo of me and KC taken in San Francisco. "Everywhere I've been, I still haven't been to California. I'll have to get my little flygirl to take me there."

He loosens his tie. There is a glint in his eye that makes me gulp.

Just in case one of my roommates comes home, I prop my suit-case against my door. Maybe all I need to do is try. Maybe when he touches me, I will feel the passion coursing through me. I will close my eyes and throw back my head and I will melt into Si-mon's body and just that easily, I will be alive again.

I sit on the bed. He stands by the window, looking out over the Thames at the spires of Big Ben and the Houses of Parlia-ment. "Nice view," he says. Then he slides the curtains closed.

"Good idea," I say, increasingly nervous about the momen-tum he is generating. I try to come up with conversation to ease into things. I start babbling on about how I am finally getting the hang of the complicated international service, that I might just make it, that I am so glad I had the courage to leave my old life behind, that I'm the happiest I've ever been.

He loosens his shirt collar.

"I like that shirt," I say.

"It's Armani."

He sits down next to me.

I try to focus on Simon's wickedly enticing smile, not on how different this feels from being with Tien, how Tien didn't like me because I was an air hostess or a hard-to-get foreigner but just because I was me. I try not to think about what I found in his mail file in Chicago.

After staring at the envelope for several minutes, I gave in and peeled up the tape, expecting letters from some other woman.

They were from me. Every letter and a printout of every
e-mail I'd ever written him. Two were torn into hundreds of
pieces and taped back together, a seemingly impossible puzzle. I
pushed them back inside, taped the envelope, and ran until I
caught up with my crew on the moving walkway.

Simon laughs and puts his hands on my shoulders, gently pushes
me down to the bed, and starts tickling me. I writhe around
laughing and gasping for air. Suddenly his lips are on mine and
his minty fresh tongue is slithering into my mouth. I kiss him
back, vigorously but without passion. No matter how hard I try,
Simon is a post-surgery ice chip. He is no substitute for water.

He moans and squeezes my breast. I don't stop him. I want to
get it over with, to have proof that I am moving on. I want it to
set me free.

He slides his hand up my skirt, along my hose-covered thigh,
and in an instant, the gentleman side of Simon is gone. He frantically unbuttons my dress, and his pants and his hands and his
mouth are all over me. I kiss him back with the same fury and
wrap my legs around him as if we were in the middle of a
bodice-ripping soap opera sex scene, the kind of sexual frenzy
that starts and stops too quickly to please a real-life woman.

Only this time, neither partner ends up pleased. He tries and
tries to force it, but he can't get hard enough to make it happen.

He runs his fingers through his hair and exhales noisily.

This is another scene I know from movies. I know it isn't me.
I know enough to say, "It's okay. It happens to lots of guys."

"Don't bloody patronize me," he says and sits up. "It doesn't
feel right."

Okay, so it is me.

He shakes his head and lies back down. "It's . . . you know."

It's that I'm not Lana.

I nod in sympathy and start to wonder what his life would be like if things had worked with her. Maybe instead of traveling and skydiving and getting wasted on pub crawls he would spend each evening standing at the Cannon Street train station with all the other suits awaiting the 6:07 to Barnehurst or Dartford or some other suburb. He'd read the *Telegraph* as he made his way home to a semidetached brick house with lace curtains and double-glazed windows. I am suddenly sure that with the right woman, that is a life he could live with passion.

"Might we just forget that happened?" he says.

"And what, just try again?"

"No." He reaches out and holds my hand. "I'm sorry. I've hurt you."

Well, I wouldn't go that far.

The thing is, I feel relieved and that disappoints me. I had hoped for more, but I imagine being pressed under his weight, naked, trying not to notice that I would like him better if he were shorter, if his accent were different. The pressure would build as I focus on each movement of his body and tell myself how good it should feel, concentrate on getting out of my head and into the moment so I could just let go. He would kiss my earlobe and pull my hair and I would think, *He is so good on paper.*

22

Girl Walks into a Bar

Kc feels like a lotto ball, puffs of air tossing her up and down and all over the world. In just the last week she's hit London, Delhi, San Francisco, Honolulu, London again, and now she's right back in San Francisco.

She steps out of the crew van and into the Victorian lobby of the Hotel Richelieu. Another day, another anonymous three-star hotel.

She goes to her room and immediately tears off the wool dress that has been aggravating her red and blistered shoulders for the last twelve hours. Of course, the sun isn't the only thing that burned her in Hawaii.

After a dab of aloe vera that does nothing to ease her pain, she remembers why she never liked this hotel. It doesn't even have a minibar.

She slips on her asymmetrical Cynthia Rowley top and heads across the street to Koko's for a cocktail, passing under the red neon martini glass to enter a near-empty bar where two older gentlemen in RETIRED NAVY caps are playing pool. She can't help but think of the last time she was here with Raj and Emily and

Tien. She figures she's just being nostalgic when she imagines Tien in the slender Vietnamese form sitting alone at the bar.

The man sips from a rocks glass and stares at a baseball game on a screen mounted in the corner. Not an unusual air-crew pastime.

She thinks about how funny it is that airlines hire people who are friendly and social and then they end up spending so much time alone.

At the interview, you're asked to bubble in a Scantron personality test that will reveal your outgoing nature. You speak in front of groups and answer questions from a podium to prove you have charisma. You playact scenarios with mock passengers to show that you will be a people person under any and all circumstances. Then you get a job that will send you out into the world alone—alone in a hotel room, alone at home despite having six roommates, alone at the hotel bar drinking vodka and eating salad to add roughage to an otherwise airline-tray diet.

KC considers leaving the too-quiet dive—nothing playing on the jukebox, no cool kids knocking back Jägerbombs. But something pulls her to the man sitting alone at the bar. She hops onto the stool next to him and says, "Hey. I thought that was you."

Tien turns and looks at her with surprise, or perhaps embarrassment.

"You won't believe this, but I flew with Kevin last week, and now here you are," she says.

"Who?"

"He was on your crew the night we met."

A flicker of recognition crosses his face. "Small world."

"I shouldn't be surprised to see you're still enjoying the San Francisco routine."

He nods skeptically, perhaps wondering whether or not she meant that as an accusation. "How have you been?"

"Good. I'm based in London now." She quickly adds that Emily is, too. She's an obvious source of common interest, but this time KC did intend to needle him.

Instead of being flustered, he smiles at the sound of Emily's name. That pisses KC off a little.

The bartender, a middle-aged blonde who looks like she's spent too much time in the sun, finishes cleaning a stack of glasses and comes over to see what KC wants to drink. KC can't help but assume that at her age, this woman is more than a carefree bartender, a single mother probably, working two jobs to get by.

KC looks at Tien's glass and asks what he's having.

"Bourbon."

She winces and orders a cosmopolitan. "I guess you're a drinker now."

To lighten things up she decides to tell her only joke. "What separates flight attendants from the lowest form of life on earth?"

"I know that one," he says.

"Oh. That's all I've got. I'm terrible with jokes."

"So," he says. "London."

"London."

She's not sure what else to talk about, so at the crack of the pool cue, she turns around and pretends to be entranced by the retirees' game.

After a few minutes of silence, Tien says, "How is Emily?"

KC takes pleasure in describing Emily's life without him. "Great, fabulous. She loves it there, going out every night, traveling around Europe on days off."

"That's good. Really good."

"She's even got this hot English boyfriend. He's filthy rich, too."

He says, "I'm glad." But he looks away and takes a drink.

The bartender slides KC's cosmo across the bar and asks Tien if he'd like another round. He waves it off and turns back to the television.

"What are we watching?" asks KC.

"Giants versus Braves."

"I love baseball." She doesn't really know the ins and outs of the game, but her dad took her to a couple of minor-league games way back. He bought her cotton candy and Cracker Jacks. They high-fived after good plays and sang "Take Me Out to the Ball Game" during the seventh-inning stretch.

"I help coach my ten-year-old's team when I'm home," Tien says, dividing his attention between KC and the TV.

"Really? I didn't take you for such an involved parent."

"I try." Tien lets out a quick yes of approval as a pitcher outs a runner trying to steal second.

KC motions for a second drink.

"They grow up so fast. You know?"

"I guess time flies when you're having fun." She nudges him.

He looks at her out of the corner of his eye, so she knows he hears her this time.

"My daughter is pitching now," he says, refusing to be provoked. "Damn, she's good, too." He shakes his head, smiling.

KC is struck by how proud Tien seems when he talks about his daughter. All for a stupid elementary school softball game. She wonders if her dad ever wished she played sports so they'd have more in common. Of course, even if she had been standing on that pitcher's mound while her teammates chanted *hey batter batter*, he'd probably be just like Tien, sitting in a bar with some chick half his age.

For all she knows, he was sitting in a bar with a chick half his age last week when they were finally supposed to meet.

When he called, she had been lying on the sand in Waikiki, listening to college kids a few towels over talking about a party they were planning at the Beta Theta Pi house. They gossiped about friends they had in common and couldn't stop saying, "Remember the time when . . . ?" Suddenly KC felt like a cardboard cutout of a person. With her job, she only has to have one joke, one cute outfit, one wild story and she can entertain a different set of coworkers every day. It can be fun, but it isn't real. Real people have inside jokes and longtime friends and a regular table at a corner café.

She stared at her caller ID and let it ring three times. DAD. DAD. DAD. She propped herself up on her elbows and brought the phone to her ear.

"Hi, Max," she said, careful to sound upbeat but not over-eager. In less than three hours, they would be together again for the first time in more than ten years.

"Hi there," he said.

As if it were stage lights rather than hot sun boring down on her, KC suddenly forgot her lines. She sat up and pushed her toes into the sand. She heard the college kids arguing about Des-cartes and Nietzsche and the meaning of life. She wanted to tell them to get a life, go do something, see something.

After all that time, KC was so close to her dad. He couldn't have been more than a few miles away. They were both being suffocated by the same humid salt air. A new future was about to start, and she had no idea what to say.

Finally her dad started.

"God, I'm sorry to do this, honey. But something came up, so tomorrow's not going to work after all."

Tomorrow? But they were supposed to meet a few hours later.

"Can you come out Thursday instead?" he asked.

No, she couldn't fly out Thursday. She would be headed back to London in twelve hours and on her way to God knows where by Thursday—Chicago? Amsterdam? Delhi?

"Barb's slammed at work, so I really need to pick up the slack at home."

He called her Barb as if the three of them are all good friends. Ten years ago KC called her Miss Barbara. Her mom called her the big-titted bimbo so often that it became their official term for her, as if a proper name would have granted too much legitimacy.

"It's just that, well, we have kids now and there's always something, you know?"

The words hit her hard enough to break her nose. She guessed his kids don't even know about her. They probably think they're the product of an innocent, wholesome home, parents brought together by destiny, their marriage sacraments blessed from above.

More realistically though, his kids weren't even the reason he bailed. He probably just couldn't be bothered.

But this wasn't a traded weekend or a forgotten rendezvous at Peter Piper Pizza. She wasn't standing out in front of the bike racks at Pueblo Gardens Elementary. She had flown fifteen hours across both the Atlantic and the Pacific to see him. She had made the effort, made the call, lit the fuse of her own humiliation.

"Sure. Thursday sounds perfect," she said and threw her phone into the sand.

She didn't remind him it was supposed to be that day. She didn't tell him she was already there, that she had worked all night, exited the gate from Delhi and jogged around the concourse and entered the gate for San Francisco with continuing service to Honolulu. She was so excited that even after working the red-eye from hell where babies cried and no one slept and everyone wanted a constant supply of hot tea and Johnnie Walker and the vegetarian meals they'd long run out of, she didn't nod off once on the flight over.

KC pulls out a cigarette and offers Tien one. To her surprise, he takes it, but before they can light up, the bartender points to the NO SMOKING sign.

"Eh, you're no fun," says KC.

The bartender smiles at her sympathetically, probably jonesing for some nicotine herself.

"I'm glad to hear she's happy," says Tien.

It takes KC a second to realize he's still on the Emily subject. Not for the first time, KC wonders what it is about girls like

Emily and Barb that makes them worth betraying a family for. She thinks of the Bimbo, everything about her loose as an off-Strip slot—platinum ponytail wagging, boobs bouncing, hips swinging, and brown liquor sloshing from a glass that seemed permanently attached to her hand.

KC comes to a time-honored conclusion—all men are dogs. It was never about Emily or Barb. Tien would cheat with anyone, especially now that there's no way he's getting any action at home. She's tempted to prove it.

"So who's *your* new honey?" she asks.

"What?" Tien turns his head, but before she can answer, her question registers. He blushes. Then looks genuinely insulted.

"Kidding, kidding," she says, throwing her arm around him and squeezing. "You know I love you."

A cheer erupts from the television and they both turn to see a ball hit by Barry Bonds sailing into the stands in right field.

"Still," she says to Tien. "It must be nice to get out of Dodge and forget you have a family for a few days each week." She laughs like she's been there.

He shrugs. "Not really."

"Come on. It must be hard being a dad, making the kids the center of everything."

"You get used to it."

"But you make the best of being on the road obviously."

He looks at her as if he doesn't understand what she's getting at.

But she knows all about his type. She knows he's just waiting for an excuse. "You know you want another drink."

"I'm okay."

"Oh, come on. Live a little." She wonders if he'll notice if she gently rubs her index finger up and down the stem of her cocktail glass.

He looks at her in surprise and shifts in his seat.

A surge of evil power rushes through her as she realizes how easy it would be to torment this man.

She leans closer to him and lowers her eyes seductively. He sits motionless, eventually letting out a little cough. KC knows she's making him uncomfortable. In a good way.

She decides it's the perfect time to turn things back to his kids, rub salt into the wound of his guilty desire. "You said your oldest is ten?"

He nods casually.

"My parents split when I was ten."

He turns his whole body toward her and looks at her more directly than he has since she arrived. It surprises her to feel so comforted by his attention. His eyes seem open and interested, as if he actually cares what she has to say. She is tempted to tell him everything. To ask him why.

He concentrates on her face for a moment and then asks, "Was it hard?"

Was it hard? She thinks, *Are you fucking kidding me?* She looks up at the ceiling. When the danger of revealing too much passes, she smiles and repeats the lie she has been telling for years. "No, not really. It wasn't a big deal."

He looks surprised. "Really?"

She tosses her hair over her shoulder like she talks about this all the time. "I know they both loved me."

His face softens a bit and he says that's good to hear.

As he smiles, KC realizes that instead of protecting herself, she has betrayed herself. She imagines her dad using those exact same words to let himself off the hook. On the very night he left, he probably crawled into Barb's bed saying, "My daughter knows I love her."

"So how did it work?" asks Tien.

"Excuse me?"

"The divorce. I mean, did the court give you to your mom?"

She doesn't want to talk about it, so she lies. "Oh, I split my time pretty evenly, to be fair to everyone."

"So your dad had weekends or something?"

"Something like that."

"Holidays and—"

He is cut off by a ringing cell phone. He stands up and pulls a small flip phone from the front pocket of his jeans. "Hold that thought," he says and then walks toward the door to answer.

From her seat at the bar, KC watches him hunched in the bar's entryway, presumably talking to his wife or kids. *Lying* to his wife and kids while he's drinking with a hot twenty-one-year-old who could have him bent over and fucking her in under ten minutes if she really wanted to.

As if Emily was the first. Or the last.

KC sucks down the rest of her cosmo and motions to the bartender. "One more. And my friend will have another bourbon."

She watches Tien finish his call and turn back in her direction. She waits until he's looking right at her. While staring him straight in the eye, she crosses her right leg over her left and slowly moves her foot up and down.

She, too, can be an irresistible force.

Plane Change

I am gliding through Newark Airport with my rollaboard in tow when I see him, the man I have tried everything to forget. Seven months after the cold January day when his wife found out about us. Seven months after he changed his phone number, there he is emerging from the jet bridge at gate A17.

My chest tightens and my grip on the handle of my bag slips. Torn between waving and pretending not to see him, I freeze. He turns from the other flight attendant he was talking to and sees me. He says something into her ear and walks quickly in my direction.

I smile though I want to cry.

We stand there saying nothing.

I can almost smell the vanilla shampoo that always clings to his hair.

The thought of touching that thick, black hair, feeling his lips against my skin, fills me once again with the love I'd give anything to escape, the same love I would give anything to keep.

He shifts his weight from one foot to the other. I push my hair behind my ears.

"Well," he finally says. "It's good to see you, EmLee."

I've always loved how his accent makes my name sound new.

"Guess what?" I say. "I have a new name. The divorce is final. I'm back to Emily Crane."

He leans forward the tiniest bit and I think he's going to hug me. I can almost feel the voltage in his touch. But then he stops himself.

I want to reach out to him. But I don't.

"You sound happy," he says.

"I am. I'm happier than ever." I stand taller and try to look like I mean it.

Travelers pass us in both directions. We pretend to watch them as we stand still trying to think of what to say.

"I'm based in London now," I finally offer.

"You were always so adventurous. I shouldn't be surprised."

I tell him I can see Big Ben from my bedroom window, that I know all of the coolest clubs and I've been to India and to Paris three times.

"I'm happy for you. This is what you've always wanted. To fly away and see the world. It's every twenty-four-year-old girl's dream."

No, I think to myself. *You're what I've always wanted.*

He glances over at the departure board. "I guess it's good that you're not wasting your time sipping noodle soup with a man thirteen years older than you."

He smiles, as if he's done me a favor, as if this is how things were meant to work out, as if I'm happier this way. I want to scream at him and tell him I hate him and tell him I miss the noodle soup, tell him I would give everything for the damn noodle soup.

He reaches out to me. He puts his hand on my arm, and I want to block out everything but his touch, to pretend for just a moment that he's still mine. I can't help but close my eyes.

He squeezes my arm and it feels so easy to hope that it isn't over, that something has changed and we have a chance, that there is a reason my heart has been waiting. But when I open my eyes, I notice he's still wearing his ring.

He notices me notice. He drops his hand.

I shouldn't have expected anything different.

"You cut your hair," he says.

It isn't a compliment. I am hit with an embarrassing thought—to me he is a constant presence, but to him I'm just a girl he used to sleep with.

"Well, I have to go," I say. "I'm on my way back there." I tilt my head toward the gate that says LONDON, HEATHROW.

He opens his mouth but doesn't say anything.

I wait for him to speak even though I am desperate to walk away before my face can reveal any emotion.

"I just came from San Francisco. I ran into your friend KC." A strange look comes over his face when he says her name.

"Did she say something about me?"

He contemplates for a moment before speaking. "She said you have a boyfriend."

I don't have a boyfriend, but do I want him to know that? When I hesitate, he quickly says, "Anyhow, like I said. I'm glad you're happy."

He reaches in for a hug. I feel the warmth of his body and want to press my head against his chest and squeeze so far I slip into him like a ghost. But his arms circle me loosely and he pats me on the back before pulling away.

I turn toward my gate. If I'm going to cry, he will not be the one to see it.

But then he says, "Wait." He grabs my hand, and I feel him trembling.

I turn back toward him.

"I have to know something," he says.

I move closer, hoping to decipher what is different in his voice. In his touch.

"I need to know if you're serious about me. If you could even handle it?"

I must look confused because before I can respond, he starts up again.

"I keep asking myself if you could really accept things like Chicago winters and a flight attendant salary and two children."

He may as well be speaking Vietnamese because I can't make sense of what he is saying. This isn't what he wants. He wants to stay with her. He wants his family. He wants me to fly away and see the world.

"I'm sorry?" I ask, needing to hear him again.

"Nothing. Forget it," he says, perhaps thinking I said, "I'm sorry" with a period.

I am about to assure him I can handle the winters and the salary and the kids, that I've been ready for all of it for so long now. But he's still talking hypothetically. If that's all he can offer, I would have to tell him no. Wouldn't I? For my self-respect?

The woman from his crew is out in front of gate A15 motioning for him to get on the plane so they can start boarding.

He nods his head to her. But wait, I had raised my voice at the end, clearly indicating a question.

He begins to move in the direction of his crew. But wait, I need him to explain.

"Emily," calls a voice from behind me. I turn around and see a girl from my crew approaching us. She hands me the paperwork she printed with our passenger manifest, special requests, list of movies, and mechanical write-ups.

I take the papers and try to turn from her, but she starts in about departure time and a missing crew member. She wants me to tell her where David went, but I don't even remember a David on our crew. She grabs my elbow to steer me in the direction of the food court where she thinks we may find him.

I look back to see Tien with his hand in the air in a motionless wave as he walks backward toward his flight.

24

Late

Five more minutes," says the mechanic as he pops through a panel normally hidden beneath the Boeing 777's carpet. He ducks back into the hole and the sound of a drill starts back up.

KC stares six feet deep into a mess of wires in the airplane's innards and wills her flight to get off the ground tonight. She's scheduled to work United 928 from Chicago to London and needs to get to Heathrow in time to catch the last flight to Hong Kong where she'll then connect to Tokyo for Jake's show. He's probably not worth twenty-four hours in a plane. But like it or not, KC needs him now that her recklessness has caught up with her.

The mechanic pops up from the floor to say, "Actually, it'll be about twenty more minutes."

He resumes drilling and KC steals a ramekin of nuts from the snack drawer in hopes of settling her stomach. She's been to India three times in the last few weeks, so it's probably Delhi belly. Almost every flight attendant based in London has been living with the bug since the route opened. At least the carnage is predictable, about twenty minutes after the crew has scavenged the leftover first- and business-class meals, it hits. For a brief window of time, every lavatory is occupied and there is not a crew member in sight.

Three pilots strut onboard, and they are all named Bob, which is actually not that surprising. It's possible that half of the pilots at United are named Bob.

"About time you guys showed up," says a flight attendant named Callie. "We're ready to get out of here."

"Thirty more minutes," says the mechanic.

The flight attendants prop their feet in first-class sleeper suites and pop open beverages.

"About forty-five minutes," says the mechanic.

The purser turns on the in-flight entertainment system and the crew members watch various movies on their seat-back screens as the delay rolls on for two more hours.

A customer service rep with a long white beard eventually leans into the plane from the jet bridge and says he's going to start sending them down in five. He says it doesn't matter if the plane is still broken because there is no more room in the gate area. He figures it'll pacify most of the passengers just to think they're going somewhere tonight.

As soon as the wheelchairs start rolling up to the door for preboarding, the PA clicks on and the welcome cycle begins. "Ladies and gentlemen, we welcome you on board United flight 928 with Boeing triple-seven service to London." . . . "*Meine damen und herren. Willkommen an bord den Boeing sieben-sieben-sieben von Chicago O'Hare nach London.*"

KC moves to the door to start greeting.

"*Mesdames et Messieurs, bienvenue à bord du vol United numero neuf deux huit pour Londres.*"

Double-chin Bob comes up from behind and puts his hand on KC's shoulder. "Hey, I'm gonna sneak off for a bit," he says. "Can I get you anything?"

Suspicious, she shakes her head.

"Coffee?"

"No, thanks." A mother with a baby strapped to her chest shows KC her ticket stub, and KC points to the back.

"Come on. Let me buy you a milkshake," says Bob.

"I said no. I'm all good." By now she knows any sign of generosity from a man comes with strings attached.

"Suit yourself," he says and steps onto the jet bridge. Apparently the passengers aren't expected to notice that they might need pilots to get somewhere.

KC watches as he squeezes his way up the jet bridge against the flow.

Twenty minutes later, Bob skulks back onto the plane and hands KC a cup of Starbucks coffee he bought for her. The smell turns her stomach. After hanging hundreds of coffee bags in hundreds of lavs to at least partially mask the stink, she can't smell coffee without conjuring the stench of urine. She shakes her head and says, "If I wanted coffee I'd just drink the Starbucks that's already brewed in the galley."

"That shit's weak," he says. "I need the hard stuff. We're on minimum rest from our last flight, and we don't get a rest break on this baby."

He tips his head toward the cockpit. "You can blame the first officer for that. And the rest of our shitty contract since he's a scab."

"The Bob with the Michael Bolton ponytail?" Legitimate pilots still keep a book up in the cockpit with the names of all the scabs that flew during the strike of 1985. Apparently Bolton Bob's name is in it. If word gets out, no one will speak to him for the rest of the night.

Bob quickly finishes his coffee and dumps the cup in the trash cart before starting on the cup intended for KC. "One time," he tells her, "I did the landing and a half hour later on my way home, you know those orange barrels full of water on the interstate off-ramps?"

She shakes her head.

"Well you'd know them if you hit them. I fell asleep at the wheel and plowed right in. Twenty minutes before that I was landing a triple-seven with more than two hundred people. Fuck!" he said, clearly still terrified at the thought of causing a fatal air disaster.

Thanks to the delay, they have all been awake for almost twenty-four hours, which according to an article she just read in the *Daily Mail* is equivalent to a blood alcohol level of .10. But no matter how tired she'll be when she lands, KC is determined to make her way to Asia.

Jake is expecting her. She told him last night that she's coming and that they need to talk, a really stupid thing to say. If he wasn't planning on cheating before, he probably is now.

Fuck him. She doesn't need him.

The purser dims the lights and they brew pots of decaf for anyone requesting coffee. Most of the passengers in first and business are chilling out watching their personal TVs or trying to doze, but a few keep asking for repeated updates. She assures them they know as much as she does. When she pokes her head through the curtain to economy, the cabin is bright with the lights from television screens and reading lamps. At least a dozen people are standing up stretching their legs or waiting for the lav. Two children are running down the aisle in what appears to be a game of tag. Lately whenever kids run by, KC fantasizes about sticking her foot out and sending them flying. She's never done it, but still. She'd be a god-awful mother and she knows it.

That's why it can't be true. Nausea? Check. Fatigue? Check. But these are all side effects of flying for a living. But the uber-sore breasts, way past PMS level—what in the hell is that about?

She bought a pregnancy test, and she stares at it every time she opens her suitcase. But she isn't about to pee on it. It's obvious that she's just five days late because of wacked circadian rhythms and all of her recent stress. She's sure she's just making herself later by worrying about it.

Instead of thinking about it, she grabs a stainless steel pot and starts from the top of the aisle.

"Tea? Tea? Tea? Tea? Tea? Tea?" she asks until it starts to not even sound like a word but just a senseless letter. "T? T? T? T? T?"

"Yes, I would like some," says an Indian man by the window who wiggles his head and holds his cup over his lap.

"Can you put the cup on the tray?" she asks.

He sits there with the cup over his lap. KC pushes the little black tray in her left hand closer to him. "Can you *please* put the cup on the tray so I don't burn you?"

"What?"

She is reminded of a guy she saw walking around in Soho with a T-shirt that said, PUT THE FUCKING CUP ON THE TRAY. So obviously a flight attendant. She'll never know who he flew for, but in that moment, the world felt comfortingly small. Now on particularly lonely layovers, she imagines a fleet of others like her exploring the same streets.

"Cream or sugar?" she asks the man.

He says his wife requires hot tea as well. *His wife?* He looks over to a woman across the aisle who sits with two children to her left, one to her right, and a baby on her lap. KC thought the woman was traveling alone because she came on hauling two diaper bags, a baby, and a stroller, not to mention the three kids who trailed behind. Now KC wishes she had spilled tea on his lap.

This is why she knows there is no God. If someone like her can get pregnant, despite being on the pill since eleventh grade, and the girl she flew with last week can fuck her husband by a timer, drop more than ten grand on fertility treatments, and still not get knocked up, something is wrong with that asshole upstairs and his sense of humor.

She thinks about the pregnancy test lurking in her bag but still doesn't feel ready to face its revelation. If it's positive, her life is pretty much over.

She can't stop thinking about how Jake might react. He once told her about a "close call" with an ex-girlfriend. "But then she finally got an abortion," he said, sounding more relieved than remorseful.

The stupid thing is that she'd be just as disappointed to find out she isn't pregnant. First off, she is willing to admit she's drawn to the drama of the predicament. Harder to admit is that she's also drawn to the restrictions it would impose. Good or bad, her life would take a permanent and predictable shape. She wouldn't have to choose what to do next or stare blankly into a future of bright cities and limitless possibilities.

She looks down at a kid in the last row. He's about ten and has no shirt on. His bulging chocolate-milk belly is tanned and he's wearing gold chains. She wishes there were a dress code to reference, but she isn't aware of one.

He asks for coffee with lots of cream and seven sugars. His dad nods.

Holding down her vomit, KC realizes that being pregnant would mean spending the rest of eternity following Jake around the world.

KC drops her teapot on the counter of the business-class galley where Callie is whining to another woman about her husband of ten years. He is apparently leaving her for another flight attendant.

KC thinks of Tien. His wife isn't a flight attendant, is she?

"The philandering douche bag is toast," says Callie.

The phone in the galley rings and Callie picks up. She relays the Bobs' message that although the plane is just about ready, if it takes more than nine more minutes, the projected landing time will put them over their fourteen-hour duty day limitation. So basically, after spending the last three hours with passengers, they're going to go illegal and cancel. "Cute Bob wants to know if we'll all go out for drinks if the bars are still open," says Callie with her hand over the mouthpiece.

Cute Bob? KC wonders which one they could be referring to.

Callie tells the Bobs she's down for drinks and then slides right back into her marriage drama. KC is tempted to tell them about her dilemma. She's sure they'll just suggest she head off to Planned Parenthood and have the thing sucked out.

They wouldn't understand. It might be the only family she has left.

"Ladies and gentlemen," says a male voice over the PA. "We're all set. We just have to wait to get the paperwork signed off and we'll be on our way to London."

Finally. She was afraid they'd go illegal.

In business, seat backs and tray tables fly up and carry-ons get shoved under seats. A cheer erupts from economy. Callie groans and KC starts calculating their arrival time, which if everything goes smoothly, could give her just enough time to sprint through Heathrow and make the Hong Kong and then connect to Tokyo.

Fifteen minutes later, the brakes are released and they back out of the gate in a hurry. As they begin the taxi out, the flight attendants are positioned in the aisles, holding up safety cards.

The plane quickly turns to the left and KC taps a seat back to stay steady. With her free hand, she continues the safety demo.

There is a loud bang and the plane lurches right. KC slams into the bulkhead. The brakes chirp and the plane comes to an abrupt stop, throwing her onto the floor. Pain hits her tailbone and shoots up her spine. The side of her face burns and throbs from where it smacked the bulkhead. She hears screams and cuss words and shouts to God. Overhead bins pop open and jackets and briefcases and wheelie luggage carts—all of the things that should be under the seat in front of you—come tumbling out.

From her position on the floor, KC knows everyone is waiting for her and the rest of the crew to react. A surge of energy hits her in the gut. This may be it—the evacuation she's trained for. She pushes herself up and runs to her door. She presses the back of her hands against it to feel for heat as she scans out the window. No fire, no structural damage that she can see. The evacuation alarm is not sounding and the captain is not yelling "evacuate, evacuate, evacuate" as in the hundreds of training scenarios she's been through. She takes a breath and stops herself from automatically swinging the enormous door handle and pulling the slide's manual inflation cord.

When she turns back to the aisle, she sees the now-silent passengers staring straight forward. The captain comes over the PA and says they've been hit by a fuel truck.

Passengers gasp.

"There is no risk of fire. We'll just head back to the gate."

KC feels her eyes starting to water.

The captain instructs everyone, including the flight attendants, to take their seats and remain there.

Before heading to their jumpseats, the bruised and scratched-up flight attendants walk through the cabin looking for injured passengers. Two people request oxygen, but most want to cause injuries to the flight attendants, the pilots, the mechanics, the fuel truck driver, anyone at the airline that is sending them back into O'Hare. KC would tell them to stop their bitching and be glad they're alive, but she's more pissed than they are. There's almost no chance she'll make it to Tokyo now.

She straps into her four-point harness, rubs a bump on her head, and tries not to think about what might be a baby inside her. She imagines walking off the plane with her new Victoria's

Secret hip-hugger underwear soaked in blood. It could just be her long-anticipated period.

The second they hit the brakes and before the seat belt sign can go off, KC throws off her harness and jogs to the space behind the last row of seats where her bag is stowed. She pulls her bag out into the aisle, unzips it in front of the passengers who are squeezing into the aisle, and whips out the sealed pee stick, stuffing it up the sleeve of her sweater like she would have if it were a tampon. She says "Excuse me, pardon me," as she pushes her way up the aisle and into the lav. Let them think she has raging Delhi belly.

She locks the door, rips open the package. She hears bodies brushing past the accordion door, which bends just a little with each deplaning passenger as she tries to produce a large enough sample. Nothing doing. She sets the stick on the counter and looks at herself in the mirror. Then laughs. She has to wait a full five minutes, so she closes the lid and, appropriately grossed out, sits atop the toilet to wait.

She looks at her dual-time-zone watch. It's 12:41 P.M. in London, 8:41 P.M. in Tokyo, 8:42 . . . 8:43 . . . 8:44 . . . 8:45 . . . 8:46. She stands up and without touching it, she looks down at the stick resting on the counter. She can't see anything, so she leans down closer to it. Still nothing, so she picks it up and holds it to the light. There may be a faint line, so faint it can't be a line, but it could be a line. Is it a line?

This is not happening. She's been making fun of the dumbasses who can't read pregnancy tests since she was twelve and first saw a commercial hawking the plus/minus thing. Why did she go for the eight-dollar Walgreens brand rather than the fifteen-dollar EPT?

Jesus Christ, what is she going to tell Jake? It's not like he's going to say let's get married and raise a little family from the back of the tour bus while the rest of the guys in his band do lines and bang bleach-blond sluts with Hell's Kitsch baby-tees and too much eyeliner and mascara. Who is she kidding? Right this minute, Jake is probably screwing one of those blondes.

Fuck him. What if it isn't even his? It better be his. The alternative is just unthinkable.

There is only one thing she knows for sure. If she *is* having a baby, giving it a happy family will be her life's mission.

25

Tempting Fate

I don't want to tell you how you die. *But*," says the Japanese fortune-teller as she grabs my hand and looks into my eyes. "Quit your job. It's bad. Very bad."

I see myself offering hot towels on a 747 as we plunge into the sea. I pull my hand away, but hoping comedy is a part of her act, I let out a small laugh.

"Quit your job," she says.

I look at KC, who sits on the red plastic stool next to mine. She shrugs her shoulders.

Six thousand miles away from our lives in London and we ran into each other in the lobby of the airport hotel. It's rare to have more than two out of six roommates home on the same night, but after a year of flying, it's getting more and more likely that I'll cross paths with someone I know.

I found KC sitting on a tiled ledge next to an indoor fountain and staring at a phone she bought from a vending machine across the street. She hoped it would make it easier to meet up with Jake, who is here for a show. Unfortunately, he isn't trying to find her.

I dragged her out of the hotel, and when we came across a

silk-draped booth, an old woman with milky eyes held out a dry crinkled hand and said, "See the future."

There is nothing either of us wants to see more.

After the Newark run-in, I checked Tien's schedule online and saw that he was on vacation for more than a week. It has been killing me that I can't track him down at a hotel and ask him what he meant. I had been working so hard to move on, and then he suggests he's leaving her. Or did he? He never speaks directly.

But now I am scheduled to fly to Chicago tomorrow. My flight back home will leave just after his, guaranteeing an airport run-in if I time things right. I tell myself it's fate.

I breathe in the jasmine scent of the joss sticks burning behind the fortune-teller and ask her if she sees anything else. I want her to give me answers. Against all odds, I'm hoping to find some wisdom in Tokyo that will help me stay away from Tien for good. Or even better, find something to justify being together.

Are Tien and I *meant to be*? Would that make everything okay? The ends justifying the means, as they say? Plenty of people are able to view things with that much single-minded selfishness. It would be easier if I could become one of them.

"You will marry a rich businessman," says the fortune-teller.

Tien is not a businessman.

"You will divorce him but keep his money," she says.

"Ha," says KC. "Take him for all he's got."

I want to shake the fortune-teller and tell her to get to Tien. Am I supposed to find him in Chicago? It has been easy to love him from afar as long as our future was up to him. As long as I was powerless, I was also harmless. Now, if he was indeed suggesting he'd leave if I am serious about him, he has pushed the burden of choice to me.

The joss smoke obscures the fortune-teller's face as she tells me I will then marry and divorce again. Only this time, the man will swindle me out of my money.

Clearly happy endings are not required in Tokyo.

"My turn," says KC as she drops a pile of yen on the folding table in front of us. She is told she will marry a fat man and kill someone while trying to defend him.

She grabs my elbow to pull me away. "That obviously had nothing to do with anything. I was really hoping she'd tell me what to do."

"About what?"

"Nothing, just wondering whether or not Jake's 'The One.' If he's reliable and trustworthy and if he'll be there for me." She laughs hard, harder than seems appropriate, and I start to wonder what is wrong. When she finally stops laughing, she says, "I'm not sure I want to know."

"Pissed that he's here for the show and still hasn't called?"

"I've got way bigger problems than that."

"At least you're not in love with a married man. Hating yourself for half hoping he is actually about to leave his wife."

KC stares at me.

"I know. I know. They never leave their wives."

"Men ditch their families all the time, Emily." She turns and starts walking away. At five foot nine, she towers above most people here, a blond head bobbing above a sea of black hair.

I jog a few steps to catch up.

Dusk begins to fall and the streets change. They are no longer lit by sunlight but by towers of neon. What looked like 1950s America—housewives in knee-length dresses pushing prams, modest couples picnicking in the park—is gradually overtaken by the night—skinny girls in miniskirts and Frankenstein boots, stunningly feminine ladyboys, platoons of American Marines. I stop in front of each jam-packed club, expecting KC to choose the best one for dancing on tables and flashing strangers, but she just scrunches up her nose and shakes her head.

We pass a bar with karaoke and see a Japanese girl with long bleached-orange hair jumping up and down in front of a microphone and singing unintelligible English-sounding words to the tune of Blondie's "The Tide Is High."

"She looks happy," says KC with a sigh.

"Maybe it just seems that way."

"Everywhere I go, no matter how rich or poor or clean or dirty the city, I see people who look so rooted and safe and at home. Nowhere is like that for me."

"We're flight attendants, KC. We're not supposed to stay home."

"I know this will sound stupid, but I guess I expected to find myself."

It doesn't seem stupid, but it does seem funny. She wanted to find a home and I wanted to escape mine. Now we've both been flying for more than a year, we know every airplane in the fleet, every service in all three classes, we've been to dozens of countries and have trendy haircuts and a few stylish outfits, but still neither of us knows who we are or where we're going.

A hunched-over old man stands behind a homemade stand at the edge of the sidewalk, but instead of selling lemonade, he's selling magic mushrooms. I pretend not to notice and hope that KC actually doesn't. I'm afraid she's going to try to talk me into experimenting. No matter how hard I've tried to be more fun and spontaneous, I will never be able to keep up with her.

"Want to just get dinner?" KC eventually asks.

I follow her into my first real Japanese sushi restaurant. I was expecting to sit on tatami mats in a room divided by rice-paper doors, but instead we are greeted by cold blue lighting and modern industrial decor. We choose a seat at the stainless steel bar, which has a constantly moving conveyer belt of sushi on plates of various colors. The chef standing behind the bar welcomes us with a bow.

We pluck a few entry-level plates off belt—tuna rolls, unagi— and then KC points at a bright red craggy one. It looks kind of like tuna, but much more creased. "What's that one?" she asks, pointing and shrugging her shoulders to mime a question to the chef.

He looks at it for a moment and then up at us.

He says something that sounds like *fess.*

"Excuse me?" asks KC.

He pinches his cheek and wiggles it, and what he is saying becomes clear. "Face, face. Cow face."

"Why not?" says KC as she takes it off the bar and eats it before she can give it too much thought.

I love her.

I am suddenly confident that one of these days we will know what we're doing. I think of the old Southern ladies I saw gathered in the hotel lobby in street clothes with matching Delta Airlines purses. With twangy Georgia accents, they loudly talked about frequent shopping trips to Asia, dream trips now so easy to come by that they could choose to go to Hong Kong on "Mond*ees*" instead of "Sund*ees*."

One day that could be KC and me, buddy bidding our trips, buying knockoffs in China and perfume in France while our mystery husbands hold down the fort at home. We'll have the best of both worlds—this amazing job, access to the world's best cities, and a decades-long friendship that produces albums full of memories.

KC squints and grimaces as she chews the cow face and swallows with a big disgusted gulp. She swipes a bottle of water from a robotic drink cart that rolls in our direction just in time.

"Just water?" I was expecting to turn up to my flight tomorrow with a raging sake hangover.

She shrugs her shoulders and stares at the sushi chef as he places a sheet of seaweed onto a bamboo mat.

"Is something wrong?" I ask.

"It's nothing." She reaches for a few more plates. "I probably shouldn't be eating this. Nothing really tastes good anyway."

From the moment I saw her in the lobby, sad face staring at silent phone, I have been concerned. I can't tell if she wants me to drop it or if she's waiting for someone to drag it out of her.

Eventually she stops eating and carefully sets down her chopsticks. "There's just something I need to talk to Jake about before I tell anyone else, you know?"

"He gave you an STD and he needs to get tested?"

She laughs for the first time tonight. "Kind of."

I feel my eyes ready to pop out. "Really?"

"No, not really. It's not that." Changing the subject, she says, "Did I tell you I ran into Tien in San Francisco?"

In the wake of Tien's potentially game-changing suggestion, I had almost forgotten that he mentioned seeing her. I want to ask her how he looked, if he said anything about me. I'd like to tell her I think he might be leaving his wife, but knowing I couldn't say that without a smile, I am too ashamed to say it out loud.

"He loves his kids."

I nod. I know she's right, but I hate that she has to point this out. What business is it of hers?

"Even though he and his wife must have their problems—it's obvious that he loves his kids."

"Yes, KC. He does."

"That's what I want."

"Kids?"

"A family man. I want to be with someone who values kids, family."

The same thing has always been one of the ironies in my relationship with him. I was so attracted to the devotion he showed his kids—staying home during the week, coaching softball, dedicating his life to flash cards and Barney—but it was exactly what I was undermining. What I am still undermining.

KC lifts up her United-issue purse and starts shuffling through keys and receipts and packs of gum.

I grab my matching purse so she doesn't think I was going to let her pay the tab.

"You have to tell me what to do," she says, shaking and on the verge of tears. "I can't figure this one out on my own."

"What? What are you talking about? You're scaring me."

"Tell me, Emily. What the hell am I going to do about this?" She pulls out a Ziploc bag and points to what's inside. A pink-and-white plastic cartridge. A pregnancy test. With two very distinct pink lines.

"Oh," is all I can think to say. I've imagined finding those fateful lines many times and tried without success to predict what I would do. Or more importantly, what Tien would do.

"Have you told him?" I ask.

KC gives me a strange look, and says, "Who?"

"Jake, of course." I thought that was a given.

"No, not yet."

26

Straight Kevin

After finally tracking Jake down at his Tokyo hotel, KC is on her way back to London, working this time. Fortunately they let her volunteer to pick up the flight from a girl who got sick on her layover. She has to be a breadwinner now.

She punches a code into the keypad of a hidden elevator near the ANA duty-free shop. The second she walks into the briefing room, she sees Straight Kevin sitting at one of the fifteen school-room desks and flipping through his handbook. Fucking hell. This is the first time she's seen him since their trip to India when she made it clear that she was with Jake and he shouldn't call her.

He says, "Hey."

She ignores him and takes a seat on the other side of the room. He looks up at her and then back down at his meticulously shined shoes. No doubt there is another long-winded story about boot camp there.

"*Konichiwa*," says a red-eyed flight attendant as she shuffles into the room adjusting her disheveled ponytail.

Still sitting down, Kevin extends his hand toward ponytail girl and says, "I'm Kevin by the way."

KC rolls her eyes. She can see it now. Kevin will find this

chick alone in the galley in the middle of the flight when half the
crew are on break and most of the passengers are sleeping. He'll
stand closer than is necessary. She'll wonder how a strapping guy
like him became a flight attendant. He'll tell her how he has his
private pilot's license and that once he has enough hours, she'll
be bringing his coffee to the cockpit. The flight attendant thing
is just a foot in the door and a way to stay in hotels with a new
batch of hot chicks every day. He thinks girls like that kind of
talk!

Fortunately, the girl doesn't seem taken with him. Maybe
she's not into Kevin's hard edges. KC hates to admit it, but lately
she's found herself kind of attracted to the stiff posture and
close-cut hair. His soldiering days may be in the past, but he still
projects an air of protection and security.

She hears a few other crew members audibly yawning or
sighing as they type away on the check-in computers, dot matrix
printers screeching out the details of the trip.

A guy with heavily gelled, platinum hair walks in and laughs
when he sees Kevin. "You made it. Late night?" He keeps
laughing.

KC watches Kevin clench his jaw and turn away.

The Billy Idol look-alike takes a seat next to KC. She acknowledges him with a half smile and smells the cigarette he
must have just smoked. There is nothing she would love more
right now than a cigarette, but she quit smoking and drinking
cold turkey as soon as she suspected she was pregnant. It's been
easier than she expected, now that she has a genuine reason to,
something bigger than herself, bigger than a self-defeating wish
to be a better or stronger person.

Billy motions his head in Kevin's direction and says, "You'll
never believe where I saw that guy a few hours ago." He and
Kevin lock eyes.

The staredown lasts a full minute, and when it ends KC asks
where.

Billy Idol shrugs his shoulders and says, "Nowhere. Just a club."

She wonders why he thinks she cares about Kevin's whereabouts. Kevin wouldn't have told people anything about their little thing in India, right? She didn't tell Jake about it. Of course, now she wishes she would have.

She didn't tell Jake about the pregnancy either. But he must have known. He invited her up to his room at the Four Seasons. He poured himself a scotch and soda from the minibar and when he asked her what she wanted, she said water. Maybe that was all it took. She was also quieter than usual. He kept asking her what was wrong. She said nothing, but he must have suspected. Eventually they started messing around.

As he felt her up he said, "If you ever got pregnant, you would take care of it, right?"

By *take care of it*, she knew he didn't mean stay home and cook the kid three squares a day.

She said of course, but then picked up her stuff and left shortly afterward. She could have gone after his money, but she didn't want her son or daughter to be legally connected to a man that would have let them die for him.

A supervisor steps into the room and interrupts the introductions to inform them they don't have a gate with a jet bridge and will have to take a bus to a remote hard stand.

KC knows that means they'll be standing out in the rain, which is all she needs right now after almost no sleep and three rounds of morning sickness. If she were to grumble about the rain, though, she's sure she would hear Kevin saying, "What's a little water?" He'd remind her that he was a Marine and had low-crawled for miles with his face in the mud and humped 150 pounds through a hail storm at boot camp and hunted for mines in three feet of snow in Bosnia.

If he'd had a rifle, she's sure he would have been spinning it to show off for her when they were in India. Why did she have to knock on his door after her trip to the Taj Mahal?

As the purser hands out paperwork, KC watches Kevin. He lifts his computer bag to the desk and his biceps flex. She hates that it makes her wish she could see him drop to the floor for a series of perfect push-ups. She just admires his strength, that's all. She could use some of it right now.

The funny thing is that she can admire his badass façade even when she knows it's at least half fake. India wasn't just about lonely bodies sweating together in the dark. She saw his vulnerable side and has to admit they bonded—though they haven't spoken since.

The sex itself wasn't exactly filled with magic. It started out hot and heavy but ended quick and angry. She suspected an ex-girlfriend had really screwed him over and he was taking it out on all the women he so aggressively flirts with and selfishly screws. When it was over, she expected him to look at his watch and point at the door. She planned to deny it ever happened.

But then he wrapped his arm around her, pulled her into the nook of his shoulder, and stroked her hair in the exact soothing way her mom had when she was sick.

They started talking and she learned that Kevin grew up in the desert, too, near a Marine base in the Mojave called Twenty-nine Palms. He told her he wanted to be like the men he saw at the bar where he'd take his fake ID after working at some dollar store his mom managed. He watched them drinking Jack Daniel's and throwing darts, their biceps branded with the Eagle, Globe, and Anchor. When he was feeling brave, he'd pull up a stool and ask a friendly-looking guy where he came from. It was inevitably somewhere green and quaint and just plain normal compared to the Mojave Desert.

KC knows just how he felt. On TV, the picture-perfect

families always seemed to live in lush and proper places back East, like Connecticut or Long Island.

He told her his idea of the good life meant chewing Skoal and wearing Drakkar cologne, becoming a good-looking, confident, ass-kicking conqueror with an expert rifle badge on his shirt and a family of brothers that had his back.

She ran her hands over his powerful arms and told him he looked like a confident ass-kicker to her. He shook his head and said she should have seen him back when he headed to boot camp still a virgin. He felt like a freak when the drill instructor compared every new skill—rifle cleaning, range shooting, grenade throwing—to female anatomy and sexual intercourse.

By the time he graduated though, he was corps and no one could take that away, a U.S. Marine just like his dad, who died a hero in Vietnam.

KC gasped at that. "Your dad was an actual hero? How cool."

Kevin snorted and said that was his mom's story. "She's so full of shit. She probably just won't admit he bailed when she got pregnant."

They both agreed that if they ever had kids, they would do things all the way, not like their dads.

The flight attendants start picking positions. KC's the most junior, as usual, so she gets stuck running the economy galley on the 777. Somehow Kevin got a spot in business, so at least she won't have to work closely with him. She's afraid that would make her too self-conscious. While she should be organizing special meals by seat number or cramming entrees into steam ovens, she'd be thinking about what to say to him and how to say it. Hint until he asks? Gradually build? Blurt it out?

Everyone stands up and starts gathering their bags to head down to the bus. Kevin bolts out of the room before she can even try to tell him about her predicament. She hopes he'll see it as their predicament. And maybe it is. Timing wise, it's more likely to be his than Jake's.

She thinks of how she almost slept with Tien, too, and although she felt rejected at the time, she's now relieved that he didn't respond to her advances. In fact, the tenderness with which he spoke about his children and his wife, despite his obvious love or lust for Emily, now gives her hope. She had long assumed he was just that kind of guy.

She overhears Billy Idol laughing with three other flight attendants and is certain she hears the name *Kevin*. So he's not a typical flight attendant. Why can't they leave him alone?

KC follows him to the elevator, where she finds him repeatedly pressing the down button. By the time the elevator doors open, the entire crew has assembled and has to squeeze in. She watches as the chick with the ponytail slides in right in front of Kevin, so close she's almost leaning against his chest. KC knows it shouldn't make her angry since she's the one who was seeing someone else.

As she hears Billy Idol continuing to whisper and snicker with some kind of gossip, her anger builds. By the time they reach the terminal, she's determined. She grabs Kevin's arm as he exits the elevator. "We need to talk."

He brushes her hand away and says, "Not now. Really, it's not a good time." He turns toward Royal Coffee and focuses on the menu.

KC figures it's probably better to wait till they have more privacy anyway so she weaves her way through the crowds who are looking at departure boards, hustling to gates, and shopping for last-minute souvenirs or gifts at the Ginza Shop and Burberry and the ANA duty-free store. She takes the stairs down to the flight line, and when she steps outside she's hit with the smell of jet fuel.

Ponytail girl is smoking under the awning, sucking so fast her cheeks must hurt. KC stops for a moment, tempted to bum a cig. But she can't. She's going to be a good mom.

KC runs across the ramp, her bag rolling behind her, splashing dirty water onto her legs. As she steps onto the bus, she's hit with the hot dry air being blasted from the heater. When Kevin boards, he throws his bag into the rack with one hand and takes a seat a few rows away from her, but she's not disappointed. It's not like she expected him to sit next to her and hold her hand.

She tries to rest for a few minutes in preparation for the long day ahead. International trips were hard even before she was so completely exhausted all the time from the hormones. She hears the wind whistle through the door as she closes her eyes.

"You know, I have this friend," Billy Idol says so loudly that KC can hear him from six rows away.

Why does he have to yell? People are trying to rest.

"This friend of mine was so gay that everyone knew it, even his mom, but he couldn't admit it."

"Why not?" a female voice asks.

"Because he grew up Catholic," says Billy.

KC tries to ignore his high-pitched, whiny voice and focus on the sound of the windshield wipers.

"You see. When he was only ten years old, his mom told him if he ever turned out to be gay, she'd disown him, kick him right out on the street."

"She said that?" asks the voice. "To a ten-year-old?"

"Yep. That fat whore. Anyway, I flew with him a few months ago and—"

"Wait, he's a flight attendant?"

KC gives up and turns around in her seat to give Billy a "shut the heck up" stare. He just smirks at her. When she faces forward again, she sees Kevin clenching his teeth, no doubt also irritated by the noisy gossip.

Billy continues. "Yeah, he's based in Boston. Anyway. I just wanted my friend to know that it's okay. That we've all been there."

"Maybe, but Jesus." The girl laughs. "If you can't come out of the closet as a flight attendant, there's something really wrong with you."

KC sees Kevin close his eyes and bite down on his lip so hard it draws blood.

27

Answers

After moving through an aisle lined with souvenir folding fans, silk kimonos, and intricately carved confections, I pass under a paper lantern that must be as tall as I am. I reach the ancient Japanese temple, a five-story red-and-gold pagoda, and am filled with awe at how far I have come from Bakersfield. Following in the footsteps of pilgrims, I drop a hundred yen, the equivalent of a dollar, into a donation box, shake a numbered stick from a metal container, and find my printed *omikuji* fortune in the corresponding wooden drawer.

KC has already left for London and I am only hours away from the Chicago trip that will reveal my destiny. For now, I'm hoping for a hint.

Around me, people smile and hug each other after reading their blessings.

The English translation printed below the Japanese characters of my fortune says this:

> The person you wait for will not come. The lost article will not be found. All is darkness and thunder.

Tokyo does not seem to like me. Another English-speaking tourist sees my shock and explains that there are only twelve fortunes, the first being the Great Blessing and the last being the Great Curse. I had drawn the curse.

It may be cheating, but I shake out another stick and move to another chest of drawers to pull this:

> The person you wait for will not come. The lost article will not be found. All is darkness and thunder.

I try one more stick, yet another number, another drawer three bureaus over.

> The person you wait for will not come. The lost article will not be found. All is darkness and thunder.

I tell myself that fortunes are bogus, but then I bend over a bronze cauldron of incense and wave the smoke toward my face, inhaling it in asphyxiating gulps in hopes of getting my luck back. Somewhere in the tornado of smoke, as I fend off what I don't want to hear, I am drawn to the dark truth. There is no fate. If I want him, I will have to fight.

I will find him in Chicago and I will tell him: Yes, Tien, I am serious about you and the winters and your salary and your children.

I will make him choose, once and for all.

Eighteen hours later, I land in Chicago. Travelers of every nationality swarm the customs hall. An immigration officer folds open my passport and looks at the picture of the former Mrs. Emily Cavenaugh and then at me.

"Makeover?" he asks as he flips to page 23 for my amended last name. "Welcome home, Ms. Crane."

I spend a night at our hotel on Michigan Avenue, but the next day instead of maximizing my shopping time like so many of my crew members, I spend my time carefully applying makeup and fixing my hair. This is, after all, the first time I'll knowingly see Tien since our breakup. I put on a fresh uniform and head to the airport nearly two hours before my check-in. My crew thinks I need to meet with a supervisor—the same lie I used the first time we crossed paths at SFO.

When I reach the domicile only a few minutes before his check-in time, a nervous energy surges to my stomach. I look around me, afraid that he'll see me and know why I'm here. I am sure I look like a stalker as I do a quick walk-through. When I don't see him, I quickly chicken out. I head back to the elevators and press the down button, eager to get back to the terminal.

I press the button again and tap my foot. It feels like ages before the elevator doors open. I half expect him to be in there.

But as the first few flight attendants exit, I can see that he isn't.

I think of the agony of not knowing and decide I am not going to walk away.

Eventually, I build up the nerve to wait for him outside of the briefing room his flight is assigned to, but when I reach it, no one is there. I take a deep breath, both relieved and disappointed.

Then I notice that according to the departure boards above the crew desk, his flight is delayed.

I pass time looking at a few of the old "stewardess" uniforms on display in a glass case. Back at the training center, we had a hall filled with mannequins in some of the same golden-age uniforms—the powder blue suit with pillbox hat of the early sixties, the orange minidress with hot dog–stand hat from 1968, the Hawaiian muumuu from the late seventies. Perhaps someday a new crop of trainees will wander the halls admiring our shapeless, militaristic navy blue dresses.

I sometimes wish I had been part of an earlier era, back when

I would have been seen to epitomize feminine grace and bold independence at the same time. Of course, I'm glad that I don't have to step on a scale every time I show up to work, fearing that if I tip one pound over the limit I'll be sent home. And I don't think I would have liked the billboards depicting stewardesses in hot pants saying FLY ME, or knowing that my airline hoped to profit from the idea that in-flight "service" had a special meaning for important male passengers.

As I walk past the crew mail files, I am pulled toward Tien's. Although I am fully aware that I am a crazy ex-mistress worthy of daytime TV, I reach in, dying to know if he still has the letters I wrote.

He does.

The photos of us?

Yep.

I also find a stack of blank postcards from Vietnam. Did he finally go there? I am filled with warmth as I imagine him rediscovering the home of his youth, finally embracing his mother after decades apart.

There is a notebook, a journal of sorts, maybe from his vacation. I flip through it and see my name at the top of one of the pages.

I reason that if he is writing about me, it's fair game. Then I think, who cares at this point anyway? So what if this makes me seem crazy. I look around for witnesses nonetheless then tear out the pages and stuff them into my bag.

Only seconds after zipping my bag and standing up, I feel a tap on my shoulder. I turn around. It's Tien. I desperately try to remember my cover story, but nothing could explain why I'm standing over his mail file.

Instead of asking what I'm doing here, he smiles that same enormous warm smile that has always greeted me.

"What a coincidence running into each other again so soon,"

he says. I fear he is expecting an explanation for the snooping, but there is no hint of suspicion or sarcasm in his voice.

I glance down at my bag half expecting the pages to be sticking out and revealing my crime. Whatever composure I had has been thrown into a tailspin. In gearing up for this moment, I had planned to address his Newark suggestion directly, but all I can do is stand and stare, too stunned to speak. Finally, I say, "I was just headed down for my flight home."

He looks around the domicile and then motions toward the stairs. "I can walk you out."

I follow him into the stairwell. The door closes behind us, and my heart accelerates. I don't know what to say.

We walk down the stairs toward the terminal in silence, each step charged with anticipation. When we reach the bottom floor, instead of opening the door, he turns around and looks into my eyes with an expression I can't read.

"How are you?" he asks.

I know it's been weeks since we left off, but I somehow didn't expect us to start with small talk.

I shrug my shoulders. "Fine? I guess." I look at him directly, almost aggressively, hoping he'll take the hint and turn the conversation back to the future he hinted at.

Instead, he just says, "That's good."

I came here to fight, and after all this waiting, I am frustrated and ready to steer toward an answer. "I've thought about what you asked me last time."

"EmLee." He puts his hand up as if to stop me.

I look around the stairwell even though I know we're alone. I shouldn't need to elaborate, so I simply say, "Yes."

Self-defeating or not, I am relieved to have put it out there instead of continuing to wait for him to move. A calm comes over me. For one delusional moment, I am completely certain that everything is about to fall into place. I wait for him to wrap his arms around me and tell me that we will be together.

He is still looking at me with emotion, but it is not joy. I think it might be something more like concern.

My calm begins to evaporate. "That question you asked me," I say, as if he has innocently forgotten. "I'm serious."

"EmLee, you have to understand."

I have to understand what? Now he is making me feel like I am the one chasing him, the one starting this back up after months without contact.

"It's just that—" He stops.

"What?!" I ask forcefully, tempted to stomp my foot like a stubborn brat.

He looks surprised, even though he is the one who has left me hanging for weeks, given me no choice but to spill my heart into a dingy stairwell that smells like rubber flooring and take-out Chinese.

He looks toward the door to the terminal. "I can't talk. My family is here. At the gate. They're coming on my layovers now."

His family. His wife. They're here?

He must sense my curiosity because he says firmly, "Don't come to my gate."

"Of course not," I say, staring at him without moving, foolishly waiting for more. There must be more.

"I'm sorry," he says. And just like that he opens the door.

With the crowds of the terminal rushing behind him, he stands in the open doorway. Half in and half out.

"Is that it?" I ask.

Infuriatingly, he says nothing.

"Tien." I stop. I don't even know what else to say. I realize I am looking at him with the imploring eyes of a child who isn't getting what she wants. Finally, I quietly ask, "What do you want?"

He leans back and looks at his shoes. When he looks up, he says softly, "Does it matter?"

"It matters to me."

"There's more to it than this moment, EmLee."

I nod as if I finally understand, but it isn't true. I hear his words, but I know it matters to him, too. I weakly try to convince him he's wrong. "We would be happy."

"Yes, we would," he says with such conviction that I am caught off guard. "But at whose expense?"

He seems to want me to say it out loud, to personalize the trade-off I am asking him to make. It feels like an accusation as much as a question, and there is nothing redeeming I can say.

When I don't respond, he asks the question I have long tried to ignore. "And for how long?"

He turns, letting the door close behind him.

I am left with nothing more than the hope that his journal will reveal what his heart keeps hidden.

28

Dear Emily

I'm writing to you from Vietnam, not too far from the home I last saw in 1975. I'm ashamed to say it took my mother's death to get me here.

I watch the rain streaming from the tin roof. Water pours to the ground and merges into a current that flows down the dirt road in front of my brother's house. The air is even hotter and wetter than I remembered, humidity you could swim in.

My wife is in the kitchen wrapping spring rolls with the rest of the women while I sit on the porch drinking whiskey with four of my older brothers.

"Our baby boy Tien finally come home," says my brother Binh, who has lived in Vietnam all of his life.

He hands me a bottle of oil that he promises will repel mosquitoes. He would cringe if he knew that before the trip, my wife and I were vaccinated for typhoid and hepatitis and have been swallowing malaria pills for the last few days.

The funeral music blares from the living room where it will play for another two days. It sounds like a marching band. My ten-year-old daughter would love it. I think I mentioned that she is in band, like you were. She plays the flute and lives for Friday nights when we take her to watch the halftime show at Winnetka High School's football games.

As we smack mosquitoes, Binh laughs at me and Hao, our other brother who lives in Paris. *"Viet Kieu,"* he says, pointing at us. Overseas Vietnamese. I'm sure we do look like outsiders, especially with the sweat dripping from our every crevice.

He slaps his knees and stands up. "I have the thing," he says, and when he returns he is holding a near gallon-sized bottle of snake wine with two intact cobra heads floating in the murky liquid.

While Hao holds out his glass, I shake my head. This only makes Binh laugh harder. "Boost sexual prowess," he says. I can't tell him that sexual prowess is the most dangerous thing he could be selling right now. My sexual prowess has turned my family and my insides to ruin.

To think just a few days ago my mother was alive and I was in Newark talking to you.

Through the front door, I see Linh place a tray of mango and papaya at the altar and bow to my mother's photo. She catches my eye and quickly turns away.

I haven't told you much about my wife. I suppose I thought I was protecting her, though she was more sickened to know that we didn't speak of her while we were dismantling the life she spent ten years building.

I feel my mother shaking her head at me from beyond. "How could you?" she asks. She will never let me forget that I have brought shame to our family.

Twenty-five years in America or not, I was raised in Vietnam. I know I'm expected to put the good of the family above myself. In my mother's eyes, I am certain that I have become a self-centered foreigner.

Although I met Linh in Chicago, she is also from Vietnam. We rarely talk about what happened here when we were kids. We just know. I know that, despite my flight benefits, this is the first time she's been on an airplane since she squeezed into the cargo hold of a C-141 with five hundred other people on her way out of Saigon.

Myself, I don't like boats.

I hate that I'm bringing her back here for the first time under these circumstances. On the plane she said she feels ashamed to face my family after what happened. I keep telling her she has nothing to be ashamed of.

Binh pours a glass and hands it to me. I don't take it. He pushes it toward my lips, so I grab it from his hands, say "Fine," in English, and toss it down my throat. Turns out if you swallow quickly enough, it tastes just like rice wine. I hold out my glass and Binh refills it so high the alcohol sloshes over the side. "*Mot, hai, ba, yo!*" I say before I slam it down.

Binh buckles over in his laughter. I use my sleeve to wipe the alcohol that drips from my lips and wonder if I pronounced the toast wrong. It's like American middle school in reverse. I wish I could just say one, two, three, cheers.

I watch my wife in the kitchen carefully slicing the cucumbers into even strips, arranging them next to the basil and mint on the salad platter. She looks over her shoulder at me and then brings out a pot of tea. She sets the tray on the table and slowly pours five cups, filling them exactly without spilling.

It's disarming to see her this way, so domestic. At home I do most of the cooking because she works ten- or twelve-hour days at Motorola. When we finished college and wanted to get married, Linh asked me to follow her to Chicago. She was sure I could get a great job with United, one of the area's largest employers. She meant management, but they weren't hiring anyone for that track. I hoped to get my foot in the door, so I chose to start on the front line. A few years later, she was making so much money analyzing networks she asked me to stay home with the kids as much as I could.

I've been disappointing her ever since. I know you thought

my being a flight attendant was perfect. You thought it meant I was interesting and a people person, and taking care of the kids showed that I was sensitive and responsible.

Believe it or not, I threw that in Linh's face one night when I should have been groveling.

"Well that's because she's twenty-four and doesn't have to help support two kids with you on that salary," she screamed, royally and rightfully pissed.

"No, she doesn't," was all I could think to say. I never talk back to Linh. When she comes home from work upset that the dishes are in the sink or the trim on the house is peeling or one of the kids was a few minutes late to music lessons, I just eat my thoughts while she blows off steam. I won't tell her I'm doing her job. I won't tell her I don't want to be her wife. Because she could throw that back, too. I know she doesn't want to wear the pants. Better a lean peace than a fat victory.

But that night, I felt like telling her that she is lucky you don't have two kids by me, that for all she knew you could be pregnant with my baby. Why the hell I would even think to say something like that is beyond me. Except that, as you know, it was a possibility. After I confessed to spending time with you, my wife went through my bags and found a box of condoms. She was livid and waving it around in the air. I told her that I hadn't slept with you and to prove it I pointed at the box's unopened seal. I didn't tell her it wasn't open because we simply didn't bother.

If only it had stayed the sexual fling it started as. I can't even bring myself to say the word for what I feel now. At least I'm wise enough to know it could never last. We would have to grow tired of each other eventually. Wouldn't we? More likely you would grow tired of me. Of course you would. You're so young.

I think of your new short haircut. Clear proof that you're becoming someone too worldly and independent to want an old guy like me.

When the spring rolls and the pho and the crepes are eaten

and the snake wine is emptied, my sister Phuong shows my wife and me to the room we'll be staying in. Linh clenches her teeth and breathes deeply through her nose when she sees the small bed we are expected to share. She brushes past me without a word and places her suitcase in the corner.

We lie together in bed without a child between us for the first time I can remember. I can feel her shifting and trying to get comfortable. I move my arm over an inch at a time until it's brushing against hers. She doesn't move her arm away, so I place my hand around hers so slowly that it's as if I thought she wouldn't notice. But she does notice and she squeezes my hand. My heart warms. A few moments later, she pulls her hand away from me and rolls to the far edge of the bed.

"It's hot," she says.

We lie in silence for so long that I assume she has fallen asleep. I try to keep completely still so I don't wake her. She has always been a light sleeper. It was both a blessing and a curse when our daughters were babies. If one of them had a single rasp in her breath or became too quiet, Linh was awake and checking on her. She may have been tired, but we always knew they were safe. We often joke that it will come in handy if they ever try to sneak out of the house as teenagers.

After an hour of complete stillness, I feel a tickle in my throat and am unable to hold back the cough.

Linh, of course, stirs in the bed.

"Sorry if I woke you."

"I'm up. Just thinking about things back home."

"Missing the kids?" I ask.

She sighs. "It is a change being alone together."

"Yes."

"That's why, isn't it?"

"Why what?"

She turns to look at me. Instead of anger her eyes are filled with pain. I can barely stand to face her.

"No. It isn't your fault," I say again, knowing she will never be convinced.

The next morning cousins and aunts and uncles and neighbors and old family friends arrive for the funeral.

Phuong lights incense on my mother's altar. My cousins begin rhythmically banging drums and clanging cymbals while the priest chants. He is speaking so quickly, I can hardly follow his Vietnamese. We burn the money and the incense. My mother is looking down her nose at me, grinding her teeth. I have no right to be here.

We are way past losing face. As I stand here in real yet self-conscious mourning, I am tasting the bottom of the earth.

My oldest brothers pick up the coffin, and I step in line behind them for the walk to the grave site.

The procession follows the dirt path along the bay. When I was a kid, my mother used to wake up early, cast our little basket boat out into this bay to fish. I can see her waving at me and pushing herself out of the sand with the long oar. I can see less peaceful days, too, see the contrails of the B-52s passing above, hear the buzzing of their load on its way down. I can see the ground exploding from underneath, trees and homes being blown apart, people diving for cover. I can hear tanks rumbling and machine guns firing, the ever-present sound of distant mortars.

A flock of birds whizzes by in a blur. My eyes are fixed on the horizon. I see nothing and I show nothing, but inside I am drowning. I wanted a peaceful life for my children, but now I have gone and waged a different war on their childhood.

We couldn't even keep it from them. A few weeks back Samantha, my oldest, found Linh crying over the kitchen sink as she peeled carrots. "Mommy, Mommy. What's the matter?" I heard her say. My wife didn't answer and my daughter found a peeler and cried and peeled along with her mother.

Now as I chant for my mother's safe passage, I also pray that this funeral will be a scapegoat for the children. I can only hope that when they look back on this confusing and terrifying time in their lives, they'll think their parents must have been upset about their grandmother's death. Right now they're at home with my cousin An, the woman who raised me from the age of eleven. After the camp in Thailand, I was sent to Minnesota to live with her and her husband, a U.S. Army sniper our family never forgave her for marrying.

Although she was asked to come, An didn't feel welcome here after the trouble she caused all those years ago. I choke out a small laugh. If anyone should have stayed away it's me.

I look from the bay back to where our old house once sat. I see what might be the same mango tree out front and remember the last time I saw my mother. I was ten years old and I watched with confusion as she shoved clothes and food into a bag and then pushed me out the door in the middle of the night. She didn't hug me or kiss me. She hid. My dad set me on the back of his scooter and brought me to this bay. He said, "Go" and pushed me even harder than my mom had, toward a scrambling group of people I barely knew and the South China Sea. I have always wondered how long they had been planning to send me away.

We spend days with family and friends, everyone an uncle or an aunt, whether related by blood or not. Some of them I remember from the old days, some of them I do not. They tell me how much I loved eating candies, beating drums, playing soldier in the tall grass when I was a boy. They recall my mother and me holding hands as we skipped toward the river where she taught me how to fish. They remind me of the time my father dropped me off at the dump when I talked back to my mother. That

I remember. He said only a piece of trash would speak to his mother like that.

I am now told what I didn't know—that he hid around the corner and kept an eye on me as I cried.

I have long used that memory as proof that it was easy for them to leave me. I was too much trouble. There were too many mouths. Too little food.

Before they died, I should have admitted what I knew was true. They didn't throw me away. They stamped out their own hearts and gave me a better life.

That night in bed, my wife leans her head on my shoulder.

"What if this trip could be a second honeymoon? It could be like when we stayed at that resort on Lake Michigan."

When I look back on our honeymoon, it is usually with regret that I couldn't take her somewhere more extravagant. Thinking of it now, I have to admit that it really was beautiful. We sat out on the balcony of our resort, watching the sailboats drifting on the lake and the sunbathers resting on the sand, the water gently lapping at the shore. "Yes, and we took the ferry out to that island in Wisconsin to see that lighthouse."

We thought life could be that peaceful forever. I had just been given a training date with United, and we fantasized that we could use the flight benefits to show our future children the world—pop over to D.C. when they studied the Constitution or Beijing when they did a unit on China. Linh was determined to get over her fear of flying.

It seemed natural that I could move up from working the front line to working in management, and then she could take a break from her career to stay home with the kids. Neither of us could have known that airlines don't work that way, that there is an invisible barrier as impenetrable as the Great Wall between the managers and the workers.

At some point, we stopped having dreams together. For so long, though, we did stick to creating a safe and stable home for our kids.

Linh starts laughing. "Remember when you tried to pick those flowers for me and that crazed environmentalist threatened to have you arrested?"

I laugh with her and she puts her hand on top of mine. She says, "We could choose to see what happened as a wake-up call for our marriage."

She's been saying things like this since it happened, but she hasn't seemed to believe it. It's probably just a pressure to stay positive that she picked up in America. Regardless, I admire her strength.

"We could go see the sights," she says. "Maybe stay a few nights at a nice hotel." She smiles for the first time in months.

"Of course. That's a wonderful idea," I say, thankful for a concrete opportunity to make her happy.

First thing in the morning, I find myself at a shop filled with tourist trinkets. I fumble through their laquerware trays and multicolored silk scarves and ask the owner if he sells maps or tourist guides. Although I say it in Vietnamese, he pulls out an English guidebook. I buy it without haggling because I feel guilty for being a rich American. But perhaps that was arrogant. I flip through the postcards at the counter. I can't help but consider sending you a postcard. I don't want to lead you on, but I do want to show you my homeland.

I set the postcards down.

The next afternoon Linh and I hire a car and wind our way to a beach that the guidebook calls the country's hottest beach destination. We pass rice fields dotted with hunched-over workers, thatched-roof hamlets, motorbike-congested towns, posters of Ho Chi Minh, and billboards of the Spice Girls. I watch this

landscape pass by the window almost the way any Western tourist would. It was once real for me, but now I can't feel it. It's like
a history book, totally devoid of emotion. Or filled with too
much emotion to touch. I know if I look at this as anything other
than a photo from a guidebook, the people will start moving and
yelling and running and falling and I will smell the smoke and
hear the helicopters and then I will start to cry and never stop.

The book was right. Enormous luxury resorts do indeed line
the beach. It must also be true that top-of-the-line rooms have
private pools and twenty-four-hour butlers. It's remarkable and
disgusting at once.

"It's beautiful," says Linh. Fortunately, I follow her gaze not
to the penthouses above but to a palm tree–studded cove. Thank
goodness. Even in Vietnam, I can't provide her with that kind of
luxury.

I take in the sea air and the smell of the local fish sauce factories. I watch a cyclo driver pedaling through traffic with two
oversize tourists in back and wonder if that is what I would be
doing if I had never left here. Perhaps I would have been a street
vendor selling coconut juice and Coca-Cola.

We consult the guidebook for what to eat. It says, "Thanks to
Chinese, French, and Japanese occupations, Vietnam is a hotbed
of fusion cuisine." For the first time in my life, I realize that even
if I had never left Vietnam, I still wouldn't have an identity.

We sit at a table by the beach eating oranges and mango. Linh
puts up the umbrella because she doesn't want her skin to
darken. No doubt her mother warned her not to play in the sun
when she was a kid. Mine always said it would make me look like
a peasant.

She waves the waitress over and orders an iced coffee, Vietnamese style with condensed milk.

"You never drink coffee," I say.

"Sweet like this, it was my dad's favorite. We used to have it all the time when I was a little girl. Somehow, it just fits the moment."

"Make that two," I tell the waitress.

I had forgotten what it was like to get to know Linh. It makes me wonder what else I don't know about the person she was before we met and the person she has become as we've let in the distance.

We discuss what to do with our time in the area and consider a bike ride because windsurfing isn't our style. The nearby Ho Chi Minh museum—"which offers a glimpse of Uncle Ho's white tunic, walking stick, sandals, and helmet"—is not on our list of stops. We will not be snapping pictures of Victory Monument, a cement tower that "depicts machine-gun-toting patriots gazing expectantly into the future." And no matter what we do, we will not take advantage of a chance to "play guerilla" and shoot AK-47s.

Down near the water I see a threesome of Western girls in bikinis staking out a spot for their towels. I listen but can't quite hear whether or not they are speaking English. They look to be in their twenties, backpackers most likely. I wonder if you have made it to Vietnam yet. I always told you you'd end up in Asia before I did. You're much more adventurous than I.

If I squint just a little I can see you in the shorter girl of the threesome who just threw her towel onto the sand. Wouldn't that be something if we ran into each other here? Just as I'm tempted to get up and walk to the water to cool off, to discover if the girls are American or English or what, I see a dark-skinned local guy circling around them like a shark. I assume he's local because he is wearing a black Speedo with his little pecker sticking straight out. No *Viet Kieu* would do that.

After three circles, the girls pick up and move. As they pass by, I hear the girl, who from up close looks nothing like you, say, "Vietnam is the new Hawaii."

I look up at Linh, who is studying the guidebook with her silky black hair gently blowing across her face in the breeze. I am reminded how lovely she is when she's happy. It wasn't so long ago I knew how to make her happy.

I am startled by a sudden hope that I might be able to do so again.

She must feel me staring because she lifts her head and meets my eyes for the first time in what feels like decades.

Maybe it isn't too late to give my children peace.

"Do you love me?" I ask her, surprising myself.

She closes the guidebook and straightens it on the table in front of her. "What kind of question is that?" she asks.

"Do you love me? Are you in love with me?"

She laughs an airy startled laugh. "I'm your wife."

I place my hands on the table and look straight at her. "But Linh, do you love me?"

She leans back and pushes her hair behind her ears. "You sound like a teenager. An American teenager."

I take a deep breath and look up at the umbrella. "What if we were to move home?"

"Home where? Here?"

"Maybe if we lived a simpler life, things wouldn't be so hard."

She stirs her coffee and looks out at the ocean. Then she says, "It is lovely here, isn't it?"

Emily, if you could see the softening in Linh's eyes, you would understand what I could never explain. I have flown so far from where Linh and I began. I don't know if we can ever make it back there, but maybe while we're trying we can stumble our way to someplace new.

29

The Wife

I am humbled to find that with a few pages of writing, I can know him more intimately than I did in all the time we were together. Buried beneath my longing, a part of me is even moved by their relationship. But it's a change to know her as more than an obstacle standing in our way.

I remember that she is somewhere in this airport, only steps away, and am overcome by an irresistible urge to learn more.

Maybe he had it right. If I could only see her, maybe then I would better understand.

I take a breath and swing open the door to the terminal. I stand in front of the departure monitor, deliberating. The San Francisco is about to board.

I break my promise and head toward his gate.

I spot him in his blue United suit and tie talking to his crew. He's holding up a finger to tell them to wait. He walks to the podium, picks up a stack of tickets, and looks around the boarding area, presumably for his wife and kids. He sees me and freezes. I duck behind a pillar. Before he can say or do anything, I slip into the ladies' room at the next gate.

I close my eyes, take a breath, and then get in line behind a woman in a lumpy beige sweater. She starts to speak to someone in one of the stalls. She has an accent, his accent. It could be her. It must be her.

I'm standing close enough to touch her. In case she turns around, I hide the United ID that is hanging around my neck revealing my name.

"Nearly done?" she asks.

A child's voice calls out from inside one of the stalls. "Almost, Mommy."

She's simple-looking, homely even. She's shorter than me, heavier than me. I begin to feel sorry for her. On top of everything, after a long week at work, she has packed up to fly standby across the country with two children, undoubtedly wondering whether or not there will be room on the flight. And if there isn't, who might be there to take her place.

She has no idea that the woman who caused all this is right beside her.

I stare at her hair, each thick strand of long black hair, her discount-store jacket and sensible Naturalizer shoes.

A stall opens and a girl who must be her daughter, his daughter, comes out. The mother turns toward me. I look at her. She raises her eyebrows at me as if to say, "What are you looking at? The stall is free."

"I, I, excuse me." I try to think of what I can say to her. Remember me?

I push my way out of line, slamming into a trash can being steered by a cleaning woman. She pushes me right back with her rolling gray can. I jog to the center of the concourse and am about to take the moving walkway to my gate, but the fever of curiosity proves irresistible. Like a stalker, I stand behind a pillar at the gate across from his. It takes me a second to find him. He is standing by a row of seats. A beautiful woman in a red silk shirt stands up, smooths her pants, and then touches his shoulder.

She's put together, refined, elegant. Her biceps are the size of my wrists, her waist the size of my thighs. She must come to my chin. Suddenly, I feel big. At five foot three, I've never felt large. It's unnerving.

I am embarrassed by my arrogance, assuming all this time that she had let herself go. I never imagined that she was prettier than me. Her hair is tied back in a bun. She has dramatic angular eyes and high cheekbones. With her black slacks, shiny black pumps, and heavy streak of blush, she looks professional, like my mom, I think. I am hit with a memory of being three years old and watching her get ready for her job at the bank. I can almost smell the drugstore perfume and Aqua Net hairspray that signaled it was time for day care.

Tien and his wife speak matter-of-factly about something. His younger daughter runs up and grabs his legs.

Next to them, their older daughter spins around in circles with her arms out. Tien boards the plane with his crew and they all wave.

Now that I've seen her, I should be done. But I keep watching. An agent announces that zone one is boarding, and the entire boarding area stands up to crowd the quickly forming line.

I remember that she doesn't know what I look like. I could speak to her and she wouldn't know the difference.

I take one step into the busy walkway between our opposing gates. I dodge my way through a stream of travelers, trailing oversized luggage behind them.

My nerves begin to spark. She walks toward the edge of the huddled masses. I am freezing cold and shaking as I move into the open space beside her.

She turns to me and offers a smile of polite acknowledgment. I hear myself speak. Through my anxiety it sounds muffled and far away. "Do you know if they've called standbys yet?"

She shakes her head and says sorry. She looks right past me. If she knew who I was, she would look at me differently.

Perhaps she looks at all women differently now, now that she can't trust her husband.

A part of me feels for her. A larger part is unbearably jealous. A poisonous thought surfaces—it is not too late to tear them apart.

How easily I could tell her why I flew all the way around the world to see her husband. If she knew we were still in contact, if she knew what he said in Newark, maybe she would end it right here in the gray-and-white linoleum halls of O'Hare.

Her older daughter looks up, bouncing up and down with a smile on her face, and asks if she can buy a piece of candy at the nearby kiosk. Both of his girls seem completely oblivious to anything that is troubling their parents. I can almost feel the innocent childhood joy emanating from their smiles.

I imagine what would happen if she were to kick him out. Would he sit his kids down on the sofa in the only living room they've ever known and tell them he has an announcement? Would one of them bite her lip in fear that he found out about her unfinished math homework, and would the other bounce up and down thinking she's going to Disneyland?

His wife says, "Yes, sweetie. Quickly." She looks up at me and shrugs her shoulders as if I have kids of my own and know what she's dealing with.

"So you're not working this flight? You're standby, too?" she asks.

"Right. Standby." I am painfully aware that she is making idle chitchat with a fellow passenger, completely blind to the fact that I am analyzing every nuance of her voice, every one of her elegant movements. She is passing time, and I am sizing up my lover's wife.

"Is San Francisco home for you, or Chicago?" she asks as she checks her watch.

I nervously clear my throat. "Neither. There's just someone

I'm hoping to see." I feel the power of the words I could follow up with.

She raises her eyebrows and gives me a little smirk like she knows by "someone" I mean a man.

If we met under different circumstances, I wonder what advice she would give me about men. Would she warn me that all men are dogs? Would she tell me to check phone records? Or would she say that when you find the right person, you can get through anything together?

"Well, the flight looks pretty full," she says. "Let's hope they let standbys on."

When I fantasized about a future with him, I saw us walking side by side through airport terminals, wheeling our matching suitcases around the country.

Now I am looking at our future. If he were to leave her, I would chase him around the country, accounting for his time, checking his phone records while he tries to make things up to his kids by buying them toys and candy.

His words run through my mind—we would be happy, but for how long? The challenges would no doubt build, and what would we do when the initial excitement wears off? Would he even have the energy to fight for us after having given up once before?

I have always thought that by picking her, he would be choosing the safe route. But for the first time, I realize it may take more courage to stay.

She waves at her daughter to hurry up, but the girl is painstakingly weighing her options at the kiosk.

His wife sighs and gathers her things to go after her girl. "Good luck getting to see your 'someone,'" she says.

"Thank you." I watch her take the hand of her youngest and walk toward her older daughter. I watch this mother and wife on her trek around the country, struggling to keep her family together, and I finally know it's not that simple. Neither luck nor love will resolve this.

I walk away. Not because I *should*, not because it's expected, but because it's right for a reason.

The person I wait for will not come. And that's finally okay.

I work the next flight home to London. When I land, my suitcase isn't at the carousel. The man at the baggage desk says they have a record of my bag getting on in San Francisco, so it should be in here. But it isn't. He takes down the contents of my bag in case it lost its tag and is being held at a place he calls Tag Off. My black rollaboard held a miniature Buddha, my favorite blue layover shirt, my uniform, my crew handbook. He admits that I'm not the first flight attendant to lose a bag in the last few weeks. *I* didn't lose the bag, I tell him.

The lost article will not be found.

I count my misfortunes and relax a little, realizing that it's over. My dark future has been lived out. In just a few days, each of the prophecies has come true. I decide to see this as an omen of good things to come, an incentive to unveil a new me. When I sweep through the airports in D.C. and Chicago and London and Delhi, it will be with a newly issued bag and a new uniform. I am a new woman who will not check his schedule just to make sure he's still alive. I will be too busy living my life.

Simon rings. I am surprised to hear from him, but I pick up. He tells me a United plane has been hijacked.

"Yeah, right," I say.

"Darlin', I'm not kidding."

SEPTEMBER 11, 2001

Darkness and Thunder

30

Early Departure

I wind the plastic tubing of the oxygen mask around my hand and let it drop from above 5B. I tug it to demonstrate initiating the flow of oxygen then pull the mask over my nose and mouth, adjusting the straps as necessary. Any other day, perhaps, I would hold the little yellow mask in front of my face to avoid germs as so many of us do. But this morning, they're all watching me, unfolding safety cards instead of newspapers. No rustling, no conversations, just hundreds of eyes staring straight at me. Besides our purser Annabelle's voice on the PA, the only noise is the hum of the air-conditioning and the *tap tap* of the wheels over cracks in the tarmac. I sway back and forth as we turn toward the runway. *Don't cry.* I tell myself. *Don't You Dare Cry.*

I take comfort in the demo's ritual, keeping in sync with Sue in the right aisle and Callie up ahead at row fourteen. At training, we practiced this dozens of times until we could all make our seat belts click in unison.

Still they stare—almost as intently as I stared at each of them as they boarded, my "How are you today?" more than a rhetorical question this time. I analyzed each answer for any hint of terrorist threat.

It's September 18, 2001, exactly one week after we lost two of our aircraft and sixteen of our crew, and I am back in the air for the first time. International flights bound for U.S. airspace only just resumed the day before yesterday.

I check my watch, 8:05. Twelve and a half hours to go. It will be a long, long, flight. We're on the 767, and its slow flight time is almost two hours longer than it would be on the 777 or 747. Most days on this flight, United 975—London to San Francisco, we make a note at some point during the initial beverage service. "Oh, the triple-seven just took off." Then when we set up the prelanding snack somewhere over Colorado, about the time when we run completely out of water and only air comes out of the taps, we point out, "The triple-seven just landed."

Twelve and a half hours to go and I can barely keep my eyes open. I got up at 3:30 A.M. to take a cab to Trafalgar Square where I caught the night bus, as the Tube doesn't run in time to make a 6 A.M. check-in. But it's not as if I was sleeping anyway. Since it happened, I've been fighting nightmares.

When I found out what happened last Tuesday, September eleventh, I was at home in London, the last flight attendant on call. My roommate had been called out for the 8 A.M. L.A., leaving me next in line for a trip. When the crew desk hadn't called by lunchtime, I started feeling lucky—the only flights left were the late New York and D.C., and those were so popular reserves never needed to fill in. Then the phone finally rang, Simon, calling to tell me about the first plane.

We didn't have a TV at our flat because there was always something better to do. I still thought he was joking and wasn't sure whether or not to laugh. My phone beeped and I clicked over. Before I could even say hello, another flight attendant said, "There's been a hijacking. Have you heard anything?" Even before I could process her words, I felt electricity fire through my body and slam into my feet. I fell to my knees. The rational part of me scoffed at such a melodramatic reaction. I wasn't sure what I was doing—was I planning to pray? Or did I just want to hold on to the ground and stay out of the air?

The voices and faces from our annual security refresher videos filled my head—flight attendants who had been hijacked in the eighties detailing every moment spent with their captors. I plugged KC and Tien's faces into these reenactments and imagined them calmly serving coffee to terrorists while the pilots nosed the plane toward the requested foreign country. Comply, comply, comply. This was our terrorist strategy.

I met twenty other flight attendants at a flat that had a TV. We saw what the rest of the world saw, but to us it wasn't just an airplane, that fuselage carried our company's livery, our coat of arms, our mascot, our country's flag. That same United logo was plastered to our uniforms, our handbooks, our badges, our luggage—the only constant in our lives.

We agreed on one thing—the newscasters had things wrong. What they were calling a narrow-body 737 was definitely a wide-body '67 with twice the capacity for passengers, crew, and fuel. We had all done the flash card drills at training and could instantly name any plane in the UAL fleet by its exterior characteristics. We knew the inside, too. We had all worked that Boston to Los Angeles flight and knew the exact 767 200-series model in question, an older model with user-unfriendly galleys and gray-and-white-flecked partitions in business. We could all smell the jet fuel that pumps through the 767 cabin on the first flight of each morning. Once an annoyingly outdated workspace—now the soundstage of our violation.

It may have been a national tragedy, but for us it was an intimate crime. As personal as if those thugs had broken into our family home, burglars rifling through jewelry boxes searching for valuables, finding only mementos to be tossed aside. They destroyed the photos of us at training, our heavily made-up faces glowing with excitement for our new lives. They destroyed the hope lingering in every sentence of our love letters.

The flat had become a boiler room, twenty of us simultaneously punching redial on our cell phones and taking shifts on the landline. "All circuits are busy. All circuits are busy." We couldn't get a line to the U.S.

We were desperately trying to find our roommates, friends, lovers. Unimatic, the United scheduling software, was shut down, so I couldn't check Tien's or KC's schedules. Since she's on reserve and could be anywhere in the world, I didn't even know where to start looking for her.

My thoughts again turned to Tien. He couldn't have been on that plane—he wouldn't have flown to Boston again. That's where he was the night she found out about us while calculating their phone bills.

I wished I had checked his next trip. Could it have been Boston? I didn't have his phone number, she'd changed it. So I just kept redialing the Richelieu, hoping he would be in San Francisco again.

The BBC told us United officials were "deeply concerned" about another flight, United flight 93, Newark to San Francisco.

He had been working that route for a month straight last time I checked.

"All circuits are busy. All circuits are busy."

We saw the towers collapse, but we didn't yet care about the buildings.

United confirmed two planes down.

A 767 from Boston with nine crew and fifty-six passengers and a 757 from Newark with seven crew and thirty-seven passengers. Extraordinarily light loads. Inconceivably light loads. We began to speculate. It had been a busy summer, months since any of us had seen an empty seat. The hijackers must have had access to those numbers. They could not have arbitrarily picked the flights with the fewest passengers to resist. They either knew UAL employees or were UAL employees.

The possibility of terrorists plotting this from inside our ranks was sickening. But the alternative was unspeakable—that luck or fate or God was with them.

A call here and a call there were connected. Most of the people we got word on had been diverted to Canada when U.S. airspace was shut down. Five hundred international flights were diverted, hundreds instructed to land immediately at the nearest airfield.

As we dialed, we watched news reports on rumored bomb threats and car bombs, other hijackings, evacuations of government buildings, America's inevitable retaliation. Someone ordered a pizza, but we weren't able to finish two mediums between us. Filched liquor minis and splits of airline wine appeared. A laugh slipped from inside the kitchen. Arguments erupted between those who felt it was wrong to be laughing or drinking and those who believed we were each entitled to our own reactions. Some of us stared at the TV. Others acted as if the world was ending and all bets were off. Recovered smokers lit new cigarettes before finishing their last. Several of us reached out to long-banished exes. Muffled moaning and thumping came from the bathroom where a woman I didn't know had entered with a complete stranger, not her husband.

Finally, a ring. The Richelieu's operator thanked me for calling. I spelled out Tien's last name, and she said, "I'll connect you."

He said hello quickly, almost a whisper. He was alive.

"Hi, it's me."

Silence.

"Hello? Are you there?"

He took a deep breath. "I knew it was you as soon as the phone rang. I promised myself I wouldn't pick up."

"It's not so bad. You wanted to make sure I was safe," I said, still in the habit of coming up with excuses.

"You know you're the devil, right?" he said with a laugh. "Not really, but it is good to hear your voice."

With all flights canceled or indefinitely delayed, Tien and his crew were determined to rent a van and drive all the way to Chicago.

"My wife is worried. My kids are scared. It's hard to be away right now," he admitted.

I could hear a distance in his voice. I realized we were sharing one of those obligatory post-disaster phone calls. He was relieved to know I was alive, but there was nothing left to say.

I thought of his wife with her kind demeanor and of the tenderness with which he wrote about her. Of course he would want to go home.

As we spoke, I could feel his commitment to her, not just legally but emotionally. Yet there was a small part of me that would rather he wanted to spend a few more days at the Richelieu, a few more days talking to me on the phone.

"I'm glad you read it," he said.

"Read what?"

"I wrote to you."

I flushed with embarrassment. He may not have caught me that day, but of course he would figure it out.

"I never meant for you to see that. But now I'm thinking maybe it helped and I'm glad."

"It did."

We said goodbye. Yet again.

I called our obvious layover hotels in places like Chicago and D.C., New York and L.A., hoping to find KC, but she was nowhere to be found. Then I headed back to my flat.

As I walked along the Thames, I saw a beggar huddling in a corner under the Hungerford Bridge. He looked up at my red, tear-soaked face and said, "Chin up, girl."

I stopped at the liquor store for milk. The Pakistani owner and I said nothing during the exchange. On past occasions we'd laughed together about being immigrants. Perhaps after what happened he was as self-conscious about his accent as I was of mine.

Once home, I sat on the couch with the phone at my side, unable to do more than stare at the blank yellow wall across from me.

My dad called and said, "Thank God. I've been trying all day."

I had been so concerned about my friends and coworkers that I hadn't yet thought of people worrying about me.

"Are you okay? Can you come home?" he asked.

I told him I was fine and I wasn't coming home.

Hesitantly, he said, "We can come out there if you need us."

He sounded relieved when I said it wouldn't be necessary, but I was touched by the gesture, and even a little proud of him for being willing to leave the country for the first time.

Over the next few days, London police who normally carried batons shouldered machine guns. The American embassy was surrounded with bouquets of flowers, along with new barbed-wire fences and concrete barriers.

I went to St. Paul's Cathedral for a memorial service and a three-minute silence that was observed throughout Europe. Businesses were shuttered, phones were silenced, the London Eye stopped turning, cabs and cars and buses pulled over to the sides of roads. Thousands of us stood side by side in the middle of central London. Where we should have heard sirens and yells, honks and construction, for a full three minutes, the only sound was the flapping of pigeons' wings.

KC finally called. Her flight to Chicago had been diverted to Toronto, where they spent three days before being welcomed back to O'Hare by cheering rampers who waved them into the gate with American flags.

KC heard that Straight Kevin and his crew were stuck in Gander, Newfoundland, for five days. They spent the first night on board the plane in an airport so small it had no facilities for processing international visitors. It took more than thirty hours to deplane six thousand passengers aboard the thirty-eight commercial jets that had descended upon Gander when the diversions were ordered. Apparently somehow, during all that time, the small local ground staff serviced the lavs and boarded meals, which the flight attendants of each plane served before cycling the same movies over and over and then spending the night in their jumpseats.

When they were finally let off the plane, cramped, sweaty, and confused, the passengers and crew stayed on cots at Salvation Army centers and churches in nearby towns. They woke up every morning hoping to go home, but only a few planes made it out each day.

Other flights that were less than midway over the ocean turned back. Some flight attendants said their pilots shut off the airshow maps and turned their planes around with a bank so shallow no one noticed that halfway over the Atlantic they were dumping fuel and returning to Europe.

"Liqueur? After-dinner drink? Liqueur? After-dinner drink?" I ask while pushing a cart through the aisles of a 767, an identical twin to the one that left Boston a week ago and barreled at maximum cruise speed into a 110-story building.

When I reach the galley, the phone is ringing. It's the captain—he needs a bathroom break. Brand-new cockpit security measures mean they can no longer do their business in private. The rest of the crew must be notified, all first-class passengers must be seated, a two-hundred-pound beverage cart must be set up as a barrier between the cabin and the aisle leading to the cockpit, and two flight attendants must stand guard.

I call to tell them we're ready. As I knock the secret knock on the cockpit door, I hold open the lavatory door with my foot so the light will help the pilots see my face through the peephole and know I'm not a terrorist.

The captain opens the door and apologizes. He says he'll try to make it to San Francisco without pissing again. But before heading back to the cockpit he admits he needs another cup of coffee. He hasn't been sleeping well.

We've got six more hours until landing. I'm dying for a nap, but we've agreed not to take rest breaks. Haunted by visions of colleagues being murdered with box cutters, no one can stomach the thought of pulling a curtain, donning a sleeping mask, and leaving the rest of the crew alone in the cabin.

I keep moving, handing out blankets and mini Toblerone bars, Bloody Marys and ginger ales. How will I make it to the end of this flight? How will I survive this job?

On the ground in San Francisco, I doze while the crew van brings us to the city. All four lanes of the 101 are packed with cars flying American flags. I want to shield my eyes from their glare. I am in mourning, and the people of California have team spirit. They are rallying for revenge, but I'm not ready for more violence.

The door to the Richelieu opens and I am accosted by the familiar smell of the lobby, that curious mixture of Pine Sol and lavender. I slide my key into a door upstairs and with an electronic click and release, I enter a room as familiar as my own.

I flop onto the bed still in uniform, then flick on the TV and throw the remote onto the shiny quilted bedspread. *Law and Order, Murder She Wrote,* Kron 4 News "reporting live from San

Francisco International Airport, where United Airlines has just announced the layoff of twenty thousand employees. Only one week after the World Trade Center attacks, the economic fallout has begun. Once again, we are live from SFO where United Airlines has just announced the impending layoff of five thousand flight attendants."

Five thousand flight attendants? The hit is so strong it knocks my organs loose. I am in the junior-most one thousand. There were twenty-six thousand of us this morning. Now there are twenty-one thousand of *them*. We find out on the news? To United, I'm already gone, blown out of existence, as if I never was.

I call the crew desk. Evil Debbie says, "I'm so sorry. I swear, we had no idea either."

I can hear Debbie's long fingernails frantically typing, matching flights with crew members. "Am I already laid off?" I ask. "Am I working my flight home tomorrow?"

"I told you. I don't know," says Debbie. "Report to your briefing. I've still got tonight's flights to deal with."

This is my first, and probably my last, postapocalyptic layover. If I could, I would cocoon myself in the hotel and eat room service in bed. Unfortunately, the Richelieu doesn't serve food. If this is my last time here, my final night in one of these overly floral rooms, I'm going to do it right. I change into jeans and walk two blocks to Miss Saigon. I order the beef pho, his favorite, even though I prefer the shrimp, then cry over the bowl. Cindy delivers my meal without making eye contact. I almost believe she doesn't recognize me, until she comes back with the jar of tiny red peppers he would have requested. She sets it across from me but says nothing.

Without this job, I will lose the only thread of connection I have with him. "I'm sorry, I need to go home," I tell Cindy and leave some cash on the table.

The next morning, I go to my briefing as scheduled. Before the passengers board, my crew gathers in the first-class cabin with our pilots. Captain Don says, "If a terrorist takes one of you hostage and demands we open the cockpit door, we will have to let you die."

The first officer nods along.

Captain Don says, "If I have reason to believe that terrorists have taken over the cabin and might breach the cockpit, I will drive the plane into the ground."

Although I understand that this is the new game plan, I tremble as he performs his cruel sermon. His voice grows stronger and as he quickens his pace, he almost cracks a smile. It occurs to me that this may be his long-awaited chance to play hero. Many of our pilots earned their wings while flying over Vietnam, returning home only to be spit on.

A supervisor I've never seen moves to the front of the cabin. He takes over where Captain Don left off and informs us we will all work our flight home to London. The three most junior of us will not work again.

We will land this flight to become untethered balloons. Our visas will be voided, we'll be sent home from London. Immigration will be waiting for us to board our flights home.

I will lose my job, KC and everyone I know will scatter throughout the world back to where they came from or someplace entirely new, I will move out of my flat and the country I'm living in. I will lose my last connection to him.

"Ladies and gentlemen," the captain announces. "Flight time to London today will be approximately nine and a half hours."

The 777, it's fast, too fast.

I wind the plastic tubing of the oxygen mask around my hand then let it drop from above 5B. They're all watching me as I'm watching them. *Don't cry, don't you dare cry*, I tell myself. I still have nine and a half hours to go. Only nine and a half hours to go.

31

Rescue Op

KC pushes her overstuffed suitcase onto the luggage rack of the Heathrow Express train. This is the first time she's spent the extra eight pounds to get there in twenty minutes instead of an hour-plus. Not that she's feeling flush. She's unemployed. It was just one nice thing she could do for herself.

She sits down in a padded bucket seat, looks up at the train's TV monitor, then quickly turns away. *Footage of a 767 flying into the World Trade Center? For a trainload of airline passengers? Whose dumbass move was that?*

KC looks at the plane ticket in her hand, turns it over and over. It's no ordinary ticket. It's not standby, it's not even full fare, it's a "must ride," which means she'll be the most important passenger on the plane. Well, the most important passenger to *board* the plane. If they were short on seats, KC Valentine would be the absolute last person to get bumped, even after the million-miler and the CEO of Coca-Cola. However, once she passes through the aircraft door, proving to the UK immigration officials that she's left the country, she will be the ultimate nobody. Unemployed, unattached, homeless. And pregnant.

When it first happened, she wished she could quit, but even

then she knew she had nowhere to go. She was working a trip to Chicago, and somewhere over Canada while they were cleaning up from the prelanding snack, the interphone chimed three times, the chilling signal that something was wrong. KC picked up the phone over her seat and didn't know what to think when the captain spoke. "All I know," he said, "is that there has been some kind of security breach on American soil. U.S. airspace has been closed and we have been instructed to land immediately in Toronto."

She felt her hand shaking as she placed the receiver back in its cradle. What could have possibly closed all U.S. airspace?

Soon after clicking off, the captain's voice came over the PA. "Ladies and gentlemen. We've had an indicator light go off in the cockpit. Not to worry, the plane is still safe, but we're going to have to divert into Toronto as a precaution."

The entire cabin groaned, no doubt fretting over missed connections. KC will never know if he was trying to spare them all confusion and stress or if the lie was a security precaution.

It wasn't long after landing that they all learned the truth. Realizing they would be in Toronto for days, along with dozens of other diverted aircraft, the working crew members offered to share their hotel rooms with employees who were flying space available and couldn't find rooms elsewhere.

As much as KC was saddened and frightened by what had happened, and as uncomfortable as she was sharing a bed with a girl she barely knew, she liked bonding with the group of castaways.

One of them, a Hong Kong–based stew who had been on his way to visit family in Florida, had only packed for tropical weather. To keep warm in the Canadian fall, he resorted to wearing a souvenir he'd picked up in Delhi for his father—a traditional Indian kurta, a collarless knee-length shirt that looks like a robe or a dress. To a lot of people in the days after September 11, it also looked like something a terrorist would wear.

Wherever they went, KC saw people watching him, studying him as if he might suddenly produce a bomb from under his dress. Occasionally, someone would nudge a friend and point in his direction.

KC's thoughts turned to Raj with his dark skin, the slight dark circles under his eyes, and the ever-present hint of the beard that loomed a few hours away. She wondered what flying would be like for him going forward. *Will he spend extra time at security, have his bags searched before every flight? Will he get interrogated every time he comes through immigration after an international?*

It was infuriating to KC to see people spewing racist remarks on TV. But she also knew that later on the plane, she too would be looking more closely at passengers of Middle Eastern descent.

When KC reaches Heathrow, the gate agent shows her to a first-class sleeper suite. *Gotta get a chuckle out of being laid off and deported by way of first class.* The thing is, she doesn't even know where she's going. They gave her a ticket to LAX, connecting to Las Vegas because that's the city she was hired out of, but there's nothing there for her anymore.

"Sorry to hear about your furlough," says a female voice from somewhere behind her.

She turns around to see who's talking to her, but instead she sees a female flight attendant ushering Kevin to a first-class seat a few rows back. She can't believe he's on this flight.

He nods at her and then sits down.

All I get is a nod? I could be carrying his baby and all he does is nod?

The plane pushes back from the gate. She watches the crew do their safety demo. As they finish and start rolling up their life vests and oxygen masks, KC feels a surge of jealousy. They are wearing her uniform, living her life, and she is headed back to Vegas and God knows what.

She hears yelling and turns around in her seat. A man with a long scraggly beard and an Islamic skullcap runs up the aisle and toward the boarding door.

"I must get off," he yells.

A female flight attendant dives out of his way and into the business galley.

Kevin jumps out of his seat.

"I'm ill. I'm ill," says the man. "I must get off."

As the man charges toward the door, Kevin steps into a wide linebacker stance at the end of the aisle. KC gasps as she watches him lower his shoulder into the man's chest and drive him to the ground. The man grunts as he falls. Kevin puts his knee in his adversary's back and turns him onto his stomach as he squirms.

KC wonders if the man has accomplices. She is suddenly worried for Kevin.

"Stay down," Kevin yells. He holds the man down by the back of his neck with one hand while he pats him for weapons.

The airplane turns and then stops.

Flight attendants are on the phone with security. A pilot jogs to Kevin's side with a pair of Tuff-Cuffs.

Kevin zips the cuffs around the man's hands and KC can see him shaking in anger as he pulls them tighter and tighter. The prisoner vomits all over the carpet. Passengers gasp and turn their stares away for the first time since the commotion started.

The aircraft door flings open and a dozen security guards in neon-green vests rush up the air stairs and onto the plane to grab the potential terrorist.

To KC's surprise, Kevin walks straight over to her.

"Are you okay?" he asks.

She nods quickly.

"I wanted to throw a punch and lay him out."

She smiles.

He squeezes her shoulder. "Are you sure you're all right?"

"I'm connecting to Vegas. You going home?" She knows Twentynine Palms isn't far from L.A.

"I guess. I don't know what to do yet." He looks her in the eye for the first time since she told him she was pregnant.

Before she can think of what to say to him, a security guard taps Kevin and says, "We need you to take your seat, sir." He gently guides Kevin by the elbow. "We thank you for your help."

Kevin shakes the guy off. "I'm not a passenger. I work here." The cop looks him up and down, questioning the street clothes. Kevin takes his seat.

The entire crew expects to cancel, but since the man didn't check any bags, management instructs them to go ahead. The plane is flooded with security guards who check overhead bins and underneath seats in the area where he was ticketed. Finding nothing suspicious, they leave the London-to-LAX flight to its fate.

Before takeoff, the captain tells the crew to check the places security skipped. His last crew found a knife stashed in a duty-free cart. They dig through lavatory trash cans, open compartments meant for oxygen bottles and first-aid kits, and ceiling panels that hold boxes of trash bags and paper towels and Band-Aids. KC tells them she'll help. As she runs her hand along the insides of a cart in first, she looks down the aisle but she can't see Kevin.

Only a minute later, over the PA, the captain says, "Flight attendants, prepare for takeoff."

The plane rolls down the runway, building speed, and quietly lifts off. Away from England, away from Europe. KC doesn't know if she's headed to her future or her past. Or if she'll even get there. She grabs her armrest like a first-time flyer. She can't be the only one on board fearing there is a bomb ticking away in the baggage compartment or the electronics closet or behind the mirror in the bathroom or deep down in the toilet or anywhere they somehow missed.

"Ms. Valentine," says the purser as she kneels by KC's seat.

She hands her something from the crew. It's a bottle of champagne wrapped in white linen. "I'm sorry about the furlough."

The entire crew has signed it. Apologies, prayers, best wishes. All from people she's never even met.

If there has to be a bright side, it would be how everyone is reaching out.

The purser stands back up and smiles down at her sympathetically. "I'm sure you'll have something to celebrate before you know it."

She seems sincere, but KC can't help but suspect there are rumors about her and Kevin. There may have been twenty-six thousand flight attendants at United, but London is a small base, and she's coming to realize that gossip travels fast.

It's been three weeks since she dropped the bomb on him over curry at a place near Queensway. At first Kevin assumed it was Jake's, and she didn't tell him that she wasn't sure whose it was. She said she was concerned about Jake's travel schedule and lifestyle. Kevin said he understood, that he wouldn't want his kid being raised around drugs and debauchery in the back of a Hell's Kitsch tour bus.

"Well, Kev," she said. "It might actually *be* your kid."

He stopped chewing and swallowed his last spoonful of vindaloo whole. He went so pale, she was afraid she would have to give him the Heimlich. She told him he was off the hook if that's what he wanted. Of course, she'd prefer him to be involved.

"You know it would be impossible for us, for there to even be an us," he said.

"The rumors?"

"Yep. That."

So it was true.

She told him she's a realist, not some romantic in love with love. KC would be more than happy to settle for reliable.

He asked how early they could order a paternity test.

———

KC thanks the purser for the champagne. "I'll go to the back and thank everyone." She slips out of the first-class cabin without looking toward Kevin's seat. She wants him to know that *she* doesn't need him, that although she would give anything for her baby to have a father, she is strong enough to handle this on her own.

Most of the flight attendants are in the aisles passing out headsets and offering newspapers. When she reaches the back galley, she sees Kevin already there being congratulated by a female passenger. KC turns around to leave. But then she stops. She won't run from him. She hasn't done anything wrong. She decides to act like she's perfectly comfortable with the situation. She grabs a bottle of water off the galley counter as if it was what she came for.

Kevin pours the woman a coffee. She thanks him and heads back to her seat.

And then they are alone.

KC looks at her shoes.

Kevin says, "I was getting a little antsy sitting in my seat. I wanted to walk through the aisle and get a good feel for each passenger, look for anything suspicious."

"Did you see anything?"

"Not yet." He swallows so loudly that KC can hear it.

"So, what's new?" she asks in a pathetic attempt to sound casual.

He crosses his arms.

She doesn't know how she thought she could play things off like there wasn't a lit fuse snaking its way between them. Now she figures he'll think that was her way of demanding an answer and decide she's a passive-aggressive bitch for putting him on the spot. She may as well have asked him point-blank.

"Look," he says, rubbing his chin in thought. "About . . . things."

"Yeah, things," she says nervously, hoping she didn't come off as sarcastic.

"I just don't know." He looks apologetic.

"No, that's fine. I understand." And she does. The way she sees it, he's in a more uncomfortable situation than she is. At least she knows it's hers.

"You must be pissed that I haven't called."

She shakes her head.

"It's just, losing my job, and moving, and I, well. You know the rest."

She looks down at the floor.

"KC, I'm worried about you."

"Don't be. I can handle just about anything. You're off the hook. It's not like I'm going to sue you."

"He is going to need someone though."

"He?"

"There I go. Yeah, I guess I've been imagining him as a boy."

KC touches her stomach and laughs. She has no idea how she would handle a boy.

First one and then two and then five more flight attendants are with them in the large wide-body galley. The usual chatter is absent. Everyone silently works on a task—counting the duty-free stock, labeling special meals, brewing coffee.

The guy doing duty free breaks in. "Hey, good news, folks. Our plane hasn't exploded."

He laughs, but he isn't joking. It is good news.

KC resists the urge to say, "Yet."

There is something clarifying about living moment by moment in a circumstance you might not survive. It hits KC that she doesn't have to be prepared to handle her entire future. If she can just survive one test at a time, plant one foot at a time, she can make it the whole way.

32

Point of Return

I fly into Bakersfield on a United Express turbo-prop, holding on to the rail as I carefully walk down the stairs that fold out of the door. My dad is waiting at the edge of the tarmac, squinting into the sun, probably pissed that my flight was twelve minutes late.

He reaches out for a hug and says, "Welcome home."

I'm right back where I started, stuck, as if nothing has changed.

We drive past the dairy farm and the oil fields, and the smell of Bakersfield wraps itself around me. After living in England, everything here looks so brown and sparse. The sun rages down without a single cloud in the sky.

There is something wild and exposed about the landscape with its open spaces and miles and miles of visibility. Something many people no doubt find intoxicating. For me, though, it is numbing to be where there is nothing left to discover, to already know what's around every corner.

My dad turns into our driveway. It is still flanked by the same ice plant and lava rock. The screen door is still crooked, its

squeak a little worse than before. I breathe slowly as I enter the
house I lived in from first grade until I married Carl. I look
around at the brown carpet and the diamond-pattern linoleum.

"You got a new sofa," I say. The camel-colored La-Z-boy has
been replaced by the same model in cappuccino.

I tell my dad I need a nap. He shows me to my old room,
which is now a den.

"But the couch is a pullout," he says, proudly.

I don't bother to pull it out. I just collapse onto the springy
cushions and cry.

My dad sits down next to me and puts his arm around me.
Too exhausted to put up any defenses, I rest my head on his
shoulder, just like when I was a little girl.

He says, "It's going to be okay."

"I want to go home."

"You are home." He pulls a crocheted blanket over me and
tiptoes out of the room.

I sleep until 1 A.M. and then wander to the kitchen where I
reheat a leftover plate of Nancy's pot roast. I eat it at the kitchen
table in the dark and despite wishing I were anywhere else, I find
myself thankful for this familiarity.

I spend three nights awake like this, thinking about the life I
had until just a few weeks ago. Exploring foreign cities had become so easy—just land, follow the signs, and get on your way.
In London, I could watch a West End musical even if there was
no one around to join me. I could pop over to Brussels to see if
their Zara had a pair of pants I hadn't been able to find in London or Amsterdam.

The next day my dad wants to treat me to lunch at the Boll Weevil. As he drives there on what feels like the wrong side of the
road, I look to the sky and see the long white contrail of a jet
headed north, probably to San Francisco. I want to get behind

the wheel and follow it. But it's easier to sit under the Budweiser lamp and order a mini-Steerburger with cheese.

My dad spins the build-your-own-burger condiment tray and stops on the ketchup. "Ladies first," he says.

As I squeeze ketchup onto my burger, he brings up the inevitable. The refinery is hiring.

I'm surprised to find that the suggestion doesn't bother me. I realize it's because I no longer need his approval.

I matter-of-factly tell him I would rather work at the Boll Weevil. I mean it.

The waitress who sat us at my dad's usual booth is wiping down a nearby table. She says, "Sorry, sweetie, the economy isn't lookin' so hot. We just had to let an experienced waitress go."

On the way home, we stop by the bookstore where Nancy works, hoping to inquire about a job for me. Immediately upon opening the door, I spot the table. Right in the center of the entrance is an enormous display piled high with books and magazines and promotional items for September eleventh. One glance reveals at least seven images of a United 767 colliding with the South Tower. A stack of bumper stickers says NEVER FORGET.

I have an urge to call the manager to the floor and ask him if he would have already forgotten about the box cutters and explosions and ashes and bodies if it weren't for the handy bumper stickers. I look around the room, but no one else seems to be outraged or affected in any way. It's being called a national tragedy, but the people around me don't feel it. They are just spectators.

I understand why Tien didn't talk about Vietnam with people who weren't there.

My dad looks at me and says, "Are you all right?"

I nod.

"You don't look all right." He takes me home and walks me to the den, which I am refusing to call "my room." He brings me hot chocolate and I let him smooth my hair out of my face. I put my head on his shoulder.

He suggests a game of Battleship, which we played for hours on end when I was a kid. "We've got the electronic one now," he says, knowing just what will get me into the game. I spent my elementary school years trying to talk him into the new-and-improved version with the flashing lights and sounds, but he was a traditionalist.

We call out coordinates, hoping to hear the explosions followed by our ships' captains saying, "Radar confirms hit." With every hit, I more deeply appreciate my dad's efforts to distract me from my sadness and confusion.

Bakersfield may be the same, but we're not.

I may no longer need my dad's approval, but in spite of that—or maybe because of it—I don't need to push him away.

Even though he is the last place I should expect to find a sympathetic ear, I tell him about that day. And then I tell him about Tien.

"These things happen," he says.

After a lifetime of my dad's rigid expectations of conformity, I am overwhelmed by this caring response to my enormous screwup. I'm sure it would have been more comfortable for him to lecture me on what I deserve after abandoning a perfectly decent husband.

"Is there a chance he'll come around?"

I shake my head and explain that it will never, ever happen.

Dad asks me if I've heard from Carl. I clench my jaw and get ready for the inevitable, but then he says he heard Carl is remarried to a girl he met at work, that they eloped after the second date.

I'm not sure what to say. I am relieved that I won't be the target of Carl's frustrations and rage, but I feel genuine concern for the woman who will likely take my place as the target of his attacks.

"I just didn't want you to hear it from someone else."

"Thanks." It's sweet that he cares.

He claps me on the shoulder as he stands up. I think we're both impressed with his job well done.

"Now you can start over," he says. "You just have to let go of the life you wanted in order to live the life you have."

I wonder if he read that on a bumper sticker at Nancy's bookstore? I know he means well, but I look around the den with its grungy shag carpet and macramé plant hangers and hate that he can so earnestly believe I could give up all of my dreams and stay here. Honestly, I *wish* Bakersfield were enough for me, but I need to know what the world is made of. I need to know what Moscow and Bangkok and Rome and Cairo look like. I need to hear the accents in Portugal and smell the markets of Venice.

I shake my head. "You don't understand me at all."

He stands up and breathes in. "I thought we were getting somewhere. It's nice that you have dreams, but you obviously know by now that you can't always have what you want."

He walks out of the room, letting the door close too hard behind him.

Stubbornly avoiding the refinery, I take a job at a Mexican chain restaurant where I know I won't last. I paste on a smile and say, "Fresh, fresh, fresh," sixty times a day. We're required to say it at least three times whenever we visit a table.

For example, "So you're having the fresh fajitas with fresh tortillas. Can I bring you a fresh margarita to wash it down?"

The conversations are anything but fresh.

One Saturday, which should be Boll Weevil night, my dad and Nancy walk briskly into the restaurant while I'm on shift.

Nancy is more animated than usual, pointing at the chalkboard easel with our specials then waving at me from the hostess stand.

When they are seated in my section, Nancy says, "I convinced your dad to come experience the freshness." There is not a hint of sarcasm in her voice. She is wearing her beaded Ann Taylor blouse, which is dry-clean-only, so I know this is her big night out. I imagine she's quite proud of wrangling my dad into something new on a Saturday night.

"How about a couple of fresh margaritas?" I ask.

Nancy looks at my dad imploringly, but he shakes his head and says, "Naaah."

I bring some Cuervo Cactus margaritas anyway. "Live a little," I say and give my dad a playful nudge.

When I bring their fajitas, I'm pleased to see that the enormous cactus-stemmed glasses are half empty.

To my surprise, they start becoming Mexican-food regulars, on Thursday nights, though. Saturdays are, of course, still spent in their regular corner booth at Boll Weevil. The compromise seems to please Nancy.

One night when they come in, my dad sounds so excited that it's hard to understand him as he says he has something to show me. He pulls out a folded-up newspaper article he'd just torn out of the paper. It's about a recent college grad who got a Rhodes Scholarship and moved to England to study at Oxford.

He says, "Em, what about trying that? It would give you two more years of living abroad. And just think what you could come home to with a graduate degree."

At first I laugh at my dad's naïveté. Maybe if I'd been a National Merit Scholar, earned straight As at Harvard, and then cured cancer. Instead I'm wearing a sombrero and look like one of the Three Amigos.

But then I realize how highly he thinks of me. For weeks I've been waiting for him to get back to his "give up and give in" rant. I have played it over and over in my mind—I would put my hands on my hips and say once and for all, "God damn it, Dad. I know that's what you want, but I'm not you. And no matter what you think, I am not my mom."

Now I can see that he already knows.

I take the article. "Thank you, Dad. But I wouldn't qualify."

"Huh," he says, surprised. After a few minutes of silence, he says, "I figured that if you've proved anything to me by now, Emily, it's that you can do anything."

For the next two months, I carry steaming trays of fajitas two shifts a day to save up for an open-ended journey. My severance package may have only come with two weeks' pay, but I have flight benefits for the next six months, and I plan to use them.

Before I know it, I'll be on a ferry in Hong Kong and then a rickshaw in Beijing. Only this time, I won't be running from anyone or waiting for anyone. I'll be free.

SEPTEMBER 2011

33

Who's Your Daddy?

Standing next to KC on the flight line at Travis Air Force Base, her nine-year-old daughter drops the glittery WELCOME HOME DADDY sign she's holding and points to the sky where the landing lights of an airplane have just come into view. "That's it. That's it," she says, bouncing up and down just a little. "That's Daddy's plane."

KC spent all of last week helping her daughter, India, make signs and cards and cookies and decorate their house with red, white, and blue streamers and balloons. Six months ago they were tracking the deployment by months, then by weeks, then by days, and now finally, Kevin is home.

"My daddy's flying that plane," India proudly tells the commander of Kevin's squadron.

It turns out Kevin's plan to become a pilot was more than just a story to impress women. A hundred or so elementary school viewings of *Top Gun* made him dream of life behind the yoke. Shortly after 9/11, he got his chance when an Air Force recruiter granted him a pilot-training slot in return for a twelve-year service commitment.

Although glad to know he would have a steady job, KC was

skeptical at first. She didn't feel ready to support a war. After the shock of 9/11 and losing her job, she just wanted to heal. But then, as she waited to get called back to work, the revenues of the airline industry continued to tank and the terrorist threats continued to rise. Still-employed flight attendants told her about the bomb-sniffing dogs that came out to inspect planes each day, the terrifying rumors about attempted flight-deck break-ins. She heard that terrorists were attempting to burn holes between first-class lavatories and cockpits. Armed with fake patients and fake credentials, "doctors" would try to access the syringes and scalpels of the emergency medical kit usually kept in the cockpit.

Fighter planes were periodically scrambled to "escort" an airliner, a term that suggested protection, as if they would guide the passengers to a safe landing, not shoot them down at the first sign of trouble.

A few too many of these stories and KC decided that even if her job were restored, she would not be going back to that life.

Instead, she went to school to be a nurse. It seemed like a logical choice. There were plenty of jobs, she had always liked taking care of people, and she had experience staying calm in emergencies. That, and she knew her way around a hospital.

She and Kevin didn't plan on getting married. When they got back to the States after 9/11, Kevin only knew that if it was his kid, he would be good for more than just child support. At first, that meant keeping in touch with e-mails, phone calls, and the occasional meal. Then, as KC grew larger and little arms and legs began kicking and poking and throwing themselves across her belly like a cat in a sack, Kevin was seized with paternal pride.

He came with her to classes on labor and delivery, and on the big day, he massaged her back and reminded her how to breathe, noticed the peak of the contractions and let her know when they were about to get easier again.

She screamed, "Oh God, I changed my mind. I changed my mind. I don't want a baby!"

And he said, "You're doing great. I'm so proud of you. You can do it." They may have been straight from the coach's manual, but his constant cheerleading efforts did more than get her through, they filled her with a long-needed sense of support.

Still, KC cried for her mom. She wanted advice from her mom's pregnancy and delivery experience. She wanted her mom to hold her hand and tell her everything would be okay. As she neared the pushing stage and the contractions came one on top of the other, KC grew delirious and could almost see her mom by her side, still alive and finally married to ever-steady Rock 'n' Roll James. She could almost see the smiling new grandparents parading the baby around the labor and delivery ward, asking everyone to look at her perfect little fingers and her perfect little toes.

Kevin stayed by KC's side for the entire eighteen hours, wiping her forehead with a wet cloth, calming her down when, petrified, she was wheeled into the OR for a C-section. When India was born, KC was still shielded by a sterile drape. Kevin ran back and forth between baby and mother, taking pictures with his phone and showing them to KC. Breathless, he narrated the whole event while KC lay motionless on the table waiting to be sewn up. "Here is the cord being cut . . . Here is India being cleaned off . . . Here she is being weighed." Never in her life had she seen a man smile so hard.

At first she was too numb from the morphine and too distanced by mere photos to share his excitement, but then India was placed in her arms. Those big blue innocent eyes, slick and shiny with antibiotic ointment, stared up at her, and KC immediately understood his unbridled elation. This was what it meant to love.

The recovery was difficult. KC spent three days in the hospital, looped on Percocet and hooked to an IV. A nurse was in and out of her room every few hours to check her vitals, give her pain meds, and even help her use the bathroom. The first time she tried to get up to go to the bathroom, the pain was so unbearable that she nearly fell to the ground. She was certain she had torn open her incision. She pressed her call button, and a heavyset nurse came jogging in. As if she were KC's own mother, the nurse held KC in her ample arms and practically carried her to the bathroom, soothing her with whispered words of *there-there* and *it's all right*.

Her convalescence wasn't without benefits. Because she couldn't tend to the baby herself, Kevin changed all of India's diapers, rocked her when she cried, and patiently fed her sips of formula from a tiny cup until KC's milk came in. By the time they were ready to be discharged, any insecurities he may have had about being a father had long vanished.

That final morning, Kevin went out for snacks and came back with a teeny-tiny fleck of a diamond ring.

"Get the hell out of here. You're crazy," said KC.

"I guess I'd have to be to propose to someone with an attitude like that," he said with a laugh. But then he said, "I want her to have a family. *I* want to be a family."

It was KC's chance to have what she'd always wanted.

KC picks up the WELCOME HOME sign and nudges India, who hasn't taken her eyes off the plane since it began its approach. India grabs the sign and holds it high above her head. Bits of glitter come off in the breeze and sprinkle down onto her hair and shoulders. Though her arms must be getting tired, she keeps the sign held high all through the landing and taxi and stands on her tiptoes to make it even easier for her father to see her as the marshaller waves the plane into its parking spot.

Customs officials board to inspect the plane and clear its passengers. After what feels like hours, they finally see Kevin at the top of the air stairs. India drops her sign and begins running toward him. He jogs down the stairs in his sand-colored desert flight suit and scoops her into his arms, spinning her around and kissing the top of her head.

After six months of communicating via computer screen, they are all together again.

KC walks toward them and Kevin sets India down so he can hug his wife. They may not have romantic love, but KC is filled with warmth and joy at seeing her husband. As they stand there with their arms around each other, she looks at the other reuniting families and tells herself they're not so different. Regardless of how their relationships started, she's seen plenty of husbands and wives fall into the habit of focusing on the children and neglecting the intimate side of their relationship.

Kevin lifts India up onto his shoulders. Despite the deployments, he has been there through teething and fevers and scraped knees. He has been there to push swings and fly kites and take training wheels off bicycles, and he has provided a life, a house, and more importantly, a home.

That's why KC avoids Dr. Taylor.

He's a pediatrician who rounds at her hospital every Tuesday and Thursday morning. You always know when it's a Tuesday or Thursday because you can't miss all the nurses with carefully applied lipstick and blown-out hair.

He's not traditionally good-looking in the slick or bad boy kind of way KC was so often drawn to. His curly hair always flops into his eyes and he has an ever-present teddy bear on his lab coat. At Christmas, he wears ties patterned with Rudolph and Frosty. But still, he makes KC nervous.

"Why don't you call me Dave?" he'll ask, not for the first time.

As with any of his attempts to make their relationship more casual, she'll beg off by saying, "We work together. I like to keep things professional."

He'll nod his head, and she'll wish he would try to change her mind.

Not that she thinks it would be unprofessional to go by first names after working together for three years. He and KC have shared enough meals in the cafeteria for her to know that he is big into astronomy, both of his parents are teachers, and that his biggest regret is never studying abroad. He knows all about her former life at United and about losing her mom, and that India has moved from collecting piles of Barbies to obsessing over horses. These days she's covering her notebook in My Little Pony stickers and pinning up posters of Black Beauty on her walls. KC's afraid of the day she becomes equally crazy about boys.

The other day, she saw Dr. Taylor outside the NICU, greeting terrified parents and exhausted nurses. Instead of rushing down the hall like most doctors, he sauntered casually, offering an easy smile to everyone he passed. No matter what the circumstances, his peaceful demeanor can make the whole floor believe that everything is going to be okay.

"Good morning, KC," he said.

"Morning, Dr. Taylor," she said.

He stopped in front of her. His stethoscope swung from his neck and threatened to dislodge the teddy bear on his lapel. He looked at her in a way she missed being looked at.

"I was just headed down for a bite. Any chance you have time for breakfast?" he asked.

She looked at her watch and asked about Baby Noah. She had helped deliver him at thirty-two weeks, and he had been immediately admitted to the NICU for respiratory problems.

Instead of being irritated at her change of subject, Dr. Taylor tipped his head with genuine concern. She has always appreciated his thoughtfulness.

She said, "No matter how long I do this, it's still hard seeing a baby welcomed into the world with heart monitors and feeding tubes."

"It always will be," he said. "I'm not his doctor, but I'll check on him for you this morning and keep you updated."

He's never too busy to help his coworkers or patients. Her mom would have liked him, she thought.

He stepped toward her, so close KC was sure all of the other nurses noticed.

He put his hand on hers.

She waited a moment before she moved hers away.

"Look, KC. I know you're married," he said. "But—"

She shook her head to stop him right there. "There is no but."

Of course in her case, there is a but. There is also the matter of Don't Ask, Don't Tell. The ban may soon be lifted, but until then, talking about their private life on the military installation where Kevin is based could mean the loss of his job, the loss of their house, the loss of her and India's health insurance.

Besides that, she doesn't want to let Dr. Taylor get too close.

Over the years, there have been interested men. For her and Kevin both. Kevin almost got serious with one, but he was offended when the guy suggested they run off to live in Mexico, abandoning India as if she were a pet he was saddled with.

Whenever a man has tried to woo KC, she thinks of all the men her own mother paraded through their lives, always hoping one of them would be their savior. She imagines her daughter getting close to this man only to end up being disappointed by him.

It stops her every time.

KC's own disappointments took years to overcome, but by the time she saw her dad again, she was no longer the insecure little girl she'd been when he left. She had weathered the tragedy and the layoff at United, become a mother herself, and had helped bring countless new babies safely into the world.

When they were stationed at Hickham Air Force Base on Oahu a few years ago, KC finally found herself knocking on the door of her father's condo. It was Barb who opened the door. She had wrinkles around her makeup-less eyes and an extra ten or fifteen pounds on her hips. Her hair was twisted up loosely in a plastic claw clip. She no longer looked like a bimbo. She looked like a tired mom.

It seemed her dad hadn't warned Barb that she was coming by. Not surprisingly after so much time, Barb didn't recognize her. She looked at KC suspiciously, and KC wondered if her dad gave her reason to distrust younger women.

The three of them shared a pitcher of passion-fruit iced tea and an uncomfortable conversation about life on the island.

"The weather's great," said KC. She hoped that starting from common ground would ease them into things, even if it meant sticking to the conspicuously superficial.

Her dad shrugged his shoulders. "It gets monotonous."

"It's so green and lush," she said, amused at the irony of talking up the place he left her for.

"I'm getting sick of the isolation here. We've been thinking about moving back to the mainland."

Barb jumped in. "But not until the boys graduate."

They exchanged a look that told KC it was a point of contention.

She later saw pictures of two boys on the mantel, both of whom looked to be in middle school or early high school. KC's half brothers. She noticed that her dad rarely spoke of them, and when Barb did, he quickly moved from the subject. At first, KC thought he might be sparing her feelings, but Barb seemed so used to his behavior that KC started to question how invested he was in their lives.

If they had been home, she would have liked to tell those boys that they hadn't done anything wrong. There was just something broken inside their father. Every day at the hospital, she watches fathers instinctively fall in love with their children, and witnessing that bonding process reinforces something she had known from the moment India was born—children don't have to earn love.

KC and Kevin and India walk arm in arm across the flight line toward their car. After six months apart, they'll finally be able to settle back into normal life. Tomorrow morning, they'll probably get up early to walk their dog, Mowgli, and stop by the park on the way to the bakery where they'll get almond croissants and coffee and hot chocolate for India. Soon they'll be shopping for back-to-school supplies and carving pumpkins. KC will volunteer as a Girl Scout leader on her afternoons off, and in the mornings she'll go to the hospital. If she's feeling particularly bold, she may even arrive a few minutes early to grab breakfast with Dr. Taylor, whom she is starting to think of as Dave.

Then she'll spend her days doing the work she was meant for—bringing families together.

34

Ever After

More than ten years after we last parted, I see him again. He is standing at the corner of Pine and Van Ness in San Francisco waiting to use the crosswalk. But I remind myself that I've seen him many times over the years, and that every time he approaches, he becomes someone who doesn't even look very much like Tien.

This time, I can tell it is him by the way he slowly and elegantly brushes his hair to the left when the wind kicks it up a bit, the way he looks up at the clouds while he waits for the light.

I consider waving or calling out or walking on. I'm married now, but far from being jealous, I think my husband would be saddened if I could so easily ignore an old friend. I can laugh with him about how much the world has changed, so much that I did something flight attendants aren't supposed to do—I married a pilot. An Air Force pilot. When the Rhodes Scholarship didn't pan out and my flight benefits were about to end, I took a job flying for a charter airline.

Tourists might have been avoiding travel, but there was plenty of business in flying military charters to Kuwait in prepa-

ration for the war in Iraq. The planes were packed with camou-
flage backpacks and rifles. Instead of serving jaded business
travelers, we passed out chicken and beef to rosy-cheeked boys
who looked young enough to be in high school. It was hard not
to laugh as they mimicked me in the aisle doing my safety demo.
They thought they were flirting. Eventually, an officer who kept
his group in line introduced himself. We stood in the galley and
talked about travel and airplanes and about Kevin, who had recently finished Air Force pilot training. I learned that he was on
his third deployment and that he was an Eagle Scout who grew
up on a ranch in small-town Texas.

At first I assumed he was a raging conservative out for revenge and blood.

He laughed at that and said, "Hey, I don't get into the politics
of it. I just fly airplanes for a living."

But that wasn't completely true either. We corresponded
throughout his deployment and I learned that he wasn't afraid to
fight for what he believed in and that he wanted more than anything to help bring peace to the region, even if that had to be
achieved through war.

I admired his optimism and his willingness to risk his own
safety and comfort to do something bigger than himself. I sent
care packages, and he told me about the souks in Abu Dhabi and
the sandstorms in Afghanistan.

The day after he returned, he flew to L.A., where I was based,
and took me out to Spago. He'd heard it was the most expensive
restaurant in town. I liked that he was trying to impress me, but
we had even more fun afterward when, after spotting a roller
rink, we indulged our childhood nostalgia for roller limbo. Neither
of us could compete with the kids around us, but we cheered each
other on as we tried to skate backward and held hands for the slow
songs. A year later he took me to the same dodgy roller rink where
he got down on one knee under the disco ball and proposed.

The red WALK sign starts flashing. Tien crosses in my direction, so I simply stand still.

Halfway through the intersection, our eyes meet. He pauses, and then he smiles a crooked smile.

When he reaches me, he says "EmLee." No hello, no question, just, "EmLee."

"I thought it was you," I say.

He has a few more gray hairs. A couple of creases in his neck and around his eyes. "I'm laying over," he says.

I look over my shoulder toward what should be the Richelieu.

"We stay by the airport now," he says. "The Richelieu closed down when United went bankrupt and canceled the contract." He looks at me tenderly.

I wonder if he felt the same sense of gentle loss I feel now when he first heard the news.

He says, "I'm just in the city for the day. I always liked this neighborhood."

"Me, too," I admit, even though my memories of the area are more filled with him than with landmarks or neighborhood charm.

"Walk with me," he says, so I do. He wants to pick up some things for dinner at Whole Foods.

"No Miss Saigon?"

"They closed, too."

We walk quietly side by side and surprisingly, it doesn't feel strange to be silent after not talking for so long. Every so often, he turns and smiles at me as if checking to make sure I'm still there.

I accompany him through the produce aisles as he chooses oranges and bananas. He holds up a mango and says, "This one looks perfect," before handing it to me. "If memory serves me, you like mangos."

I'm not hungry and I don't really want to carry around the

mango, but I take it, and after he purchases his fruit and his baguette and brie, I buy it.

We walk down the stairs toward Peet's Coffee and the exit, but instead of opening the door, he sets his groceries next to a small table and says, "Join me?"

I sit.

I watch him sip his Americano. His legs are crossed rather than spread out like most of the men in the room. I've always admired his grace, something I no longer mind lacking myself.

"I still come to San Fran as often as I can," he says.

I nod and ready myself for an awkward period of small talk.

"There's another young girl I visit whenever possible."

I glare at him.

He laughs and says, "No, no. I'm just teasing you. It's my daughter. She goes to Berkeley now. I see her when she's not too busy with her boyfriend."

"That's wonderful," I say, relieved that his family seems to be doing well.

I watch him laughing, his face relaxed and joyful. I see that he is clearly happy, peaceful, so different from the months after she found out, when his expressions never revealed a thing. I'm happy for him, and for her, the woman I wronged in so many ways.

Tien tells me about life at United and how workdays are getting longer and layovers shorter. I tell him about my life as a charter flight attendant and Air Force wife, the dozens of countries my husband and I have visited, some together and some apart, the places we've lived, from Okinawa to Oklahoma. We have met friends in every corner, making the world more familiar and more extraordinary at the same time.

I grow lighter as Tien and I reconnect, and with a mixture of surprise and recognition, I realize there is almost nowhere I feel more at ease.

"I was in Bakersfield last year," he says. "We took a family trip to Sequoia National Park and spent a night there on the way."

"Sorry to hear that."

He looks at me like he doesn't get the joke. "I half hoped I would run into you. Mostly I hoped you were long gone and had found a place that made you happy."

I don't have to think long before telling him the truth. That I am happy.

I tell him I still see KC several times a year. I'm always hoping that someday we'll be based near her and Kevin and India. When KC first told me about their situation, I felt sorry for them, married but living in separate rooms of the same house. Now that my husband and I are trying to start a family of our own, I hope to be as effortlessly and glowingly happy as they are, holding hands with our daughter between us, swinging her arms and lifting her off the ground as she laughs out in joy. Like Kevin and KC, we'll show her how big the world can be and how limitless her place in it.

Tien looks at me with a focus that unnerves me. Eventually he says, "EmLee, I want to explain something."

I turn my eyes away and pretend to be distracted by the barista, who is swirling a pitcher under a hissing milk steamer. Tien leans back, tears open a sugar packet, and sprinkles a few more crystals into his coffee. As he stirs in the sugar, I breathe easier, hoping that I averted the embarrassing apology he must think I need to hear.

He sets his coffee aside and leans toward me. "During our time together, I heard one flight attendant say to another, 'You can't live your life for other people.' I admit it made me think." He puts his hand on mine. "But I came up with the opposite. At some point I realized, if you can't live for your family, what's the point of living?"

I imagine him back then, packing his children's lunches, helping them with long division, coaching their softball games, and kissing their bruises. I admired it. I envied it. I nearly destroyed it.

For years, I have tried to understand why we did what we did. Maybe I was being used for sex or I was using him to avoid a real relationship. Not too long ago, a therapist offered a low-hanging hypothesis straight out of the analyst's playbook, one that KC had been suggesting for years. "You were looking for a father."

"Please," I said. "That's so cliché."

"There's a reason it's cliché."

I thought of his daughters and thanked God that no matter how hard I prayed, their father never abandoned them.

Today, looking at Tien and feeling the warmth radiate from his smile, the why becomes clear. I loved him. Plain and simple. What I misunderstood at that age was what that meant. I thought that if we didn't end up together, it wasn't real. I now shiver realizing how easily we could have forced it to be "destiny." I am grateful that he had the foresight to stop what I couldn't.

Early in my relationship with my husband, when I realized we were completing each other's sentences and had developed our own language of inside jokes, I needed him to know who I was. I confessed my shameful secret, hoping he would love me despite my failings. Instead of turning on me, he said he understood my guilt but that he was thankful for everything that made me who I am now. He kissed my cheek and told me I should be, too.

I watch Tien as he dips his croissant into his coffee, and I am reminded of a younger me, a me who needed to see myself through his eyes in order to find the self-acceptance and independence that I now take for granted.

He tears the edge off his croissant and offers me a bite. Just like old times, yet even after all the anguish, I can see that we have both moved forward.

I look at the familiar scar above his eye and once again wonder if it's a relic from his final days in Vietnam.

Now we're in a different war and I'm married to a military pilot. Sometimes I imagine we will have a daughter and she will love a man whose parents pushed him onto a truck full of strangers that dodged mountains and armies and bullets, eventually bringing him to America. Maybe someday we will be sitting down to dinner, my husband retired and wearing an Air Force tie tack. The boy, Abbas or Fahim or Tariq, will tell us he is from Afghanistan. And my husband will say he was there once, back in the day. The boy will reply, "Oh, that was you up there, dropping bombs."

God willing, the wars will be over and the sacrifices on both sides will have changed the world for the better. When the scars have healed, this boy will be able to return to see his family and find that he is a part of each place, rather than a stranger to both. My daughter will embrace his culture, and with home planted firmly in their hearts, they will be free to go anywhere and everywhere.